This Book Belongs to

Tyrone Dotson

A WIZARD IN MIDGARD

CHRISTOPHER STASHEFF

A WIZARD IN MIDGARD

TOR®

A Tom Doherty Associates Book

New York

A WIZARD IN MIDGARD

Copyright © 1998 by Christopher Stasheff

This book is printed on acid-free paper.

A Tor Book
Published by Tom Doherty Associates, Inc.
175 Fifth Avenue
New York, NY 10010

Tor Books on the World Wide Web:
http://www.tor.com

Tor® is a registered trademark of Tom Doherty Associates, Inc.

Library of Congress Cataloging-in-Publication Data

Stasheff, Christopher.
    A wizard in midgard / Christopher Stasheff.—1st ed.
        p.   cm.—(The rogue wizard ; 6)
        "A Tom Doherty Associates book."
        ISBN 0-312-86033-1 (acid-free paper)
        1. Gallowglass, Magnus (Fictitious character)—Fiction.
    2. Wizards—Fiction.   I. Title.   II. Series: Stasheff, Christopher.
    Rogue wizard ; 6.
    PS3569.T3363W5868   1998
    813'.54—dc21   98-13776
                                                                                      CIP

First Edition: June 1998

Printed in the United States of America

0 9 8 7 6 5 4 3 2 1

A WIZARD IN MIDGARD

1

Magnus walked down the road, swinging his staff in time to his footsteps and surveying the countryside. It was a neat patchwork of green and gold, even an oblong of red here and there, depending on which crop was growing where. But as he'd seen from orbit, most of the workers in the fields seemed to be very big—six and a half feet or taller—or else very short—less than five feet or even smaller. There were children in the field, some stooping to hoe like the adults, some running around in play. If it hadn't been for their games, Magnus might have thought them to be dwarves, too. As it was, he had to look closely to see if the short people had the proportions of adult dwarves or of ordinary children. They were all dressed in worn, patched tunics and leggins, most of which were gray or tan. Some of the garments had once had some color, but were now worn almost as gray as the others.

As he watched, an overseer spoke sharply to one of the tall men, hefting a cudgel in a threatening manner. The tall man cringed and nodded quickly, then turned back to work, stooping and hoeing with renewed vigor.

Magnus was outraged. Bad enough that any man should have to fear another that way, but worse when the slave was so much bigger and stronger, and easily the master in an even fight! But he realized that was his own bias, projecting his own situation into them, for he was seven feet tall himself.

Something hard cracked on the side of his head.

Pain wracked his skull, and Magnus stumbled and fell to his knees, the whole world swimming about him even as he realized he'd let himself become distracted, lowered his vigilance—but his staff snapped up to guard position by sheer reflex. He hadn't even seen his attacker approach, hadn't heard his footsteps coming up from behind! Another stick swung at him, but he felt it coming and managed to swing his staff to deflect the worst of it. A fist hooked into his face, snapping his head up, and rage broke loose. Magnus surged to his feet, roaring. The world still wobbled, but he lashed out with his staff blindly. It connected, someone shouted with pain, and Magnus snapped back to guard, head clearing, pivoting about, ready for the next blow.

There were a dozen of them who had come up cat-footed behind him, all about five and a half feet tall, all grim and hard, dressed in tunics and bias-hosen of bright colors and stout cloth, each with a staff or a cudgel, three at the back with swords, two with bows.

Magnus read their intent by their armament alone—to capture him if they could and kill him if they could not. Half a dozen of them stepped in, sticks slashing. Magnus caught one on his staff, another, a third, but two more struck his shoulders and one his head, hard. The world swam again, panic churned up from the depths, and Magnus realized he was fully justified in using his psi powers. He projected raw emotion broadcast, a numbing fear, and swung his staff like a baseball bat. It struck one man in the ribs, knocking him into another; both fell, bringing down a third, and the rest ran, howling with fear. But pain exploded on the back of Magnus's head, a thud resounded through his skull, and as he fell, he realized that one of the hunters was a man of true courage who hadn't let his fear stop him. Then midnight claimed him.

In the darkness, one single thought rose: that he should have realized the depth of these people's hatred for anyone bigger than themselves. The thought brought a dream of memory, of watching from above as a double rank of Vikings bellowed their battle cry and charged a row of giants, four of them to each titan. The giants met them with roars and quarterstaves—steel quarterstaves, to judge by the way the Vikings' axes and swords glanced off them.

The giants fought back to back, staves whirling as they fended off blows from three sides at once, striking downward at men only two-thirds their height. The Vikings used their size to advantage, though, leaping in under the giants' guards to slash and chop at their legs. Here and there, a giant went down, and the Vikings leaped in to butcher him quickly before other giants could come to his rescue—which they did, for those steel quarterstaves cracked the Vikings' helmets and drove their blades back against their own bodies.

Suddenly it was over, and the Vikings were leaping away, retreating back to their own side, forming a ragged line that turned and fled. One or two giants roared and started after them, but their mates caught them and pulled them back.

Watching them on his viewscreen, Magnus guessed, "The

giants have fallen for that trick before—chased the Vikings to their own doom."

"No doubt," said a voice from thin air—or from the concealed loudspeakers in the spaceship's lounge. "I suspect the Vikings led them into swamps, where they floundered, easy prey for spears and arrows."

"Or led them under trees thick with spearmen." Magnus nodded. "The giants have learned their lesson. They're holding their line."

On the viewscreen, the giants were indeed standing firm, breathing hard and waiting for the smaller men to come back. Their mouths moved as they called to one another, but of course Magnus couldn't hear what they were saying. "I wonder if they're speaking Terran Standard."

"We can send down a probe with an audio pickup," the voice offered.

"Now, Herkimer," Magnus reproved, "you know I'm not rich."

Herkimer was the name he had given his ship's computer and, therefore, the ship itself. It navigated and operated the vessel, monitored his life support systems, cooked his meals, cleaned the ship, and to top it off, dredged up an amazing variety of facts from its vast memory.

"I'm happy enough with pictures," Magnus told the computer. "In fact, I'm amazed the electronic telescope can zoom in tightly enough to show a close-up of a human face from an orbit twenty thousand miles above the planet's surface."

The world was listed by the name of "Siegfried" in the atlas of colonized stars. That alone had been enough to send Magnus to searching it out. There had been a record of a colonizing expedition and the general direction in which they intended to search for a habitable home, but none of where they had landed or whether they had survived. It had been an interesting search.

"It is impressive." Being a computer, Herkimer couldn't really be impressed by anything. "But a microphone that could reach so far is completely out of the question."

"No need, when all we're trying to do is gain an overview of the situation."

The giants waited a long time as the Vikings retreated, step by step. Even when they were out of sight, half the giants stayed on guard. The other half turned to tend the wounded.

"Do you suppose some of those giants could be women?" Magnus asked.

"Quite possibly," Herkimer answered, "but it is difficult to say. They're all wearing the same armor, over similar tunics and cross-gartered leggins."

"But some of them don't have beards," Magnus pointed out, "and the ones who don't, have breastplates that bulge outward more than the men's do."

"It is possible," the computer admitted. "Odd that their men would not object to risking them, though."

"Maybe not, when they're so badly outnumbered," Magnus said, "and when any one of them is big enough to be a match for three of the Vikings. Of course, they come at the giants in squads of four. . . ."

"We must count it a hypothesis to be examined more closely," Herkimer cautioned. "We need more data."

"How strange those giants look." Magnus couldn't help thinking of them as anything but giants, when they were half again as tall as the Vikings and five times as massive. Their thighs looked to be two feet thick, and their upper arms more than a foot. Their hips were four feet wide, and their shoulders five. "They're so broad and thick that they seem short."

"Perhaps they are," Herkimer suggested. "We really have no artifact by which to judge their scale."

"True enough," Magnus admitted. "I'm assuming that the Vikings are of normal size for human beings—somewhere between five and six feet tall. If they are, the giants are nine feet tall on the average. I suppose they need such thick legs to support all the weight that goes with that extra height."

"Still, we are only assuming," the computer reminded him. "For all we know, the ones you call Vikings may be only two feet tall."

"Well, yes," Gar admitted. "But they have the proportions of normal men, and if they were shorter, they should also be more delicate—so I'm betting they're of normal size. Oh, and by the way, yes, I know they aren't really Vikings."

The Vikings of Terra's past had been ordinary Scandinavian citizens at home who had gone raiding the shores of richer countries to supplement their incomes—or, in some cases, for their whole incomes. A great number of Norwegians, Swedes, and Danes stayed home and farmed—but when they went to war, they wore the same armor and carried the same shields and weapons as the Vikings did.

"They do dress like medieval Scandinavians," Herkimer admitted, "and most people associate horned helmets, beards, and war-axes with Vikings."

"Yes, you'd almost think they had stepped off the screen of a dramatic epic," Magnus said. "Of course, they're probably very ordinary farmers and tradesmen at home, not medieval pirates. They've simply been called up for war."

There certainly was no sea in evidence, except for the coastline hundreds of miles to the south. Only one central area of a small continent had been Terraformed; the rest was desert or tundra. This battle had taken place on the eastern border of the land, assuming that the mountain range on the photographed map before Magnus was indeed a border.

"Zoom out," he told Herkimer, and as the giants dwindled in the viewscreen, the Vikings came back into sight. Sure enough, they were out of the foothills where they had fought the battle and into the meadows and marshlands beyond, carrying their dead and wounded.

"The mountains do seem to be the borderland," Herkimer said. "I think we can infer that they are the giants' homeland."

To the east, the giants finally broke their formation and brought out stretchers to carry home their dead.

"They must have scouts in the last foothills near the flatland, and some way of signaling back to the army," Magnus guessed. "How many lost their lives in this skirmish, Herkimer?"

"Ninety-eight, counting the dead on both sides," the computer reported. "Judging by the severity of their wounds, I estimate that sixteen more will die within a few days."

Magnus scowled, the sunlight of discovery and investigation dimmed by the shadow of death. "I wonder how frequent these battles are?"

"We found this one by only an hour's search," Herkimer replied. "Probability analysis indicates an almost constant state of border clashes."

"Yes," Magnus said, brooding. "If they were rare, the odds of chancing upon such a battle would have been extremely small. At least their wars seem to be confined to small battles."

Then agony seared through Magnus, and the dream fled.

Awareness returned in the form of the racking ache in his head. Then a sudden sharp pain exploded in his side, and a voice commanded, "Up with you, now! I saw you twitch! You're awake!"

The accent was strong, but it was still Terran Standard. That was bad; if the language hadn't drifted much from its origin, it meant that the government was strict, harsh, and stonily conservative. Magnus struggled to rise, but the effort made the pain spear from temple to temple, and he fell back with a groan, thinking, *Concussion. . . .*

The sharp pain jabbed at his side again, and the voice shouted, "Up, I said! By Loki, you'll do as you're told, or you'll die for it!"

Anger overode the pain, and Magnus forced his eyes open. Light tore at his brain, and he squeezed his eyelids to slits as he rolled, trying to ignore the agony in his head and the nausea in his stomach, looking for his tormentor.

The man stood above him with a yard-long wooden stick capped with a metal point—for all the stars, a cattle prod! "Up!" he bellowed. "Into the field with you!" He jabbed again. "That for your arrogance, walking down the road in broad daylight like a real man! Into the field with you, half-giant, and learn your place!"

Through the raging in his head, all Magnus could think was, *Half?*

Then he remembered what he had seen from orbit— from orbit, safe in Herkimer's cozy, luxurious lounge.

Magnus pored over one photograph, then compared it with another and another. "There's a pattern here."

"Of what sort?" the computer asked. Its injured tone had to be Magnus's imagination; Herkimer couldn't really be feel- ing miffed that Magnus had discovered something that it hadn't. In fact, Herkimer couldn't be feeling, period. It was a machine.

"Some form of slavery," Magnus said. "In every picture showing people working, the real drudgery is being done by the biggest and the smallest."

"Stronger people would naturally do the heavier work," the computer noted.

"It isn't always heavy." Magnus leafed through the pictures. "They're chopping wood, drawing water, mucking out pig-pens, that sort of thing. The medium-sized women are feeding the chickens, sweeping the steps, and tending the gardens. The medium-sized men are making barrels, driving wagons, forging iron implements—crafts and trades. The big ones and the small ones do the unskilled labor. More medium-sized men are watching them with sticks in their hands."

The computer was silent a moment, then answered, "I have correlated all the pictures we have taken, including close-ups of photographs we had not previously examined in detail. Your analysis holds."

"Some sort of slavery? Or a caste system?" Magnus shook his head. "We need more information."

Well, he was getting that information now, and there didn't seem to be much doubt about the slavery. What a fool he had been to leave that nice, safe spaceship just because he thought other people were being oppressed!

The prod goaded him again, and the overseer roared, "Up, monster! Or I'll stab you half to death!"

The tide of anger almost overwhelmed Magnus—but people were most definitely being oppressed, and his own mistreatment was proof of that. He fought down the anger and stumbled to his feet. By sheer bad luck and his own stupidity, he had fallen into the perfect situation to study their suffering—and to take a look at this society from the inside. He could play the obedient slave until he had a clear idea of what was going on. Then he could escape—he had no doubt of that; for a projective telepath, it only took thinking sleepy thoughts at the guards.

Though he might stop to beat up this particular overseer a bit on the way out. . . .

Looking down, he was amazed to see that he wore the same sort of worn gray tunic and leggins as the field slaves. "What did you do with my clothes!"

"Gave 'em to somebody who deserves 'em," the overseer grunted. "His wife will cut them down for him, never you fear. Half-giants have no business wearing such finery!"

Finery? The cloak and tunic had been of stout, close-woven wool, good hardy black travelling clothes, and the boots had been carefully scuffed and worn, but still sound and waterproof. Instead, he wore sandals, scarcely more than soles strapped to his feet.

"I am Kawsa, overseer to Steward Wulfsson," the smaller man snarled. "You'll have cause to remember my name, you great hulk, and my prod too! Now get moving, or you'll wish you were dead!"

Magnus was tempted to split the man's head with the same agony he felt—but he couldn't be sure of his telepathic abilities until the concussion healed. He turned to shuffle toward the field, fighting dizziness and nausea.

The prod whacked him across the back of the knees. Magnus cried out as he fell.

"What do you say when an overseer speaks to you, boy?" Kawsa growled.

"My mother taught me not to say such things," Magnus groaned.

The stick cracked into his buttock. Magnus managed to strangle the shout of pain.

"You say, 'yes, sir!' " Kawsa bellowed. "No smart talk to me, boy! And it doesn't matter what I say, the only answer is 'yes, sir!' You understand that now?"

"Gotcha," Magnus affirmed.

The stick cracked across his buttocks again. "What?"

Magnus steeled himself to the degradation and reminded himself that he needed to study these people up close, witnessing how badly they oppressed their slaves and how they chose who was to be a slave and who free. "Yes, sir." He nearly choked on the words, but he got them out.

"That's better. Into that field with you, now, and grub weeds!"

Magnus tried to push himself to his feet, but his leg nerves hadn't recovered yet.

"Aw, can't get up?" the overseer crooned, than snapped, "Crawl, then! That will remind you what a worm you really are!"

Magnus told himself that the slaves needed the kind of sympathy that can only come from shared suffering, and crawled into the field. Other slaves glanced up at him, then quickly glanced away.

"Well, you're close enough to the ground that you don't need a hoe," Kawsa told him. "Grub with your hands!"

He watched while Magnus pulled a dozen weeds, then walked on down the row, but glanced back frequently.

A very short man in the next row spoke out of the side of his mouth, carefully not looking at Magnus. "Whatever possessed you to go marching down the high road dressed like a freeman in broad daylight, poor lad?"

"I'm from far away," Magnus told him, "very far, beyond the borders of this land. I didn't know."

"From the North Country?" The man looked up, surprized, then remembered the overseer and turned his gaze back to his hoe. "Then your parents must have been slaves who escaped, and should have told you what it was like here! I thought everyone knew how things were in Midgard!"

"I'm from farther than that," Magnus told him, but registered the name of the country well, to remember it. Midgard? Well, it did go with the horned helmets. . . .

Again the man stared at him, but only for a second. Then studying his hoe blade, he muttered, "Didn't know there were people farther away."

"I'm real," Magnus assured him. "I didn't know what I was getting into."

And that, he decided, was nothing but the honest truth.

At least he had expected to see dwarves, too. He had seen them in the pictures from orbit, after he and Herkimer had explored Midgard's eastern border.

"Let's see how the western border compares with this one, Herkimer."

"Initiating acceleration," the computer replied, but the artificial gravity within the ship was so excellent that Magnus felt no change. "Should we examine the northern border on the way?"

"No point," Magnus said. "Your photographs show it to be a wasteland with only a few small settlements." He looked down at the pictures on the table before him, aerial photos of the planet's one inhabited continent.

Some were large-scale, some small; some showed the country as a whole, some only single villages, some even close-ups of just a few people. "Wattle and daub huts, thatched roofs, wooden wheels on their wagons, clothing limited to tunics and bias-hosen for the men, blouses and skirts for the women, hooded cloaks for both . . . yes, it looks very much like the Scandinavian Middle Ages."

"Too much so?" the computer supplied.

"Definitely. Someone set about a deliberate imitation, but wasn't a stickler for historical accuracy." Magnus couldn't rid himself of the feeling that he was looking at a gigantic stage set.

"We have come to the dawn line," Herkimer reported.

"Good." Magnus turned back to the viewscreens. "Is there a natural border?"

"Yes, a river, and the land beyond it is thickly forested."

"Scan it for signs of battle—there!"

The view on the screen steadied, showing a bird's-eye view of two straggling lines of dots facing three rings of other dots, smooth with geometric precision. Behind and between the circles were lines of dots, again straight as though drawn with a ruler. The two sets of lines faced one another between the river and the forest.

"Hold this view on one screen and have the other zoom in," Magnus directed.

On the right-hand screen, the dots swam closer. The ends of the lines swept out, and the dots resolved themselves into Vikings on one side, charging with waving axes and mouths open to shout. Across from them were three circles of armored warriors with crossbows, marching around and around. The ones in front aimed and discharged their weapons as they paced along the front arc, then wound back their bows and reloaded as they marched along the back arc. Between them stood other warriors with long shields and short swords. Long spears thrust out between sword-wielders from the second line of warriors.

As the Vikings came closer, the crossbowmen kept up a continuous field of fire. The Vikings charged straight into their storm, horn-helmeted men falling left and right, but the rest running on, shouting. Half their number survived to reach the standing warriors. They pushed the spears up with their shields so that they could chop at the swordsmen—whose heads were scarcely waist-high.

Magnus stared in amazement. "The spearmen are dwarves!"

"Relative to the Vikings, yes," Herkimer agreed.

Looking more closely, Magnus could see that the warriors in the formation had legs and arms that were shorter in proportion to their bodies than those of the Vikings—but their shoulders were almost as wide, and their heads almost as large, as those of their bigger opponents.

Magnus gave a long, low whistle. "No wonder they're fighting with such iron discipline! It's the only way they can stand against men twice their size!"

"And who outnumber them," Herkimer pointed out.

There did seem to be twice as many Vikings as dwarves—but that appearance changed as the taller men tried an outflanking maneuver. On the left-hand screen, the overview of the battle, Magnus saw the ends of the second line of Vikings split and swing out, to try to catch the circles of dwarves from the flanks—but as they did, archers rose from the bushes at the sides and filled the air with arrows. A number of Vikings fell, and the rest retreated back to the battle line. They found themselves racing the center, who were fleeing from the crossbow fire. The dwarves, apparently moved by a chivalrous impulse their larger foes lacked, held their fire. They seemed to feel no need to kill as long as their enemies were retreating.

"Reserves hidden in ambush." Magnus stared. "Some of them are almost as big as the Vikings!"

"They would seem to be traitors," Herkimer commented.

"They must certainly seem that way to the Vikings! Of course, I suppose they could be fugitives given sanctuary by the dwarves—or even political dissidents." Magnus compared the two screens. "Still, the Vikings outnumber them by half."

"At least," Herkimer agreed.

The dwarves held their ground, not taking the bait to chase—but a final flight of crossbow bolts filled the air, hurtling toward the fleeing Vikings. Several more of them fell. Their comrades scooped them up and carried them back to the river. There, they slowed to cross a bridge made up of low boats with decking laid across their centers. The Vikings tramped over those decks, carrying their dead and wounded, and as soon as the last one passed, the sections of bridge broke away and began rowing back to the eastern bank of the river. The water was indeed a border.

The dwarves held their formation until the last boat was well out from shore, then turned to embrace one another, slap each other's backs, and even break into an impromptu dance here and there.

Magnus stared at the close-up. "Some of them are beardless. . . ."

"And their cuirasses are very pronounced about their gender," Herkimer finished. "Many of those warriors are women."

"No wonder, when they're so badly outnumbered, and so

small into the bargain! We're looking at a military society, Herkimer."

"It would seem so," the computer agreed. "Holding so tight a formation under the stress of battle speaks of long training."

"Yes, from childhood, probably." Magnus frowned. "And as with the giants, if we could find a battle so quickly, they have to be common—another part of life, like plowing and reaping."

"A time to sow, a time to reap, and a time for war," the computer agreed.

But the dwarf slaves in these fields hadn't learned to fight, and the only time for them was a time to suffer.

When the sun neared the horizon, Kawsa and half a dozen other overseers lined them up with shouts and insults, then started them off in a shuffling line back to the farmstead. They went down through rows of barley and hops to a broad farmyard of clean tan gravel. Another file of slaves was driving cows into a milking barn, and three others were pouring swill into the troughs of a huge pigsty. Gar's file shuffled past them all to a long ramshackle shed of unpainted boards, and inside.

There the silence ended. Half of the slaves dropped down onto pallets of moldy straw with moans of relief. Others only sat down on rude benches, but everyone breathed sighs of relief. Even the older children sat down with groans, their dusty little faces lined with weariness. The younger children had been able to nap in the field, though, and still frolicked and quarrelled. Magnus expected some of the tired adults to snap at the little ones, but they only sighed with philosophic patience—and a surprising number of them watched the children with doting smiles. Even in the midst of such misery, they found pleasure in the innocent squabbles and joys of their children.

Magnus noticed a great lack of water, and a greater need for it.

A tall young woman came up to him with a bucket from which she lifted a dripping ladle. "Drink, lad, for you'll need it!"

"Thank you," Magnus said sincerely, and drank the ladle dry, thinking it was the sweetest drink he had ever had during peacetime—if you could call this peace. He handed it back to the woman with a sigh of relief. "I needed that."

"I'm sure you did," she said, then reached out to touch his forehead, frowning anxiously. Magnus forced himself to hold still, though the touch of her fingers hurt. "You've a right ugly bruise there," she told him, "and a few more I can't see, I don't doubt."

"I'm sure you're right," Magnus told her. "I've a dozen aches at least. Believe me, I've had hours to count them."

"Don't I know it!" she said. "My name's Greta."

"I'm honored to meet you, Greta." Magnus inclined his head gravely. "My name is Gar Pike."

She stared at him in surprise, then gave him a wan smile. "A gar pike, are you? Gar I don't doubt, and you're a poor fish indeed, to let yourself be caught like this. But why take such a name for yourself?"

The question brought a sudden wave of longing for his nice, safe spaceship lounge, and a memory of Herkimer saying, only hours before, "Why do you insist on using that abominable alias when you go planetside to start a revolution, Magnus?"

Magnus shrugged. "You never can tell when there are going to be secret agents around, from SCENT or some other

Terran government agency. I'd just as soon they didn't recognize me by name."

"Surely the name of Gar Pike must be almost as famous as that of d'Armand, by now."

"Not to SCENT, fortunately—unless they've had agents on every planet I've visited." Magnus's mouth tightened at the thought of his own brief stint as a SCENT agent, and his disillusionment with their methods. His father, Rod Gallowglass, whose real name was Rodney d'Armand, was one of the most famous agents of the Society for the Conversion of Extraterrestrial Nascent Totalitarianisms—famous because he had discovered Magnus's home planet of Gramarye with its potentially explosive population of espers. For three decades now, he had been holding the planet secure against the schemes and plots of two futurian organizations, one trying to subvert Gramarye to some form of totalitarian government so that its telepaths would be at the service of its interstellar dictatorship, the other trying to subvert the planet to anarchy so that the telepaths would help spread its unrealistically idealistic form of chaos throughout the human-colonized planets. Rod Gallowglass had short-circuited all their schemes with the help of his native-born wife Gwendylon and their four children—three, since Magnus had taken to the stars, unable to accept his father's imposing of democracy on a people who might not want it. He had joined SCENT under an assumed name, become even more disenchanted with its methods than with his father's, and gone off on his own to bring about social change in a way about which he could feel right— which meant that he sought out planets where the majority were really miserably oppressed, and the only solution was revolution.

So here he was, talking to another miserable one, and trying to explain, "The name was given me as much as I chose it." He realized he had better think of himself as "Gar Pike" for the rest of his time on this planet.

Greta's wan smile warmed a little. "Don't you ever talk like a proud lord, though!"

"Is he all right?" asked another woman anxiously, coming up to them. Gar looked down and saw she wasn't even five feet tall.

"He seems well enough," Greta answered her. "He walks fairly straight, and his limp's almost gone."

"I'm past the worst of it," Gar confirmed.

"This is Rega." Greta gestured to the smaller woman.

"Honored to meet you, Rega."

Rega smiled up at him. "No wonder the overseers set about you so hard, with your courtly ways. Where did you escape from, lad? I know Groi says you're from far away, but that can't be, can it?"

Groi, Gar decided, must be the small man who had talked to him out in the field. "It's quite true. I wanted to see something of the world before I settled down."

"Seen enough yet?" Greta asked with a sardonic smile.

They were very surprised when Gar said, "Too much—but not enough."

2

Gar was certainly seeing the world of Seigfried, and was regretting every minute of it—but he and Herkimer had tried to reason out the social conditions on the planet from the evidence of what they had seen, until Herkimer had finally said, "There simply is not enough information to justify any conclusions about this culture, Magnus."

"Other than that we need more information," Magnus said with a wry smile. "Still, we've seen two battles producing dead bodies in a very short space of time. I think constant warfare is reason enough to help these people make a change in their form of government, don't you?"

"Help, or incite?" The computer was capable of recognizing irony, if not actual humor. "Provisionally, I would have to agree. After all, you have engineered one peaceful revolution already—why not start a revolution to bring peace? But if the tallest and shortest of the Midlanders are really locked into slavery and the misery that almost always accompanies it, I would say that was an even stronger reason."

"War and slavery," Magnus said grimly. "I've helped people who were worse off, but this is surely bad enough. Yes, I think it's time for Gar Pike to conduct a fact-finding mission."

And the first fact he had to find was whether or not the people of Siegfried were really as miserable as he thought—or if he was reading his own desire for purpose into their situation.

"Where do you wish to land, Magnus?"

"Near the border of the land of the medium-sized people," Gar said. "Since they seem to be fighting both of the other nations, they should give me the best chance of understanding the whole situation at one experience."

"You might not fit in," Herkimer warned him, "and might not be accepted. In fact, they might take you for an enemy. After all, you are a giant among your own kind, or have been on every planet you have visited."

Magnus was broad in proportion to his seven feet of height, constant exercise and martial arts practice having made him very muscular.

"I shall prepare the appropriate garments, Magnus," the computer told him. "You will find them in the wardrobe of your sleeping chamber."

"Thank you, Herkimer." Magnus rose and went to his suite, to enjoy what might well be his last civilized shower for a very long time.

Dinner was served by two women from the farmhouse kitchen, from huge buckets carried by two of the oversized men. Gar expected the slaves to race clamoring to the doorway and fight one another to be first, but they only pulled wooden bowls from their pallets and lined up. Their eyes bulged and their mouths watered, but no one pushed his way past anyone else. Gar was especially surprised that none of the semi-giants kicked any of the small people out of line, and the few who tried it were shoved back into place and scolded soundly by the nearest of their fellow huge ones. Gar took his place at the end of the queue, even though his stomach growled and his mouth fairly ached with hunger—but he knew he had eaten better than any of them, and probably just as recently.

He studied the line, trying to figure out how they decided who had what place. He would have expected the smaller people to either have to accept last place, or to be allowed to go first, but they were sprinkled throughout the line. It wasn't even big person/small person in alternation, but one here, two there, even three in one place. Finally he cracked the system—the ones in front were the oldest, with the youngest next; the middle-aged came last, forcing themselves to wait, presumably because the others needed their food more.

Finally Gar came up, and the server scraped the bottom of the bucket to come up with half a ladleful for him. She started to hold it out, then stared. "You have no bowl!"

"I'm new today," Gar told her.

"Are you indeed!" She peered up at him, squinting—she was one of the small ones. "What's your name, lad?"

"Gar," he answered.

"Well, I'm Lalle." The little woman turned to her partner, a woman two feet taller than herself. "Vonna, have we an extra bowl?"

"Always." The big woman set down her ladle and fished an empty wooden bowl out of a huge pocket in her apron. She handed it to Gar. "Scrub it with sand when you've done, and keep it under your pillow! Here, now." She scraped around the bucket with her ladle and plopped a half-dipper of porridge into his bowl. Lalle added her half dipper, and Gar thanked them numbly, then turned away, staring into his bowl and wondering how he was supposed to survive to do heavy work on a bowl of thickened pea soup.

He also wondered how he was supposed to eat it, but one look at his fellow slaves told him the answer. He sat down by the door and dipped two fingers into the mess, then stuck them in his mouth and sucked off the food. It was crude, but it worked. The porridge was, at least, reasonably tasteless. He reminded himself that it could have been worse. In fact, he was so hungry that it actually tasted good—or felt that way.

When he was done, he followed the others outside to a sand heap where he scoured his bowl, then went back indoors. He was amazed to hear the slaves beginning to sing. It was a slow, mournful ballad, even as he would have expected, but it was full of the promise of the joys of tending the gardens of the gods amid the fragrance of fruits that made people always young, and where all work seemed play.

Gar listened, feeling his stomach sink. Were their lives so miserable that this was the golden afterlife that made the burden of existence bearable—an eternity of work for a kind master, in a garden where perfume induced euphoria? He shuddered inside at the thought.

Then a rough voice tore through the song. "Greta!"

The slaves fell silent on the instant, and the girl who had brought Gar his drink stood up, paling and backing away, hands out to defend. "Not me! It was only three nights ago!"

"So I find your body pleasing." Kawsa strode into the slave barracks, two other overseers behind him, grinning eyes gleaming with lust. "Out, girl, and into the barn!"

"No!" Greta cried. "It's not fair! Not so soon! Choose someone else!" She turned to her fellow slaves in appeal. "Someone who hasn't been in a while, please!"

Stone-faced, Rega started to rise, but Kawsa just pushed her back down. "It's you tonight, Greta lass, and none other! Come now!"

"No! I won't!" Greta backed away, then suddenly bolted for the window.

Kawsa caught her in two strides, wrestling her down to the floor, then catching her wrists. She screamed and kicked, then managed to lever herself up enough to bite at his hands.

He dropped her with an oath, but one of the other overseers caught her wrists and another her ankles.

Kawsa nursed his bitten hand, growling, "Take her out and tie her to the post." Then he kicked a very small boy nearby and said, "Run and fetch the steward."

Eyes huge with fear, the boy ran out the door.

"Everyone out!" Kawsa bellowed. "All of you! It's been too long since you watched what happens to a slave who disobeys an overseer!"

They moved with the speed of fear, for all the overseers were red with anger and watching closely for an excuse. They gathered around the whipping post as Kawsa tied Greta's wrists to it. She screamed and fought, of course, and another overseer had to hold her in place while Kawsa bound the rope tight.

As they finished, Steward Wulfsson came up. He was a thick, beefy man in early middle age with lowering brows and a fleshy face. "What's the matter, Kawsa?"

"This woman Greta, your lordship." Kawsa was breathing hard from binding the woman. "She refused an order, she argued."

"He had me only three days ago!" Greta protested. "Not so . . ."

Wulfsson stepped up and, quite methodically, backhanded her across the mouth. "I don't care what the order is or what your reasons—you don't refuse one of my overseers! It's the same as refusing me." He looked her up and down, and his eye glinted. "Who knows? I may call for you myself, one of these nights." Then he barked to Kawsa, "Bare her back and give me the whip!"

What followed was as ugly as anything Gar had seen, but he couldn't look away, because the overseers paced along the semi-circle of slaves, snarling, "Look, damn your hides! If one of you tries to close your eyes, we'll beat the lot of you!"

The overseers made lewd comments as they tore Greta's tunic open along the back, and Wulfsson plied the lash himself, eyes glinting hotter with every scream. Gar warred within himself, weighing Greta's pain against the freedom he might bring the whole country if he stayed undercover long enough to learn the bosses' weaknesses. He had to do something, so he tried to pull the cat-of-nine-tails short with each stroke, but it wouldn't obey his thoughts. In desperation, he tried to make the knots at Greta's wrists untie themselves, but they barely twitched. His stomach sank as he realized the blow to his head had indeed done as much damage as he had feared. He could only hope it would heal, and quickly, for he was trapped here until it did.

When the whipping was done, Wulfsson tossed the whip back to Kawsa. "Here. Tell me when she's recovered enough. Back to finish my dinner, now."

He stalked away, and the overseers stepped aside to let the women slaves untie poor Greta and carry her sobbing into the barracks. The slaves turned and filed back inside, a silent, shaken crew.

"Rega!" Kawsa snapped.

The small woman stopped in her tracks and turned slowly to look up at the overseer with utter dread. "Yes, sir?"

"Into the barn and up to the hayloft with you, quickly!"

Rega turned away toward the huge dark outbuilding with its lowing of cattle, her steps dragging.

Gar felt outrage and fury, the more bitter because he could do nothing to stop it. He went on in and sat down on his pallet. From farther down the darkened room, he could hear Greta's voice, thick with sobs, saying fiercely, "I don't care! I'd rather this than have to bed that beast again!" Then she broke off into more tears.

Gar reached out with his mind to try to speed the healing of her back, but could feel no response. In desperation, he let his awareness expand, feeling, listening, for Kawsa's mind. He felt a huge surge of relief when he found it, glowing in the mental darkness like a coal on the hearth, burning with lust and cruelty. He reached inside, found the ganglion that would give the signal to stop the the flow of blood in exactly the right place, thought hard at it—but the synapse functioned as smoothly as though his thoughts were nowhere near it.

As indeed they were not, for he could listen, could hear another's thoughts, follow the nerve-signals down individual pathways—but his numbed brain couldn't send out the impulse to change that path, to change anything. Magnus withdrew quickly, not wanting to hear anything, to feel anything secondhand, feeling completely useless, completely alone, in the dark.

Someone started a slow and mournful song, almost a dirge. Others joined in, until half the slaves in the barracks were singing, adults and children all. A cry came from across the way, but they sang all the louder for it.

A hand grasped Gar's shoulder, and his glance leaped up into the gloom, body tensing to fight—but the man's eyes were only a little higher than his own, even though Gar was sitting while the other was standing, and the gaze was gentle and filled with pity. "First time you've ever had to witness something like this, is it, lad?"

"No," Gar answered, "but it's the first time I haven't been able to do anything about it."

He had never felt so helpless in his life.

When full darkness fell, and the gloom thickened so that he could scarcely see a foot in front of his face, Gar stretched himself out on his moldy pallet, writhed about to try to find a way for none of his bruises to come in contact with the straw, and listened to the sounds of the other slaves as he lay waiting for sleep. There was the muffled sobbing of Greta, Rega, and the other woman whom one of the overseers had chosen for a few minutes' pleasure; there were snores from those who had been lucky enough to find slumber and, here and there, the gasps and little cries of delight of pairs of slaves who had found the only pleasure left to them. Gar reflected bitterly that Steward Wulfsson couldn't even afford privacy for them, though they didn't seem to need it.

A soft rustle of cloth near him made him look up to see a small woman folding her skirts to sit beside him, looking down with a quizzical smile. "I've been watching you all evening, stranger."

"I'm Gar," he whispered. "You?"

"Hilda," she said. "Life's bitter, lad. We, too, could find a little sweetness in it."

"Thank you, but after what I've seen tonight, I'd hate myself if I reached out to touch a woman." Gar groped to give her hand a quick squeeze anyway, then dropped it. "I'm surprised the steward allows his slaves to have any pleasures at all. Why doesn't he just keep the men and women apart?"

"Why?" Hilda actually giggled. "Why, he can't depend on enough free women bearing children who are too large or too small, lad. He has to make sure he'll have more slaves tomorrow."

"Breeding," Gar said sourly.

"He calls it that," Hilda told him. "We call it love." She looked off into the darkness in disdain. "Poor fools out there—two couples trying to make normal babies, one a big woman with a small man, the other a small woman with a big man. Even if the babies do grow to Midgarder size, they'll still be slaves."

"Even though they look just like the masters?" Gar asked in surprise.

"Even though," Hilda assured him. "They carry blood that might be a giant's or a dwarf's, after all. The son or daughter of a slave is still a slave."

That left the question of why she had sought him out, but Gar had tact enough not to ask. "Poor souls," he muttered.

"Aren't we all?" Hilda looked down at him again. "It surely seems to have taken you sorely, lad, watching Greta whipped. Have you never seen the like before?"

"I have a weak stomach," Gar explained.

"Well, let it heal, and seek me out when it does," Hilda sighed. She touched his hand, a light caress, then slipped off into the night.

Gar let her go, realizing why she had come, why the slaves went on making babies even though they knew the children would grow into misery like their own—because he had never felt so bitterly alone as he did that night.

By the time he went to sleep, Magnus had learned all he needed to know to justify overthrowing Midgard's government. He wasn't sure what that government was, but he felt totally justified in conquering the country—as bloodlessly as possible, of course, but he doubted how bloodless that could be. The depth of anger and hatred in the slaves was hidden, but very great.

That anger, though, was completely directed toward the masters, and only struck at other slaves in brief flashes, the sort of quarrels that are bound to crop up between people anywhere who are forced to live too closely together. Gar was amazed that the men didn't try to browbeat the women, especially seeing how the overseers exploited them—but perhaps that was why: the slave men, sickened by the bullying, were determined not to imitate it.

He was also astounded to see that the big slaves didn't try to beat the small ones—that, in fact, all the slaves seemed to cling together for comfort, regardless of size or gender. He wondered if it might be because they shared a common bond of suffering; semi-dwarf and demi-giant united in misery, and in the need to care for one another in order to survive.

Of course, it also might have been that they were simply too tired to try to intimidate one another, but Gar doubted that; he had seen people in very deprived circumstances still trying to bully their fellows.

There was no question about the overseers' power, though. Each of them took a different woman every night, and during the day, seemed to be alert for the slightest excuse to strike a slave. They always found excuses to yell, to insult, to browbeat, and seemed to enjoy every minute. As his concussion healed, Gar read their spirits more and more accurately, and realized that they did indeed enjoy their work. The position seemed to attract sadists.

He felt no compunction about reading their minds. There

could be no doubt they were the enemy, or that he was at so severe a disadvantage that he would have to use every psi power he had to escape and stay free.

He also felt no compunction about rummaging around in Steward Wulfsson's mind—there was no question that the man was an enemy, or that Gar would need every scrap of knowledge he could gain to topple the power structure of which Wulfsson was a part. He learned that Midgard was split into a dozen kingdoms, and that each king governed his own little domain as he wished—but that in practice, he followed the policies laid down by the Council of Kings. The Council ruled all year round, so the kings had to leave the day-to-day running of their kingdoms to their barons while they themselves lived in the capital. The barons, in turn, divided their holdings into twenty farms, each run by a steward.

Once a year, all the barons gathered in the capital for the Allthing, a legislative body that established policies for the Council to execute during the next year, and decided legal cases between noblemen.

Gar was amazed that there was even that much division of power, and wondered how it came to be—but Wulfsson's mind seemed to be curiously empty of history, and historically empty of curiousity.

His concussion healed quickly, but it still took days—and during those days, Gar saw sights he would never forget. Overseers prodded him whenever he didn't move fast enough to please them, which happened whenever they were bored. He talked back once, and a dozen overseers descended on him to beat him with sticks and iron-shod prods; reading their minds as he tried to block their blows, Gar realized they had been waiting for the new slave to try to stand up for himself.

Later in the day, he saw a man whipped for refusing to beat

a woman when the overseers commanded it. That evening, Kawsa ordered Gar to take a load of wood up to the steward's house, and Gar saw that the house staff, old male slaves and middle-aged women, were all hopeless, apathetic people who had only one emotion left—fear. The table servants had decent clothing; everyone else wore the same rags as the field hands.

By the end of the week, Gar decided he'd seen enough to be sure this regime had to be torn down, and had a notion that he himself would sponsor a tribunal for crimes committed under its aegis. He tested his powers, first on the weeds he was hoeing, and when the first yanked itself out of the ground, he felt a soaring jubilation. A few minutes later, he thought sleepy thoughts at Kawsa, and was rewarded with a series of yawns. That evening, when a skinny old man had to wrestle an armload of wood up to the steward's house, Gar pushed the wood with his mind, and saw the man straighten in surprise, then walk with a lighter step all the way to the back door. Gar smiled, knowing his range might not be as far as it had been, but was definitely far enough. He searched Kawsa's memories and found where his pack had been stored.

After dark, he tested his dexterity by thinking a kink into a particular tube in Kawsa's anatomy, and was rewarded by hearing a curse from the hayloft across the yard. There was also the sound of a slap, unfortunately, but only one, and a few minutes later, Kawsa came storming out of the barn, face red with fury. The woman who had been his night's choice came out soon after, dazed by her escape.

Gar lay on his pallet, tense with excitement and anticipation. His brain was healed, and he was ready.

The planet had three moons, though none was as bright as Terra's. When all three were in the sky together, they gave quite a bit of light indeed. Gar had already pegged the hour of the first one's rising, and slipped out in the full darkness of early night, while only the stars held the sky. The overseer on watch wasn't Kawsa, unfortunately, but Gar had his grudges with all of them by now, so any one would do. As the man crossed the barnyard, Gar willed him to look away from the shadow where the giant crouched, then thought of sleep, of the softness of a bed, of its warmth and coziness, of how wonderful it would feel to nod off. . . .

He jerked his head upright; it had been a long day, and his spell was working on himself. But it worked on the overseer, too; the man paused to yawn, then leaned against the side of the barracks. He yawned again and again; his head nodded, then jerked upright, his eyes blinking; but he yawned yet again, nodded some more, then slipped to the ground, not even waking enough to notice he had fallen.

Gar stepped over to take the man's cloak, hat, and prod. It wasn't much of a weapon, but it would have to do. Then he slipped into the shadows, going from outbuilding to outbuilding until he was catfooting past the steward's house. He stopped to take his pack from the toolshed, then crept onward.

When he came to the road, he paused. He had never been out this way before; the slaves always went to the fields behind the house, and Gar had a vague notion the crops across the road belonged to someone else. He called to mind the photo-map he had studied in orbit, remembered where the sun rose, and turned to his right, following the road to the east, hunched over under the cloak, tapping with the staff as though he were an old man, trying to look no taller than five and a half feet.

It almost worked. But as he passed the next farmhouse, a voice out of the night snapped, "Who goes there?"

"It's a slave!" someone shouted from the other side of the road. "A big one, trying to hide his inches!"

Then they hit him, half a dozen at least, furious blows of iron-shod prods, shouting in anger.

This time, though, Gar was ready for them. He set a bubble of mental force around himself; it wasn't strong enough to stop the blows, but it slowed them enough so that their hurt was minor, and so that Gar could block some, then return them with harder blows of his own. He parried an overhand blow, kicked the man in the stomach, whirled around and jumped high to kick another man in the chest and struck downward to crack a third over the head. As he landed, though, a blow from behind made his head ring; he fell to his knees, groping frantically for the man's mind, lashing out with the outrage and anger of a week, only a week. . . .

He heard the strangled cry even as he pushed himself to his feet. He stepped over the body toward the lone overseer who still stood, backing away from him, the whites showing all around his eyes in terror, shouting, "What did you do to him? What did you do?"

Gar reached out for the man, who turned and ran. Gar thought of stumbling, toes catching against the opposite ankle, and the man went down in a tangle. Before he could even cry out for help, Gar let a burst of illumination explode in the man's mind and savored his lapse into unconsciousness. Then he took the man's sword and hid it under his own cloak.

Lamps were lighting up in the farmhouse, and voices were calling in alarm. Gar stepped back into the shadows and thought very intensely into the mind of each man who was still alive—five out of six wasn't bad. A few minutes later, he relaxed, then slipped away to find a brook he could wade. The men would wake, he knew, and all tell the same story of the bear who had come out of the night and fought in eerie silence, striking down overseer after overseer—and if one had mysteriously died without a mark on him, well, no one could be surprised that he had died of sheer fright.

For himself, Gar wouldn't mourn the man. It was a week for firsts in his life—he felt not the slightest hint of remorse.

.

3

Alea was just managing to begin to drowse when a crow
of triumph jolted her awake, and the tree shook. She
grabbed at the limb to her right in a panic, then remembered
that she had tied herself to the trunk and couldn't fall.

"Come down, my pretty!" a hoarse voice called, and the
tree shook again.

Looking down, Alea saw two boys standing by the trunk
and joining their strength to shake it.

"Come down and play!" one of them called. "Rokir and I
are tired of our own games!"

Their games hadn't been much fun, from the look of
them. They were gaunt from short rations and hollow-eyed
from lack of sleep.

"Pretty legs, Jorak!" Rokir said. "How would they feel?"

His voice broke on the last word. Judging by the sound
and by their pimples, they weren't very far into adolescence.
Alea tucked her skirts tight to hide her legs from below, trying to ignore the panic that hammered in her breast as she

examined them more closely. As ordinary boys, they would have seemed well-proportioned and muscular, but as young giants, they were gangly and scrawny—and giants they were, for their heads reached above the branch she had had to jump to catch on her way up. That made them eight feet tall or more, definitely giants, but with a foot or two of growth yet to come.

"Pretty indeed!" Rokir answered. "I'll touch and see!" He swung himself up on a limb—and it broke, spilling him to the ground.

Jorak guffawed. "You can't go climbing as you used to, Rokir! It takes grandfathers of trees to hold us now!"

"All right, so I've a lot to learn." Rokir scrambled to his feet, red-faced. "So have you, Jorak!"

They hadn't been raised as giants, then, for if they had, they would have known what size of trees they could climb, and which were too small for their weight. That meant they were Midgarders, boys who had been cast out of their villages for being too tall, obviously on their way to becoming giants. In spite of her fright, Alea felt a rush of sympathy for them, even tenderness, for she was twice their age at least, and had just learned what they had learned—that the self-righteousness of the Midgarders hid an unbelievable intensity of cruelty. She wished she couldn't believe it.

Then the boys shook the tree again. She hugged the branch to hold herself upright, but her skirts fell loose once more. Rokir whistled with an admiration that held a mocking echo, Jorak leered up at her, and the sympathy drowned under a flood of fear. Alea knew the sound, knew the expression, and was determined never to let a man catch her again, even if he was a fuzz-cheeked boy.

An eight-foot-tall, three-hundred-fifty-pound boy.

"Come down, pretty!" Jorak called. "Or I'll shake you down!"

"You?" Rokir scoffed. "You wouldn't know what to do with her if you had her!"

"Just what I've done before!" But Jorak's voice struck an echo of uncertainty. "What would you know about it anyway, pie-face?"

"I'll show you, as soon as she falls into our arms!" Rokir said with some heat—too much heat, Alea thought; it struck a false note.

Then the tree lashed about so wildly that Alea cried out, hugging the limb to her right, afraid the trunk would snap—but it didn't. She thought frantically. If they had to egg each other on with jibes and insults, that meant they were really reluctant to try to grapple her. . . .

"Do it like a whip!" Jorak called. "One . . . two . . . three. . . ."

The tree abruptly lashed back, breaking Alea's hold and spilling her off the limb. She cried out in panic, a cry that was choked off as her rope caught her with a painful pinch on the stomach. Her makeshift staff fell clattering, and its tether jerked painfully against her wrist. She dangled, kicking and flailing, trying desperately to get back on her perch.

"She tied herself on!" Jorak called in disappointment. "But what a pretty fruit she makes, doesn't she, Rokir?"

"She does that." Rokir was working hard to sound gloating, as he'd probably heard older boys do. "Let's pluck that tasty plum!"

"How, if the branches won't hold us?" Jorak said, then brightened. "Come to think of it, she's not all that high up! Give me a boost, Jorak, and I'll have her down!"

Alea pulled her staff up quickly, before they could think to pull on it. She held it in both hands, ready to strike and wishing she'd learned how to do it right.

"So, she'll give us a drubbing!" Rokir hooted. "Not much good that'll do her! Come on, Jorak, make a step."

"Wish I'd thought of it first." By his tone, Jorak was glad he hadn't. He cupped his hands, and Rokir stepped into them, steadied himself on a limb, and climbed up to Jorak's shoulders, where he reached up and snatched at Alea's ankle. She jerked it out of reach and chopped at his knuckles with her staff. He yanked his hand out of the way in the nick of time, grinning. "So our plum has a thorny stem! But you can't hit me when you're swinging about like that, pretty plumkin!"

The rope was biting into Alea's midriff so hard she could scarcely breathe, but the thought of falling into the boys' hands galvanized her with fear. "I'll learn," she promised Rokir.

"It talks!" Rokir crowed. "Did you hear that, Jorak?"

"I heard," Jorak grunted. "Hurry up and get her down! I can't take your weight much longer!"

"Bear up," Rokir told him. "Life's gone sour, so I need something sweet."

Alea's thoughts raced. Their big talk showed that they feared sex as they desired it, shying from the unknown as much as craving the ecstasy promised by the gossip of the older boys. If they hadn't been hiding such reluctance, she probably would have been their victim already, even though she was high above them and armed with her staff. If they were still virgins, and as filled with misgivings as with eagerness, she should be able to talk them out of it.

"There's no fun in taking what's not given," she told the boys. "I've seen it, and I know."

"Seen it?" The boys stared, and she could see in their eyes that they were wondering if she had watched, or been part of it.

"Well, unless you enjoy hearing people scream," Alea told them. "If you're the kind of boy who thinks it's fun to torture little furry animals, maybe you would think it's fun." She shuddered as she said it, remembering.

Rokir jumped down, wide-eyed and taken aback. Jorak groaned with relief, rubbing his shoulders, then grinned up at Alea. "Come on! You know you'd love it! All women do!"

"No we don't," Alea said sharply—or as sharply as she could with the rope digging into her. She caught as much of a breath as she could and told him, "Women hate being forced, b . . . young man. If we could get revenge on a man, we would—the very worst revenge we could take, I promise you!"

She said it with such vehemence that both boys recoiled. Jorak's eyes wide with surprise and apprehension. "But . . . but the big boys said . . ."

"They said what they thought others expected to hear!" Alea snapped. "Have you asked a woman? Believe me, even if we're willing, there are precious few men who are good enough lovers to make it much of a pleasure to us!"

"You're lying!" Rokir protested. "Everyone knows it's fun, that the pleasure just happens!"

"It takes patience and skill," Alea contradicted, "and that means years of learning—not that I'd have a chance to know!"

The bitterness in her voice surprised even herself—not that it should have. That bitterness made the boys recoil again, though, wide-eyed and with guilt shadowing their faces.

Alea throttled back her anger—if they could feel badly about what they'd tried to do, they were good boys underneath. If she could reach that goodness . . .

"It's true, lads," she said, more gently. "Ask any woman. In fact, ask as many women as you can. You might do it well when you get the chance, that way."

The boys glanced at each other, then looked away. Rokir sent a quick look at Alea, but couldn't hold it and looked down at his toes.

"You can come down, then," Jorak said gruffly. "We won't hurt you."

"Come down?" Alea couldn't help smiling. "That'll take a bit of work. Turn away, please."

Jorak frowned. "Why?"

"Because I'm going to have to kick high to get a leg over that branch, if I'm going to get back up on it—and I have to, I can't just untie myself while I'm hanging."

The glint came back into Rokir's eye, though it was faint. "Why should we turn away for that?"

"Would you want me looking up at you if you didn't have your leggins on?" Alea asked, and at the looks of horror and embarrassment that crossed their faces, "No, I thought not. Be good lads, now, and turn away for a minute or two."

Shame-faced, they shuffled around to face away from the tree.

Alea kicked high and managed to get a leg back up on the limb—she'd been hanging right next to it, after all. She managed to swing herself up, blessing her tomboy days, and clawed her way up the trunk until she was sitting again. She hugged the trunk, arms tense while the rest of her went limp with relief.

But she couldn't afford to let the boys see her weakness. She pulled herself together, swung both feet up on the limb, and tucked her skirts around her. "All right, you can turn back now."

They turned, then stared. "But you're still up there!"

"I'll come down when I'm feeling strong enough," Alea told them. "Hanging from a tree wasn't the worst fright I've ever had, but it was bad enough."

"Why?" Rokir frowned, really not understanding.

"Because the rope could have broken, or the knot could have worked loose," Alea said, her tone tart, "and you two ungainly louts might not have been able to catch me!" Worse, they might have.

They winced at the rebuke, and she was instantly sorry. "I don't really mean to be sharp, lads." She mustn't call them boys, not when they were beginning to think they were men. "It's just that you gave me a bad scare."

"I know," Jorak said, surly but looking at the ground.

"You can come down," Rokir told her. "We'll be good."

"I will, lads, when my heart slows down." Alea knew that she would have to take the chance—you have to keep promises made to children, or they lose all faith in other people. The thought gave her a glow of strength. She was an adult, after all, and if they'd lived in the same village and she'd been their neighbor, these boys might have been put in her care now and again, only a year or two ago. They were children still, no matter their size. Boys that age still looked to their mothers for reassurance, though they didn't like to admit it, and therefore to most older women, too—at least, if they'd had good mothers, and she guessed these two had. It must have been a cruel wrench indeed to have their own parents turn them out of the house—though she suspected the village had turned them out and shouted down the mothers' weeping. "Are you both from the same village, lads?"

"Huh?" Jorak asked, surprised by the change of topic.

Rokir, quicker to catch up, said, "No. We never met until a week ago."

"Odd how strangers can become friends so quickly, isn't it?" Alea asked, and added mentally, *Especially when they're lost and lonely, feeling their lives are ended.* "I fled my village only two days ago."

"Fled?" The boys stared, astounded that anyone could actually *want* to leave home.

"Ran away, yes." Alea's tone hardened again. "My parents died, and no boy had come courting because I was too tall. The baron's man told the Council to take my parents' house and lands and goods and give them to someone else, and give them me into the bargain."

A sick look crept over the boys' faces. They'd seen such things happen before and joined in the vindictive cries that the victim deserved it, for being suspiciously like a giant or a dwarf. It didn't look so right and just now, though.

Rokir tried for bravado. "At least they didn't cast you out for being a giant!"

"I'd rather they had," Alea said, her tone grim. "Do you have any idea what people do to slaves? Or try to—especially women."

The boys winced and looked at the ground, sullen again. They had heard, well enough. Jorak muttered, "There are good masters."

"There are," Alea agreed. "Mine weren't among them. The baron's man gave me to a family that had always hated my parents."

Rokir shuddered at that, and Jorak grudgingly admitted, "No wonder you ran."

"No wonder," Alea echoed grimly.

"You can come down, miss," Rokir told her. "We wouldn't hurt someone who's been through as bad as we have."

"At least you realize it would have been hurting." Alea frowned at a sudden doubt. "You do realize that, don't you?"

"I've heard screams from houses where they kept slaves," Rokir admitted. "I should have guessed."

"We didn't know you'd been a slave." Jorak's eyes were still downcast. "Thought you were one of them wild women they talk about."

"Wild or not, it would have hurt just the same." Alea still eyed them warily. "Do you promise?"

"Cross my heart." Jorak actually drew an X over the left side of his chest.

Alea's heart went out to them in spite of what they'd tried to do—or tried to work themselves into doing. They were still children inside, after all, and children who had been heart-hurt very badly. But they were growing up fast.

She had to help them grow up right. "Very well, I'll come down. Turn your backs again."

The boys did, and Alea climbed down, staff still dangling from her wrist—she wasn't about to let it go. She dropped from the lowest limb. "All right, you can look."

The boys turned around as she slipped the loop off her wrist and leaned on the staff to look up at them. Heavens, they seemed huge! Almost two feet taller than she was, and already hulking with muscle. "You'll have to learn to stand very straight," she said automatically. "You don't want to grow up hunching over."

The boys straightened up on the instant, but Jorak frowned. "Who made you our mother?"

Something in Alea cringed at the thought, but she answered gamely, "It's just that I've been down the road ahead of you, my lad. A girl as tall as I am starts hunching her shoulders forward and stooping a bit, so people don't see how high she stands. My mother stopped me from that, or I'd be a hunchback by now. Stand straight! Stand tall! Be proud of your inches!"

"Proud?" Jorak stared, confounded.

"Proud!" Alea declared. "Half the reason they threw you out was jealousy, you know, and the other half was fear. They wished they could be as tall as you, and were afraid what you might do to your enemies when you were grown. What you are is grand, and don't ever let anyone tell you otherwise!"

"She speaks truth," rumbled a deep voice behind her. "I've never heard a Midgarder speak so honestly."

Alea whirled in alarm and stared up—and up, and up. She'd thought the boys were huge, but she hadn't known what size was. The giant towered four feet above her head and was so wide he seemed to fill the whole world. He wore the same tunic and leggins as the men of Midgard, with leather armor sewn with rings and plates. But there was so much of it! She wondered dizzily how many cows had gone to make his hauberk, how many sheep had been shorn to make his clothes.

"Nay, don't be frightened, lass," the giant said, his voice oddly gentle. "We'll not hurt you."

We? Alea glanced around him and saw half a dozen more, one or two even bigger than he! But the strands of gray in his hair showed him to be the oldest and most experienced, so it was he who spoke for them all.

Alea stood her ground, squaring her shoulders and lifting her chin in defiance so the giants wouldn't see the fear inside her. If Midgard women went to battle, she might have seen one of these behemoths before, but since they only went as nurses, half a mile behind the fighting, she never had.

"I'd best talk to her, Gorkin," a lighter rumble of a voice said, and a shorter giant stepped up beside the leader. Alea took in the long hair flowing out from beneath the iron cap, the huge steel cups sewn to the leather of her armor, and realized with a shock that this second giant was a woman! She was scandalized—how dare the giants risk their women in battle? But hard on its heels came envy—this huge woman could share in the glory of war and had been trained to face its dangers. Most importantly of all, she could defend herself against attack! Alea wished sorely for some of that training now, when she had to face the world alone.

"Aye, speak with her, Morag," Gorkin agreed, and the giant woman actually smiled with sympathy as she looked down at Alea.

"What do you hear in the wasteland, lass?" Then she lifted her gaze to Rokir and Jorak. "And what do they?"

Alea glanced back and saw the boys huddling together. Tall they might be, but nowhere nearly as tall or massive as these grown giants. She could see that all the nursery tales they'd been told of horrible titans crunching on children's bones, and the horror stories they'd heard from returning soldiers about the savagery and cruelty of the Jotuns, were storming their minds.

"Come, lads, it's not wartime, and we won't hurt you," the giant woman said kindly. "You're more our kind than theirs now, anyway."

The boys stared wide-eyed, horrified at the idea.

"They've told you lies about us, haven't they?"

"A rain of lies," Alea said, her voice hard.

All the giants glanced at her with approval. Then Morag turned back to Jorak and Rokir. "Were you cast out, then?"

"We . . . we were," Jorak stammered.

"The cruelty of it, casting out their own children!" Morag let her anger show, but the boys cringed back, and she smoothed her face.

Gorkin and the others didn't, though.

"We're one of many patrols who scour this no-man's-land watching for Midgarder raiders and for outcasts like yourselves." Morag glanced at Alea as she said it, including her in the term. "If you're big enough, we take you home to grow up among your own kind."

"But we're not . . ." Rokir caught himself and gulped, his eyes filling.

"Nay, you are," Morag said, all sympathy. "How old are you? Thirteen? Fourteen? You've a great deal of growing before you, my lads, and you're giants for sure—but I warrant you'll find us kinder than your own folk." She spread her arms. "Come to us, then, and you'll find you've a home once more!"

The boys stared, wavering.

Alea realized they needed a bit of encouragement. She let the envy show in her voice. "You lucky, lucky lads! A real home and a kind one, and you young enough to grow into it! Oh, if I had your chance, I'd sip every drop of it!"

That was all they needed, approval from a Midgarder. They both stumbled forward into Morag's arms and let themselves lean against her. She folded her arms about them, saying, "Now, then, the nightmare's over, you've waked into a hug, and you'll always have folk who care about you for the rest of your lives!" She went on with other soothing murmurs, and little by little, the boys let themselves go limp. Alea heard a choking gasp from one, and knew they were letting the tears brim over as the fright and the horror sank down.

She looked up at Gorkin, her face hard, guarded. "Did I guess right? Is there no such chance for me?"

Gorkin's gaze was all pity as he shook his head. "No, lass, I'm afraid you guessed right. How old are you? Twenty-five? Thirty?"

"Twenty-eight," Alea said through stiff lips.

"Aye, that's what I feared," Gorkin said sadly. "You've grown all you're likely to, and you'll never be big enough to call a Jotun. You're only a Midgarder to us, lass, like all the others."

"But the Midgarders made me a slave because I was too big to be one of them!" Alea cried. "They beat me for every mistake and . . . and did worse things to me! I tried to submit, I tried not to protest or fight back, but I couldn't help myself, and they beat me all the harder for it. I tried to accept my fate, to submit to the lot the Norns had spun me, to give myself to the weird that had found me, but I couldn't help my anger at the injustice of it! I fled, I escaped, I ran, and I'm sure they're on my trail with their hounds and their whips! Please, can't you hide me?"

Morag's face reflected every ounce of Alea's pain, but she only said to the boys, quite severely, "Don't you ever treat a woman like that! Giant, Midgarder, or dwarf, no lass should ever have to fear a man's attentions! I'd be ashamed of you forever if you did!"

They both gulped and looked up wide-eyed, shaking their heads, but Jorak gave a guilty glance at Alea. She seethed, and the anger and hurt almost made her blurt out what they had tried to do—but they'd backed off when she rebuked them, and she couldn't find it in her heart to take away from them the sanctuary for which she herself longed. She only said to Gorkin, "It's not right!"

"It is not your weird," he countered. "It doesn't find you, lass—you find it. You must read your weird, and if it's not to be a meek slave among the Midgarders, then that's not what the Norns have spun for you. You were right to run—but we're not your weird either. You must keep seeking until you find it."

"But what if the Midgarders find me first?"

"Then escape again, and again and again as long as there's breath in your body," Gorkin told her. "Never give in, never give up!"

"Where am I to go?" Alea cried, near tears. "The real people make me their slave and their whore, and you won't take me in! Where could I go?"

"We are real people, too." Gorkin's voice was very gentle again. He smiled at her shocked stare. "Aye, that surprises you, doesn't it? But there's not a giant alive whose grandmother or grandfather or ancestor somewhere wasn't a Midgarder, lass, an ordinary person like any of them. How could their children be any less real? Nay, we have sorrows and joys like any of you, angers and delights, loves and hates, all of them, and we worship the same gods as the Midgarders and try to hold back the worst of our angers and hatreds. Oh, we're real people too, right enough."

Alea could only stare, stunned by the revelation. All the horror stories of her childhood seemed to echo inside her head, all lies, lies!

"But we can't take you in, you see," Gorkin said sadly. "You've said yourself that they didn't cast you out—that you ran away, as you should have. You can see, though, that we can't be sure you're not a spy, that you might not slay your host in her bed and creep out to open the gates at night and let in a host of Midgarders to slay us all." He raised a palm to forestall her protest. "No, I don't accuse you of that, and I don't really believe it for a second—but I can't be sure, you see, and it's possible."

Alea couldn't hold the tears in any longer; they began to trickle down her cheeks.

"Och, I'm sorry, lass," Morag said, as though her heart were breaking. "If you'd been born to a pair of us, it would have been a different matter, but they're the only small folk we can allow among us. If we let more Midgarders in, the day would come when there would be more of them than there would be of us—and you may be sure there would be spies among them. Oh, one or two of your folk might come among us and be glad and grateful, but if there were a hundred, the old fear and hatred of their cradle-songs and granny-stories would come boiling up, and we'd find ourselves fighting for our lives in our own towns. Nay, much though it grieves me, we can't take you in!"

"We can wish you well, though," Gorkin said, as kindly as he could. "Here, we can leave you drink, at least." He took his aleskin from his belt and laid it on the road, then straightened and turned away. "Fare you well—and may the gods smile on you."

"Fare you well." Morag's voice was thick with tears. "Here, take something to defend yourself!" She laid her belt knife by the wallet and aleskin, then turned away too, arms still around Jorak and Rokir. Jorak looked back, eyes swollen. "Goodbye— and thank you. I wish I could stay to keep you company, but I can't, if I'm going with them."

"No, you go!" Alea cried, though the tears flowed freely now. "I'd hate myself forever if you lost your true chance because of my selfishness! Go, Jorak, and the gods smile on you!"

She turned away then, and managed to hold back the worst until a glance over her shoulder showed her that the giants had gone out of sight through the trees. Then she dropped down on the road and wept and wept, wondering if her heart would break—and wishing that it would.

4

Magnus had to suppress the impulse to project a call to Herkimer on radio frequency out of sheer loneliness. If it hadn't been for the road, he'd have found it hard to believe there were people on this planet, never mind the photographs he'd seen from orbit. Even then, the road might have been only an animal track, if it hadn't been ten feet wide. It seemed unusually broad for a medieval road until Magnus remembered that giants might have laid it out. That gave him a strange chill down his spine. He found himself trying to believe giants were only fairy tales.

Well, true enough, these weren't forty feet tall, and no human being could hide in their beer steins or spend the night in one of their gloves—but they were big enough to call giants. From what Magnus had seen in the orbital shots, though, this buffer zone between Midgard and the giants' country might very well have had ordinary-sized people as well as giants walking about. It was barren enough, Heaven knew—a broad plain with knee-high grass, and a line of trees to his left that presumably shaded a watercourse. But there was genuine forest to his right; it seemed that the road had been built along some sort of natural boundary.

Then some people came around the bend, half a dozen in armor and with battle axes at their hips, with two adolescents along. Magnus was surprised that the bend was so close—it had looked much farther away, but the people made it seem much nearer.

Then he realized that it wasn't the bend that was so close, it was the people who were so tall.

He stopped and stared, eyes wider and wider as the strangers came nearer and nearer. For the first time since his adolescent growth spurt, he found himself looking up at someone—up higher and higher. As they came close, their sheer size overwhelmed him—not just their height, though he only came up to the chest of the shortest grownup, and was still a head shorter than the boys. It was their mass that made him feel so small, for each of the grown giants was easily twice as broad in the shoulder and hip as Magnus was. Their legs were virtual tree trunks, and their arms would have shamed a gorilla.

They weren't looking any more friendly than that gorilla, either. The oldest man—at least, to judge by the gray in his hair—rested his hand on the haft of his axe and demanded, "Who are you, Midgarder? And why are you here?"

"My name is Gar Pike," Magnus said, trying to imitate their accent.

The leader couldn't help it; his face quirked into a smile. "Your parents didn't really name you that!"

They hadn't, so Gar decided on belligerence. "And what's wrong with my name, I'd like to know?"

"Why, a gar pike is a big fish, and you're scarcely a minnow!" the leader said.

It was the first time in fifteen years that anyone had called Gar small. He found he didn't like it, especially since it was true, given the present company. "All right, Gar is short for Edgar, and Pike has been a family name for centuries." He carefully didn't say whose.

"Well enough, and pardon my rudeness," the leader said gruffly. "I am called Gorkin. Why have you come to this no-one's-land, Gar Pike?"

For a moment, Gar stood amazed by the giant's courtesy—after all, it was himself who was the intruder. But he pulled himself together and answered, "I've come from far away, and the . . ." What had the giant called him? Midgarder, that was it! ". . . the Midgarders enslaved me. They said I was too tall, too close to being a giant." He managed a sour smile. "They seem to have been mistaken."

"Not so much as you might think," Gorkin said. "We've children who grow no bigger than you, some even shorter. But you're no child of ours, and far too small to become one of us." He clapped one of the boys on the shoulder. "Jorak, now, he's only fourteen, and already taller than you by a head. He's due to grow two feet more at least, and fill out to a proper size—but how old are you, foreigner? Thirty, if you're a day!"

"Well, I'm more than a day, that's true," Gar said slowly, "and you guessed well. I'm thirty-one."

"Two in one day!" the woman beside Gorkin said—and Gar was amazed to realize she was indeed a woman. But her face was more finely featured than Gorkin's, her hair flowed down around her shoulders, and her armor bore two huge bulges that Gar found not at all stimulating. He did wonder who the other of the "two in one day" was—and what.

Gorkin shook his head sadly. "We can't take you in, foreigner. For all we know, you might be spying for the Midgarders—and you've surely grown as much as you're going to, at your age. Why, you're almost small enough to *be* a Midgarder, and certainly as skinny. Besides, if you're like the rest of your kind, you've been raised to hate and fear giants, and you're too old to have a change of heart there."

Both boys glanced up at him, then looked away, sheepish and guilty.

"They were both raised as Midgarders," Gorkin explained, "but they're young enough to learn they've had lies poured into their ears from their cradles."

"But I never saw this man before, not in my village or anywhere in the barony!" Jorak protested.

"Nor me," Rokir said, "and my barony was one over from his."

"His accent is strange," the woman pointed out.

"It is that," Gorkin admitted. "Might be you're from far away indeed, foreigner."

"Yes, and you believe it, Gorkin," the woman said, "or you'd be calling him 'stranger,' not 'foreigner.' "

"Peace, good Morag," Gorkin grumbled. "What I believe of him and how I may treat him have to be two different things. You know the law."

"Yes, and know there's reason behind it," Morag sighed. She said to Gar, "I regret it, foreigner, but we can't risk a spy coming into our town to creep out and let a Midgard army in. Besides, if we took you, we'd have to take that woman we just left on the road, too, and the next one we found, and the next and the next. First thing, there'd be more Midgarders than giants, and we'd have to flee our own homes."

"I understand, I understand." Gar stood amazed at the kindness of these people, who actually apologized for not giving hospitality to a potential enemy!

"You go on back to Midgard, and tell them the giants threw you out," Gorkin said gruffly. "Likely they'll find you a place among them then."

"Yes, as a slave," Jorak said darkly.

"Might be, might be," Gorkin agreed heavily. "Still, that's better than wandering the wild lands with everyone's spear against you, isn't it?"

"No!" both boys said together, and Gorkin looked down at them, amazed.

"They're right," Gar said. "I've seen what slaves go through in Midgard. I was lucky to escape. Better to have everyone's sword against me in the wild. After all, out here, I'm allowed to fight back."

"Is it so bad as that?" Gorkin asked, shaken, then shook his head in sorrow and anger. "And they call themselves the only human folk, these Midgarders!" He look down at Gar, deeply troubled. "We'll bid you farewell, then, foreigner, and wish you well, but that's all we can do."

"Why, fare you well too, then," Gar said, "and may your gods smile upon you."

The giants all stared at him in surprise. Then Gorkin broke into a smile. "A Midgarder wishing a blessing on us! Might be hope for this world yet! Well, stranger, may all your gods smile on you, too!"

They went past, and some turned back to wave. Gar returned the wave, staring after them, feeling numb and very unreal. He had to remind himself that he hadn't just lived through a dream, that these were genuine people who had talked to him, actual giants, or as close to the fairy-tale variety as anyone could ever be.

He forced himself to turn away and start walking again, in the direction from which the giants had come. Go back to Midgard? That would have been extremely foolish. Still, Gar very much wanted to do just that—go back to Midgard, and start preaching. If he were going to have a chance of ending the constant wars, he would have to gain the acceptance of all three nations. The giants had been so polite that he thought they would at least listen to any ideas he gave them, but if the Midgarders were so fanatical as to cast out their own children for growing too big, seven-foot-tall Gar was going to find it almost impossible to manage even a parley.

He reflected that Dirk Dulaine, his erstwhile companion, would have been welcome in Midgard society, and could have brought Gar in as his simpleton slave, a role Gar had played with Dirk more than once—but Dirk wasn't here, and Gar would have to find a way to the Midgarders' ears on his own.

That reminded him of good times with his friend, of shared dangers and shared glory, and of his bittersweet joy at seeing Dirk marry the woman he loved, then the poignancy of their goodbye as Gar left their planet, alone. He felt a pang of loneliness, and wished he could find love as Dirk had, but knew he was too big, too taciturn, too ominous, too homely, and too reticent.

He wondered what had happened to the cheerful outgoing teenager he used to be, then remembered the kaleidoscope of women who had used him as targets for cruelty, or to make their lovers jealous, or for social climbing. On reflection, he wasn't surprised the cheery boy had gone underground, and was more sure than ever that he would never find a mate.

The wind of alienation blew through him—he was an absurd figure, for what purpose could he have in life? He remembered his boyhood on the medieval planet of Gramarye and his leave-taking, then the aimless wandering that had led him to join SCENT, his outrage at the team's heartless manipulation of a backward planet's culture without regard to human rights, and his own decision to work for those rights among oppressed people, solo, then with Dirk, now solo again.

But he also remembered the planets he had put on the road to forms of government of their own choices, the lives he had saved that he knew about and the many, many he had probably saved but didn't know about, and felt a renewed strength to go plodding on toward old age and death. His life would serve some purpose, after all, and who knew? There might still be some bits of pleasure in it, too.

Alea dried her tears, telling herself that she had to go on, that life would somehow prove worth living. She didn't believe herself, but generations of women had drummed that idea into their daughters, and old women had told them it had proved true for them. Life had good times and bad times, and sometimes it was so bad that you couldn't believe it would ever be good again—but it would, if you could just hang on.

She sighed, braced her tree-branch staff, and pushed herself to her feet again. At least the giants had left her food and drink. She couldn't believe how kind they had been, how horribly the grown-ups had lied to her as a child!

Could they have lied about the bad times passing, too?

Alea shoved the thought to the back of her mind—it wouldn't bear thinking about. You had to go on, that was all, because if you gave up, if you just crawled into a hole and died, then life certainly couldn't ever get better, could it? No, all in all, it was worth the gamble. She decided to go on a little farther yet.

At least the giants' wallet and aleskin had strings for holding them to the belt—strings to them, but straps to her. She slung them over her shoulders and set off down the road, determined to find some place she could be happy, some place where life could have meaning. She couldn't be the only slave who had ever escaped, after all—in fact, she'd heard stories about escapees who'd fled to the northern wasteland, and never been brought back. Of course, those stories also said the runaways lived by robbing travelers, even by eating them, but considering how badly the tales had lied about the giants, there was every reason to think they'd lied about the escapees too. She decided to take a chance on the North Country.

She stopped to look at the sun and take her bearings. It was ahead of her and off to the right, still well before noon, so her road was angling toward the north anyway, and away from Midgard. She saw a bend to the left in the distance, which meant the road would turn even further toward the north. She set off, resolving to find people of her own kind if she had to walk ten years to do it.

After ten minutes, the exhaustion hit her. A dizzy spell seized her, and she stopped in the roadway, leaning on her staff and waiting for the world to steady itself, hoping it would. She realized she was worn out both emotionally and physically, for she'd been walking all night. Daylight was her time to hide and sleep, and she'd just started dozing when Jorak and Rokir had shaken her awake. She knew she should find another tree and hide for the day, but she didn't want to stay where the boys had gone crashing through the roadside brush to find her, and the Jotuns had refused her. What with their tracks and the boys', her trail was far too clear—any band of slave-hunters would see her footprints in the roadside dust, and would follow her to her tree.

The dizziness passed, and Alea forced herself to start walking again, down the middle of the road where the clay was packed hard and wouldn't show her tracks. There was a chance that the slave-hunters would find her before she found another safe tree, but it was less than the chance that the marks of her struggle with the boys, and the tracks of the giant patrol, would reveal her old hiding place. She had to find another tree large enough to hide in and a quarter mile or more from the scene of the scuffle. She watched her feet, forcing them to move until she could trust them to keep going, then looked up and was surprised to see that the bend in the road was there already.

She was even more surprised when the half-dozen Midgarders came around that bend and saw her.

Their dogs started baying and howling on the instant, and the men shouted and came running, hands out to catch her. They didn't ask her business or her name—her size alone was enough to tell them what she was, easily a head taller than any of them, so she couldn't be anything but a runaway slave. They would worry whose she was after they'd bound her. They swarmed around her.

Alea swung her staff desperately, managing to knock one man in the head and jab another in the belly before one of them chopped viciously with a cudgel, and her staff broke with a loud crack. She swung the butt of it in despair, but another man seized her wrist and a third caught her around the waist, crowing with victory. Alea screamed and kicked back.

The man's crow turned to a howl, and the hands let go of her waist. She lashed about her with the butt of her stick and kicked at the shins of the men in front of her. One went reeling, hands pressed to his head. Another fell back, hopping and howling. More hands seized her wrists and her waist, though. Then a rope whipped about her torso, pinioning her arms, and another man caught her leg. She howled in anger and horror, kicking at him, but he stepped to the side, holding the leg up.

A heavier man, with a bruise from her staff already purpling on his forehead, shouldered his way through to her and cracked a slap across her face. Alea screamed and, as the hand came back, bit at it, but the man yanked his hand aside and slammed a fist into her stomach. She doubled over in agony, struggling for the breath that wouldn't come, but he yanked her chin up and stared into her face—face to face, for he was a good foot shorter than she.

"Six and a half feet, big dark eyes, straight nose, brown hair—this is the one that ran from Karke Village, right enough," the slave-hunter said. "Back you go to your owners, woman, and harshly may they punish you."

Breath came back in a rush. Alea used it for a wordless shout and lunged at the man, lashing out with her free foot.

He cracked another slap across her face and snarled, "We can hurt worse than you, my lass!"

"We should, too," one of the other men growled. "She's given me a harsh knock, and I'll be limping for a week!"

"You're right there, Harol," the leader said with an ugly glint in his eye. "After all, we have to take her back to her village for judgement, but no one says what kind of condition she has to be in when she gets there—and she has to be taught not to run, doesn't she?"

"She does!" One of the men moistened his lips, eyes greedy. "And what's the worst hurt you can give a woman, eh?"

The others answered with a shout of agreement. Someone caught at Alea's free foot, but she screamed in terror and kicked, wrenched a wrist free, and lashed out with a fist. It connected, but the men roared and descended on her in a body. She fought desperately, afraid of death but suddenly not caring, as long as the nightmare didn't happen again.

But they were falling back away from her, something was making dull thudding sounds, and men were crying out in rage and alarm. As breath came back, Alea saw a huge man laying about with a proper quarterstaff, knocking her tormentors aside. They shouted with anger and leaped away from the madman, and she saw her chance. She scrambled to her feet and ran toward the trees.

"Catch her!" the leader bellowed.

Alea heard feet pounding behind her, but she heard something crack too, then heard the knocking of wood against wood, and the trees closed mercifully about her as she ran, gasping and sobbing, trying to find a tree big enough, a cave deep enough, anywhere to hide, to be safe.

Behind her, Gar laid about him with his staff, taking his share of knocks but dealing out five for each one he received. More importantly, though, he reached out with his thoughts and struck terror into the minds of each of the hunters. One or two had the courage to come back at him a second time, though dread was surging up from their stomachs. The rest ran, howling in sheer terror, away from Gar and from the poor woman they'd been wrestling.

"Giants!" someone shouted. "Giants!" But none seemed to remember that they'd been trained to fight the huge man.

Gar lashed out at the last two with virtual explosions of panic as his staff whirled to strike first one, then the other. They spun away, fear finally mastering them, and ran down the road, back the way they had come.

Gar stood watching them go, chest heaving with exertion, filled with the elation of victory, even if he'd had to cheat a bit—but when it was one man against half a dozen, using projective telepathy to scare them into running was fully justified. He was quite willing to let them think he was a small giant. After all, by the time they reached home, he would have grown three feet in their memories anyway.

They went around the bend in the road and were gone from his sight, and from his mind, too. Gar looked around for the woman they'd been manhandling. He didn't see her and, all things considered, he didn't blame her, either. He went on the way he'd been going, noticing where her tracks ran off the road, then where her steps began to shorten. She had run to hide in the woods—wise, under the circumstances. He hoped she was good at covering her trail, for the hunters had dogs. True, with the scare he'd given them, they might not stop running till they were home—but then again, they might. In fact, they might even try to cover up their fear with anger, and come back to take revenge on the vulnerable one.

Of course, they wouldn't try to attack her if Gar were with her, or even nearby.

He had a notion he'd have to settle for nearby—after the shock the woman had just suffered, she wouldn't be likely to trust any man again. She'd seemed unusually brave, though, fighting back every inch of the way. She hadn't caved in for a second.

Gar was surprised at the admiration he felt, and told himself he would have admired that kind of heart just as much in a man. Nonetheless, he decided to dally a while, to stroll down the road and take his time pitching camp. The woman would make an excellent ally, after all, if he could win her friendship. On every planet on which he'd landed, he had always tried to team up with a local—how else was he going to learn all the details that had developed since the last computer entry about the world? In most cases, that last datum had been entered hundreds of years before, and almost everything had changed since.

He definitely needed a local, and the woman was at least aware that he was on her side—if he could find her. In addition, if he really wanted to try to heal the wounds of this world, she might be the key to the puzzle of making peace between the three nations—dwarf, giant, and Midgarder.

He remembered how the situation had looked from the bridge of his spaceship in orbit, when he and Herkimer had been surveying the world via telephoto scanners, and he'd still been thinking of himself as Magnus. They'd watched Vikings battling giants, then dwarves battling Vikings, all in so short a period of time that Gar could only think the warfare was constant.

"So we have a land of pseudo-Teutonic Viking-type people of normal height," he'd summarized to Herkimer, "with a land of dwarves to the west and a land of giants to the east, tundra to the north and an ocean to the south."

"The Teutons seem to outnumber both other nations by a considerable margin," Herkimer pointed out, "even if we don't count their slaves."

"Rather odd to leave your biggest men at home when you go off to war," Magnus mused, "but the Teutons might figure that the big ones would be apt to desert to the giants—not surprising, considering how they're treated at home. By the way, Herkimer, what was the name of this planet? Other than Corona Gamma Four, that is."

"The records of the plans for the original expedition are more scanty than usual," the computer told him, "but they do include the information that the intended local name for the planet was Siegfried."

"So somebody was planning on the Teutonic theme from the beginning," Magnus said. "Were they planning on breeding three separate sub-races, or was that an accident?"

"It could hardly have been an accident, Magnus," Herkimer reproved. "The Terran government insisted on very stringent safety precautions for colonial expeditions, including having a gene pool large enough to prevent inbreeding."

"Yes, even private expeditions had to pay lip service to the regulations, at least," Magnus agreed. "If they didn't have enough colonists, they had to bring frozen sperm and ova— but once they had landed on a new planet, there was no one to guarantee they would use what they had brought."

"Surely you don't think the original colonists actually planned this state of affairs!"

"No, I think it far more likely that they had a horrible accident," Magnus said, "something that killed off half the colonists or wiped out the gene bank—or that in spite of their precautions, genes linked up to cause unusual effects."

He thought of his home planet, whose original colonists had contained an extremely high proportion of latent telepaths and other kinds of latent espers, though nobody had realized it at the time. Because of that, their descendants had more operant psi talents than all the rest of the Terran Sphere combined.

Magnus was proof of that himself. "Nature has strange

ways of achieving remarkable surprises, and you can't always foresee every problem. I'm voting for no malice intended by the original colonists, just inbreeding reinforcing genetic drift. After all, it makes sense that if a few giants were born, they'd want to marry other giants."

"And dwarves would wish to marry other dwarves," Herkimer agreed. "But why would they seek out separate territories?"

"That, I leave to normal human cussedness," Magnus said.

Now, Gar reflected that he had guessed more rightly than he knew, in using the word "cussedness." Maybe "perversity" would be more fitting—but either way, if he really wanted to bring peace to this world, he needed a local ally, and Gar thought he might be able to forge an alliance with the woman he'd rescued—if he could win her confidence enough to talk with her. She would be a valuable information source and a possible peacemaker—but even if she weren't, she was a person who needed help. He didn't usually make a practice of adopting waifs and strays, but he had a notion this one needed a friend more than most.

Besides, he needed a friend, too—preferably one whose brain wasn't made of silicon.

From her tracks, their direction, and the rate at which she'd been going plus the panic that had impelled her, Gar estimated where she would have gone to ground. He strolled along the road for another fifteen minutes, then stopped and looked around as though judging the place's fitness for a campsite.

In reality, of course, he was listening with his mind.

5

There. He could hear her thoughts, quite loudly and clearly—but only surface thoughts. *Monster's looking for me hurt me have to freeze so he won't see me be ready to run if he does.* Then a sudden undercurrent of doubt: *Why'd he help me?* But suspicion overwhelmed it in an instant: *Wants me for himself.*

She was watching from somewhere, absolutely still and watching him, trying not to breathe, ready to run at the slightest hint of pursuit—but under her tension, Magnus could feel an utter bone-weariness and a massive dejection, an impulse to just sit down and die.

He couldn't let that happen, of course, and was absolutely determined not to give it a chance. He started walking again, went on another hundred feet, then stepped off the road. He could feel the sharpness of her burst of panic, but also the caution that went with it and held her frozen in place, terrified at the thought of making a sound or a movement that might attract his attention. Deliberately not looking in her direction, Magnus stopped in the center of a small clearing and surveyed it. Fifty feet of leaves and underbrush hid him from the road, but the open space was wide enough to light a fire safely. He nodded and started searching for rocks, picking up one in each hand and carrying them to the center of the clearing to build a fire ring.

When the ring was made and the plants and dead leaves cleared from it, he found the driest sticks he could and kindled a fire. All the while he was aware of the woman's thoughts, wary and watchful, wondering what he was doing, testing his every movement for menace, trying to puzzle out whatever trap he was laying for her. She hadn't yet thought of the trap called friendship, which could hold her more surely than any snare.

Magnus made a frame of green branches, notched one to make a pothook, took the little kettle out of his pack, filled it with water from his skin canteen, and hung it over the fire. Then he took out two tin mugs with wooden handles, crumbled tea leaves into each, and waited for the water to boil.

While he waited, he took out bread and cheese and slowly, carefully cut his slices and laid a thick slab of cheese on the bread. He ate slowly, too, savoring each morsel, and feeling the answering pang of hunger in the watching woman. He guessed she'd had very little to eat in the last few days.

The water boiled, and Gar poured some into each mug, then took out salt beef and dried vegetables to add to the water. He stirred it and waited, sipping first from the one mug, then the other. The fragrance of the tea rose into the morning, strange to the woman, but to judge by her thoughts, very enticing. Soon the aroma of the stew reached her, too, and the pang of hunger became a stab.

Now Gar caught sight of her out of the corner of his eye. She was crouching behind a bush, peering through a gap in the leaves. Giving no sign that he'd seen her, Gar cut a thick slice of cheese and broke off some bread, then rose and went around the fire, put the wooden platter on a rock with a mug of sweetened tea beside it, and went back to his own place some ten feet away.

Alea had run as fast as she could, too frightened to consider whether the stranger was a friend or an enemy. She had nearly panicked again when she saw him coming her way, but the childhood fables of the wisdom of the rabbit had made her freeze where she hid. She had watched him, ready to bolt in an instant, and had felt great relief when he settled down to his campfire. But the sight of the bread and cheese had started hunger gnawing at her belly, reminding her that she'd eaten only handfuls of berries and a few raw roots since she'd finished the bread she'd taken when she ran away, three days before. Then the delicious scent of whatever it was in those cups had almost undone her, almost pushed her to go to him and beg a morsel—but fear held her in place. After all, it was a strange smell, and who knew what he had put in those cups? But she had watched him drink out of first the one, then the other, and had decided that whatever it was, it wouldn't hurt her.

Also, the message was clear—*Come share a cup with me, my fair!*—and when she realized it meant he knew she was watching, she had almost run away. But her fear had begun to slacken, for she had never seen a slave-hunter who tried to entice rather than pursue. Curiosity roused as strongly as her hunger, and held her watching until the aroma of the stew made her weak at the knees. Now, though, the invitation was undeniable indeed—a plate of food and a mug of drink for her, far enough away to give her a head start, and with a fire between to slow him down. She didn't trust him for a second, of course, but oh! How she needed a friend! Besides, he had chased away the hunters—and he was as tall as she, taller. Like her, he needed to fear the Midgarders, but wouldn't be welcome among the giants.

Then, too, he was wearing slave clothes.

She made up her mind; food and companionship were worth the gamble. Clutching her staff, she moved slowly around the bush, rising a bit but still crouched, and prowled around his campsite toward the bread and cheese. He gave no sign of seeing her, didn't look her way, even kept his eyes on his own plate, but somehow she knew he was aware of her every movement. Slowly, ready to bolt at the slightest threat, she came closer, then snatched the plate and retreated back among the leaves, eating while she watched him.

Even out of the corner of his eye, Gar saw her clearly, and was amazed at her tallness—well over six feet, when most of the women he had met in his life had been a foot shorter. He was also struck by the voluptuousness of her figure—she was perfectly proportioned, but on a larger scale than most women, and looking under the dirt and lines of fatigue on her face, Gar saw that her features, too, were perfectly proportioned, almost classical, like those of a Greek statue—but the haunted look, the shadows of fear and bitterness, kept her from being beautiful. Still, she made him catch his breath.

She finished the bread and cheese, and he still had not made a move in her direction, only raised his cup to drink, then poured the stew into two bowls. She came close enough to take the mug of tea and sip, holding her improvised staff at guard and ready to run. "Why did you save me back there?"

"I don't like seeing men manhandling women," Gar told her. "I don't like seeing six against one, either. I've been on the receiving end too often. By the way, my name is Gar Pike."

Either the double meaning of the name was lost on her, or she was in no mood to laugh. She stood frowning at him, but didn't offer her own name. Instead, she asked, "How did you know I'm not a murderer?"

"You might have been," Gar allowed. "But more than anything else, you might have been some sort of slave who had managed to escape."

"Think you know everything, don't you?" she said darkly.

Gar laughed, but managed to kept it low and soft. "Know everything? Enough to survive, at least. Beyond that? I don't even know why I'm alive."

The woman digested that, thought it over, then said, "Who does?"

"Married people," Gar told her, "the ones who are in love, at least. And the ones who have children."

She flinched; he could see he'd struck a nerve, and said quickly, "But I'm none of those, and probably won't ever be."

"Why?" She was suddenly intent.

"I'm too big for most," Gar explained, "and too moody for the rest. Besides, if a man hasn't married by thirty, there isn't much chance that he will."

It was more than true—in a medieval society. Again, she winced. He guessed her to be in her mid-thirties, though allowing for the medieval rate of aging, she could be younger, even in her late teens or early twenties.

"Why are *you* living, then?" She asked it with that same intensity, almost a hunger.

Gar shrugged. "Because I was born," he said, "and I haven't quite given up yet."

She thought that statement over too, then gave her little nod once more.

"Back away," Gar warned. "I'm bringing your stew to that rock."

Her eyes widened, and she darted back into the forest, but stopped when she was fifty feet away, almost lost in the leaves. Gar moved slowly, keeping both hands in sight, rising and crossing to the rock where he'd left the bread and cheese. He set down the bowl and went back to his own place. As soon as he sat, she came back, much more quickly than she had the last time. *Good,* he thought. *She's remembering how to trust, at least a little.*

She knelt, a broken branch ready in her left hand as she lifted the spoon with her right, darting quick glances at the bowl when she had to, but otherwise keeping her eyes on Gar. When she was done, they simply sat looking at one another for a while, and neither seemed to feel the need to be the last to look away. She frowned a little, studying him as though he were a problem she had to puzzle out, almost seeming not to notice his gaze, being too intent on watching him. Her eyes were large and gray and long-lashed, but haunted. . . .

Gar realized he was holding his breath for some reason, and forced his mind back to business. All this staring was getting them nowhere and yielding no information. There wasn't any need to hurry, of course, but Gar had a whole planet to analyze. Well, if she wanted help, she could ask for it.

He bent to empty the bucket and scrub it with grass and sand. "Coming to get your plate and mug," he said, and she retreated again, but more slowly, and not as far. He brought back bowl, plate, and mug, stowed the gear in his pack, and scooped dirt on the campfire.

"Thank you," she said, as though it were dragged out of her.

"A pleasure to help a fellow wanderer," Gar said, "and it's been another pleasure to meet you. You're welcome to walk with me if you want. If you don't, I wish you a safe journey." He turned to start hiking again.

Alea watched him walk away, uncertain of her feelings, then started to follow, but fifty feet behind. After all, he seemed to be a genuinely gentle man.

If he was, though, he was the only one she'd ever met—other than her father, of course. She decided to reserve judgement, but her curiosity was aroused. She told herself that she was only interested in seeing if he really did prove to be gentle in the long run, then forced herself to admit that he was the only one she had met who wasn't already taken, and he was taller than she was, too. If there was any safety for her in this wilderness at all, he was it—until he started expecting some sort of payment for his protection. But he had shown no interest in her as a woman, only as a person.

That didn't mean that he wouldn't, of course. She reminded herself that there was no real safety for her at all, anywhere. Still, something within told her that she could trust this man. She wondered why.

As she followed Gar down the road, Alea gathered berries and roots whenever she found them, so that she would have at least some food to offer in return for his. After perhaps half a mile, Gar glanced back and saw how haggard she was, how unsteady her gait. He halted, and she stumbled on for a few steps before she realized he had stopped. She yanked herself to stillness, suddenly completely awake and ready to run again.

"You've been traveling at night, haven't you?" Gar asked.

"I—I have, yes."

"And you're worn to the bone." Gar turned off the road and used his staff to thrash a way through the underbrush. "Come, sit down while I pitch camp."

Alea blinked, stupefied that a man would change his plans because of her. Then she managed to remember some realities and said, "The brush—they'll see where it's flattened. . . ."

"They who?" Gar turned back. "That rabble who were bothering you? I'll be very surprised if they stop running before nightfall."

"If not them, there will be others!"

"Is it that bad, then?" Gar studied her, frowning. "Yes, I suppose it must be. If the giants have patrols in this no-one's-land, why shouldn't the . . . what did you call your people?"

"Not mine any more!" It came out much more harshly than Alea had intended, but she wasn't about to back away from it.

Gar lifted his eyebrows in surprise, then nodded slowly— it would be very bad for him to undermine that realization. It must have been hard enough for her to admit, after all. "What shall I call them, then?"

"Midgarders," she said though stiff lips.

"Midgarders it is. There's that great a chance that another of their patrols will come by?"

"Every chance!"

"Then I'll straighten the brush so that only a sharp eye will notice it's been knocked aside. Walk carefully."

Alea watched him for a second, wondering about the readiness of his agreement, then picked her way over the underbrush, trying not to tread any more down. Gar moved ahead as she came, until she was past the underbrush and into the relatively clear land under the shadow of the leaves. "I need a large tree, lad."

"Really?" Gar looked about. "Larger than these?"

"No, that one will do." Alea went over to an apple tree that must have been at least fifty years old. She was too tired to wonder what traveler had tossed aside an apple core in her grandfather's day. She almost asked Gar for a boost up but caught herself in time, and scolded herself for being so quick to trust. She wondered why as she climbed.

She settled herself on a limb and glanced down to see Gar, thirty feet from the tree, staring up at her with anxious eyes. "Don't worry." She untied the rope from around her waist, cast it about the trunk and caught it, then tied it in front of her. "I won't fall."

"That can't be very comfortable," Gar said doubtfully.

"It's not," she assured him, "but I'll manage to sleep. I've done it for three days now."

"No wonder you're almost dead on your feet. Why not sleep on a bed of pine boughs on the ground?"

Instantly, her whole body waked to fight or flee. Was he trying to lure her down? "There are packs of wild dogs in this wilderness, lad, or so rumor says. Haven't you seen them?"

"Not yet," Gar said slowly—but what she said made sense. The continent, having been terraformed and Terran colonized, had no native predators, only breeds of Terran domestic animals. People who had tired of their pets, or found they couldn't afford to feed them, had probably taken them out into the country and abandoned them. Eventually they would have found one another and formed packs. Farmers would have killed most of them as menaces to the livestock and even people, but some would have escaped to this buffer zone between kingdoms.

"There are wild pigs, too," she told him, "herds of a dozen or more each, and the boars have grown tusks."

Reverting to the wild indeed! Gar wondered how the pigs had escaped, but he knew they were smart animals when they cared to stir themselves. "I can see the advantage of your tree."

"Not comfortable, but safe," Alea told him.

Gar reflected that she would be safe from predators indeed, would even have some measure of safety from the two-legged kind—bandits were less likely to notice her when she was up in a tree, and the height of her perch would give her an advantage if they started climbing after her.

"Hadn't you better climb up, yourself?" Alea asked.

"No, I think the fire will keep them away," Gar said. "If I see them lurking, there will be time to climb." He didn't mention that he could make sure pigs and dogs both stayed away by inserting fearful thoughts into their brains. "Are there wild cattle, too?"

"Yes, but they'll usually leave you alone if you leave them alone. What if your fire goes out?"

"It won't, if I tend it." Gar turned away. "First, though, I'll cover our trail."

Alea let her eyes close, head nodding heavily. Then a sudden thought brought her wide awake again. "What will you do while I sleep?" she called.

Gar turned back and smiled up at her. "Why, I'll keep watch, of course. When I can't keep my eyes open, I'll wake you for your turn as sentry."

Alea braced herself. "How shall you wake me?"

Gar looked about, then guessed, "Little green apples?"

Alea thought that over, then said, "That will do. Not my face, all right?"

"I'll aim for your leg," Gar assured her.

That bothered her, oddly, but she could find no reason to

complain. "Well enough, then. Good night. Good morning, I mean."

"Good night this morning." Gar grinned and started to turn away.

"Lad?"

He turned back. "Aye?"

Again reluctantly: "Thank you. For standing watch, I mean."

"I'm glad to do it," Gar said. "Journeying is lonely work otherwise." He turned and went before she could answer.

What would she have said anyway, especially since his words waked alarm in her again? She told herself that was foolish and closed her eyes, leaning her head back against the trunk. There wasn't room enough, so she loosened the rope, slid forward, then tied it again. Now she leaned back.

Exhausted as she was, her mind buzzed with questions, and sleep seemed slow in coming. Alea found herself wondering what horrors could have made a man lose interest in sex—or had he simply been raised to respect women? Or even more simply, was he just a good man by nature?

She told herself sternly not to think that for a second. There was no such thing as a good man, and that way lay the nightmare.

As a last thought, she tucked her skirts under her legs, then leaned her head back again and let weariness claim her. It came in a flood, and she was asleep.

Gar covered their trail with expert touches and settled down to meditate, reflecting that one of the predators she feared was certainly him. He wondered what traumas had made her so wary of other people—especially men. Since she'd been a slave, the answer seemed clear, but he had a notion it went deeper than the last week or two. For a moment, he was tempted to probe her sleeping mind, to sift through her memories, but he banished the idea as quickly as it had come. His parents had taught him the ethics of mindreading, and as he had grown, he had weighed their teachings and decided they were true. He wouldn't allow himself to read a friend's mind without a very good reason. He wouldn't even read an enemy's mind, unless it was necessary to save his own life, or someone else's. If the enemy were ruthless, the situation usually became severe enough to warrant the intrusion sooner or later, but even so, Gar felt he had to wait until the danger was clear and present. No, he wouldn't read Alea's mind—but he would listen carefully to what she said, put clues together, and see if he could piece out what had happened to her, so that he would know how to behave in order to help her.

Assuming, of course, that she chose to keep traveling with him.

Alea woke, feeling stiff and groggy, then saw the gloom about her. Her eyes flew wide open with panic. She throttled it, looked down—and saw him, sitting by a small, smokeless fire with his little kettle steaming.

She relaxed—he was there, but still keeping his distance. Then anger began, and she nursed it, treasuring the feeling, believing it gave her some strength. She untied herself, wrapped the rope about her waist and tucked it, then climbed down.

Gar looked up at the sound as she jumped to the earth. "Did you sleep well, then?"

"Too well!" She strode toward him, staff swinging. "You said you'd wake me for my turn as sentry!"

"I didn't grow sleepy. Probably will around midnight, but

I'll manage to keep going until dawn." He took the kettle from the fire and poured boiling water into the two mugs. "That will have to brew a few minutes."

Alea halted, glowering at him, wondering how you scolded someone for being generous. It was a new problem for her; no one had gone out of the way for her since she'd turned fifteen—no one except her parents, at least, and she certainly couldn't have scolded them. She let the issue go with bad grace, sitting on a boulder, legs tucked so that she could rise quickly, and took the mug when he offered it.

Gar saw that she was almost within arm's reach, and didn't seem to have noticed. Of course—if she had, she'd have moved farther away, and rather quickly, too. His heart sang with the elation of accomplishment.

"Where are you going?" Alea asked abruptly. "Other than away from Midgard, I mean."

"I've met the giants," Gar said slowly, "at least, a giant patrol, and that's as much as I'm going to see of them without visiting one of their villages. I'm not sure that would be wise just yet."

"Visit the giants!" Alea put down her mug, staring at him. "Are you mad?"

Gar cocked his head to the side. "Why would that be mad?"

"Because they'd kill you as soon as look at you!"

"They didn't," Gar told her. "The few I met on the road yesterday seemed quite peaceable. Ready to fight if I offered it, but ready to talk, too. They told me, rather sadly, that they couldn't take me in, though—I'm too short!" He chuckled. "I haven't been told that since I was ten."

With wonder, Alea said, "Why—they were gentle with me, too, the patrol. And you're right, they almost seemed sorry they couldn't take me—that I was too short too, and not likely to grow because I was too old." Her face tightened. "I've been told the last often enough, but never the first." Then she turned thoughtful again. "Why should I still think them monsters?"

Gar was amazed. For a medieval woman to question why she thought as she did, was almost unheard of. Alea must have been a very rare woman indeed. He suggested, "Did other people tell you the giants were harsh and cruel?"

"Oh, from my cradle!" she answered. "Everyone in the village, every traveler who came by, always spoke of the villainy of the dwarves and the cruelty of the giants. The bards' news was always of the latest battle, and how treacherous and deceitful the giants and dwarves were in their fighting!"

Gar thought of suggesting that the giants and dwarves might tell their children the same things about Midgard's soldiers, but thought better of it. Besides, the giants he had met had been wary of him, but hadn't seemed to think him a lower form of life. Instead, he said, "The lessons we learn earliest stay with us our whole lives. No wonder you think the giants are monsters even after you've met them, and they proved to be gentle. The real question should be: will you ever be able to believe the truth?"

"I've never met a man who gave a thought to what small children learned," Alea said, frowning. "That's women's work."

"Not where I come from." Gar gave her a bleak smile. Inside, though, he was shaken. What kind of culture made men ignore their own toddlers? "Some man must have been concerned about it some time, or who would have started the lies about the giants?"

"I suppose they are lies, aren't they?" Alea looked away, shaken. "Though maybe not; we've only seen a few giants."

"That's true, and we shouldn't judge the whole nation by one band."

"You're right about some man starting the rumors, though." Alea turned back to him, frowning. "I can't see a woman making up horror stories like that."

"I've known women who would do it." Now it was Gar's gaze that drifted. "Ones who wanted to heap shame on a neighbor whose son or daughter had grown too tall, perhaps, or one who wanted to make up for feeling tiny when she looked at a very tall neighbor woman."

"Yes," Alea spat, her face suddenly twisted with anger. "There are women who would do that."

"Still, I think it more likely that the fathers were trying to raise sons who would be better giant-killers because they didn't see the big ones as people, really." Gar's gaze drifted back to her. "And wanted to raise their daughters to become wives who would urge their husbands on to mayhem out of sheer terror."

Alea frowned, thoughtful again. "You don't suppose husbands and wives agreed on the same horror stories for different reasons, do you?"

Again, Gar was amazed at her ability to see beyond the confines of the culture in which she had been raised. "I think it's very likely. In fact, I don't think the ordinary grandmother could make a story sound true if she didn't believe it."

"But if our ancestors told us lies about the giants," Alea asked, "what of the tales of the dwarves?"

"Interesting question." Gar grinned. "Why don't we visit the dwarves and find out?"

Alea stared. "Visit the dwarves? Are you mad?"

6

Gar sighed, and summoned his reserves of patience—but before he could begin to explain, Alea gave a laugh. "Silly of me, isn't it? When I've just worked out that the real giants may be nothing to fear, I'm still terrified of the dwarves!"

The laugh transformed her face, bringing out all the beauty hidden by her bitterness, fear, and exhaustion. Gar caught his breath, but as suddenly as it had come, that beauty was gone in the hardness of the look of a woman trying to confront the truth—which amazed Gar still more, for she came from a culture in which superstition was accepted as fact.

"A visit to the dwarves is another matter completely, though," Alea told him, "for they live in Nibelheim, far to the west, and all of Midgard lies between us and them."

"I'm not eager to cross Midgard," Gar admitted. "Somehow, I doubt that we'd make it through."

Alea shuddered. "Thank you, no! I'm not about to walk back into slavery!"

Gar closed his eyes, visualizing the photographic map Herkimer had displayed for him, and the line where the darkness of pine forest gave way to tundra. "Who lives in the north, Alea? How far does Midgard go?"

"Well, there's a land to the north of it, if that's what you mean," Alea said, surprised. "I don't know how many days' journey it would take to go there, but it doesn't matter—nobody would want to.'

"Really?" Gar asked, interested. "Why not?"

"Well, because it's a wasteland," Alea explained, "all pine forest and high moors, too cold and dry to grow a decent crop. Besides, they say there are no rivers, and the brooks are few and far between."

"Someone must have been there, then," Gar pointed out, "or there would be no stories telling what it's like."

"Oh, travelers have gone there, yes," Alea said. "Some have even come back—slave-hunters and the like. They say there are giants there, but not many."

"Slave-hunters?" Gar looked interested. "So some slaves do manage to escape and stay free?"

Alea shuddered. "Yes, but they're as bad as the hunters. Folk speak of whole bands of runaways, all murderers and thieves—bloodthirsty men who will do anything rather than be caught."

"I know how they feel," Gar said, smiling.

For a moment, Alea was angry with him, indignant that he could seem amused at the notion of such criminals. Then, though, she remembered what she had just learned about the tales with which she'd been raised, and laughed. "It does sound too horrible to be true, doesn't it?"

"It does indeed," Gar said. "Just the kind of thing you'd tell slaves, to make them afraid to try to escape."

Alea sobered. "It might be true, though, and such men might not be too gentle with women."

"Might." Gar held up a finger. "Might not, too. I suspect the rumors have become far worse than the reality."

"Oh?" Alea bridled at his self-assurance. "What do you think is the truth, then?"

"Probably a handful of scrawny, ragged people on the verge of starvation," Gar said, "if what you say about the land being so poor is true. But if there really are a few giants there, then I suspect there are some dwarves—in fact, it just might be a country where all three nations live side by side. I wonder if they fight, or help one another?"

For a moment, Alea was scandalized by the thought of giants, people, and dwarves working together, shocked at the vision it raised—of all three dwelling in a single village in peace. Then she managed to accept the notion, or at least its possibility—if giants could be gentle, why not escaped slaves? She realized that having discovered the lie in one set of things she'd been taught, made her question all the rest. "It's possible," she said, "but what difference does it make?"

"A great deal, if we're going there." Gar stood up, swinging his pack to his shoulders.

"Going there!" Alea jumped to her feet, heart pounding. "But you can't!"

"Why not?" Gar grinned. "You've already told me that some escaped slaves manage to hide there and stay free. In fact, it looks like the only place where we'd really have a chance. Besides, if I want to visit the dwarves, I'll have to go through the North Country, since I can't pass through Midgard. To top it off, I might actually be able to meet both giants and dwarves without having to worry about permission to cross someone else's territory."

"But the danger!" Alea cried. "Those wild slaves might do anything to us!" She shuddered at the thought. "For all we know, they might even eat us!"

"Or, for all we know, they might welcome us," Gar pointed out.

"The stories also tell about wild-dog packs," Alea said darkly, "many of them. I'm sure they'll welcome us, too."

"Four-legged predators can't be any worse than the two-legged kind," Gar countered, "and they tend to run in packs, too. As to the hazards of the wasteland, I've dealt with them before, and I can deal with them again. I'm willing to take the chance. Besides, is it any safer to stay here in no-one's-land?"

"No-one's-land!" Alea stamped her foot in anger. "Why can't you say 'no-man's-land,' like everyone else?"

"Because I don't think the world has ever belonged just to men," Gar said, "though we like to flatter ourselves that it has. It's belonged at least as much to the women they marry, who raised the next generation of men, and women for *them* to marry. In fact, if there weren't any women, there wouldn't be any men, so the country has to belong to both of them—if it belongs to anybody at all."

Alea stood stiff, bracing herself against the wind that was sweeping away all her old ideas of the world. Men and women own the land together! Men and women being equals! Her mind reeled at the thought, but her heart leaped.

Then she realized that Gar's hand was on her shoulder, that she was leaning against it, and that he was looking down at her with concern, asking, "Are you well?"

She leaped away, striking out at his hand. "Don't touch me! If I'm as good as you, I can demand that much, can't I?"

"That, and a great deal more." Gar shook his hand ruefully, backing away. "I'm sorry. I didn't mean to invade your privacy."

The wind of concepts blasted her again, and Alea stood rigid against it. A man, telling a woman he was sorry when he wasn't even in love with her? Worrying about her privacy? What kind of man was this, anyway, and what kind of world did he bring with him?

Whatever kind it was, she knew she wanted it. Her heart surged, and she yearned with all her being for this wonderful new vision Gar had given her. "I'll go with you to the North Country," she heard herself saying. "But mind you, you'll have to teach me to protect myself. You can't fight off a whole pack of wild dogs by yourself, you know."

Gar's smile was dazzling. "Done! You'll have your first lesson at moonrise."

Actually, they had to wait until the moon was above the trees at the edge of the river meadow they chose for their rest. Its light was a blessing—in the darkness, Alea was forever tripping in potholes and over boulders, even in the roadway. By moonlight, though, all the old tales about ghosts came flocking back to make her fearful, and there was no assurance that the dog packs wouldn't come hunting by night, even though they were daytime animals, and so were the wild pigs. She felt much safer with Gar than she had before she met him, but the night still seemed haunted.

Now, though, Gar squared off from her and said, "European style first. Hold your staff in the middle, so your hands divide it into thirds, like this." He held up his staff to guard position. "Now from here, you can block a blow from overhead just by bringing the stick up, from below by bringing it down, and from left or right by striking." He demonstrated as he talked. "Now strike at me with your stick, and see how it works. Strike lightly, by the way—that dry branch won't stand much of a blow. We'll have to find you a better one soon."

Exasperated by his self-assurance, Alea struck, probably harder than she should have. Gar's staff snapped up to block, and at least Alea's stick didn't break. She took that to mean she hadn't struck too hard after all, and swung up from below. Smiling, Gar dropped his staff to block again.

Alea began to grow a little angry. Determined to wipe that smile off his face, she struck from the right. Gar swung his own staff as he'd said, and the two knocked together. Alea realized she'd have to go through with the demonstration, so she struck from the left. Again, Gar blocked her stick.

"Now I'll strike, and you block." Gar saw the look of fright and belligerence on her face and said quickly, "I won't swing very hard, of course, and very slowly. The point is to teach you, not to hit you. On guard!"

Alea brought her stick up as he had shown her.

"Not so high," Gar warned. "You're giving me too much target below the staff. Ready? Now!"

He moved his quarterstaff as though he were pushing his way through molasses. Alea swung hers up much more quickly, to block. Gar touched her stick hard enough for her to feel the blow, but not much more. Then he said, "From below, now. Guard!"

She lowered her stick to the level he had shown her, then dropped it down some more to catch the tip of his staff as it came up.

So it went for half an hour, with Gar showing her how to strike from left and right, then how to make a circle with the end of the staff in order to strike from above or below, then how to feint, starting a blow from above but changing it to left or right. By the time he called a halt, they were both breathing in gasps and covered with sweat.

"It's not good to let the night chill us," Gar told her. "I'll kindle a fire."

Soon after, they were sitting on opposite sides of the flames sipping tea. Alea wondered how long his supply would last, and hoped he had a lot of it—she was beginning to like the beverage.

Gar broke out biscuits and cheese and passed her some across and to the side of the flames. Alea took them, then realized how close she was to him. She felt a spurt of fright and almost moved farther away, then told herself that was silly— she'd been within arm's reach of him for half an hour, and he hadn't. Reached, that is. Besides, she was determined not to let him see she was afraid of him.

"You're a quick learner," Gar said. "and you move well. You must have danced a great deal."

"Not as much as I would have liked." The statement brought memories of village dances, and of herself watching as the boys chose other girls. But there had been the women's dances, for May or other holidays, and she had loved the movements there. She had practiced by herself in her father's barn where no one could see her, as often as she might, at least once a day. "How could you tell?"

"Coordination," Gar said simply. "You always seem to be aware of your whole body, where each hand and foot is, every second. You'll learn the staff quickly. Let the dog-packs of the North beware."

He said it with such a joking air that Alea felt exasperated again. Didn't he realize the dogs were real, genuine danger? "Why face them?" she demanded. "Why are you willing to take such a risk?"

Gar shrugged. "I can't live in Midgard, except as a slave—
I'm too tall. The giants won't take me in because I'm too
short, and I'm sure the dwarves would think I'm far too big.
Where am I supposed to live?"

The question cut deeply into Alea. She, too, no longer had
a home. Where did you go, if you fit nowhere? "Do you think
there might be more like us in the North Country?"

"If there are, they're far enough north so that word of
them doesn't seem to have come back to Midgard—unless
the runaway slaves and criminals they tell of are really people
of our own kind, too short to be giants but too tall to be Midgarders."

"Or too small?" Alea sounded a little forlorn, even to her
own ears, and wondered where the idea had come from.

"Possibly, yes." Gar seemed a little excited by the idea.

Alea felt another touch of exasperation. His enthusiasm
was infectious, but also draining. She countered it. "So there
would be bands of people our size, and other bands about
four feet high. They'd fight, wouldn't they?"

"Perhaps not." Gar gazed into the fire, face gone dreamy.
"They might be so disgusted with the old nursery stories that
they'd try to make peace. Besides, who says they might not all
be in the same bands?"

Alea looked up in alarm. "Then surely the short ones
would be slaves!"

"Maybe not," Gar said softly. "People are sometimes more
valuable to each other when there are fewer of them. Besides,
I don't think there would be very many bands of outcasts."

"They'd probably as soon rob us as welcome us," Alea said
sourly.

"That's possible, too," Gar sighed. "It might well be every

man for himself there, with all hands turned against their neighbors. No, if we want a home, we'll have to make one."

"In a frozen wasteland?"

Gar shrugged. "I suppose I could live on sauerkraut and reindeer meat if I had to."

"What is a rain dear?"

Gar gave her a searching glance, then said, "Just a dream creature from a child's story. But I suspect oxen escaped and bred there, so there should be some kind of game to hunt. After all, the wild dogs have to live on something."

Alea shuddered at the thought of the dog packs, though she had never seen one.

"Still, I'm not planning to stay in the North Country," Gar told her. "It would be much better to persuade the three human breeds here to learn to tolerate one another and stop fighting. Then, maybe, they wouldn't feel obliged to cast out those such as us."

"Even the Midgarders don't cast us out," Alea said bitterly. "They enslave us, and if we're lucky, we escape, though I've never heard of anyone who wasn't brought back—except the outlaws to the north." Then she frowned. "What kind of man are you if you don't know this?"

"One from far away," Gar answered, "very far, and sometimes I think I should never have left home." A shadow crossed his face, but he shook off the melancholy before it could take hold of him. "I did leave, though, since there wasn't much for me there, and I have to make a life for myself. How can I do that if all three kinds of people are fighting so hard that none of them will accept me?"

"You don't think you could persuade them to let you live among them even if you could get them to make peace, do you?"

"It's worth a try." Gar flashed her a grin. "And it's better than spending all my days running and hiding without any hope of being able to settle down to a real life."

"Yes, it is!" The audacity of the idea dizzied Alea, the sheer nerve of daring to try to achieve something so immense as peace between the Jotuns, Nibels, and Midgarders. She wondered for a moment where women might fit into Gar's new world, then scolded herself for silliness—women were part of men, everyone knew that. Still, the giants had seemed to treat her with greater respect than the men of her own land. . . .

Hope flowered within her with such an intensity that it almost frightened her—she had begun to accept despair, almost to clasp it to her, and she found that hope hurt. But she summoned her courage and gazed into Gar's eyes, daring the pain, embracing the hope, discovering that no matter the risk, she couldn't turn away from the idea of winning back her life. "I'll go along and try for that peace with you, lad. We're probably a pair of fools who will die trying for a dream that can't come true, but Freya knows it's better than dying in despair grubbing roots and berries!"

"Brave woman!" Gar flashed her his grin again. "That same Freya knows I'll be glad of your company—but it will be dangerous, you know."

"There's no way my life can't be, now," she told him. "In fact, there's no hope of life at all, except as a slave and whore. No, I'll face danger beside you."

"Then let's go conquer the world!" Gar shoveled dirt on the fire, put away the mugs, then rose and turned to start down the road. "Or shake some sense into it and make it see it has to be a peaceful world, at least."

Alea fell into step beside Gar, amazed at herself, but just as much amazed at him. How many men would invite a woman along if they knew they were marching into danger? He was a rare one, all right, and must be very sure of his ability to protect them both.

The thought chilled her. If he was that strong, that good a fighter, how easily might he beat her or wrestle her down?

Anger surged, and her hand tightened on her staff. He would pay dearly for that victory, Alea vowed—then realized that if he'd wanted to do it, he would have already. She glanced up at his face with its slight, serene smile, eyes bright with eagerness to face the future and the struggle for peace. Strangely, she felt safe with him—or safer with than without him, at least. She wondered why, and scolded herself—she must keep on being careful, after all.

Still, she was amazed to discover that she could trust a man again, even as little as this.

She was amazed, too, to realize that she had come to accept the idea that dwarves and giants were people just as surely as the folk of her former village. How quickly that had happened, how suddenly! Might it be because it meant that she and Gar were people, too? Still, it was a wonder.

So was he.

They wandered northward through a wild land for three nights, keeping the evening sun on their left and the morning sun on their right. Woodlands alternated with meadows, the grass filled with weeds and the trees filled with underbrush. Twice they had to hide from patrols of human hunters setting out in the first light of dawn, once from a squadron of giants on their way home in the dusk. They saw no farmers. No one dared cultivate the rich land of this border region, when armies might clash in any field on any day.

Since the only predators they needed to fear hunted by

sunlight, they kept to the pattern Alea had established, traveling by night and sleeping by day, Gar always by the campfire, Alea always in a tree twenty or thirty feet away, one of them always awake. The tree limbs were uncomfortable, and Alea began to find herself tempted more and more to sleep on the ground while Gar kept watch for danger, but she snapped herself out of the notion whenever she realized it had crept up on her. She reminded herself that no matter how gentle he seemed, he still couldn't be trusted. After all, he was a man.

The fourth night, the wild dogs found them.

False dawn had come, the sky pale and the world filled with the ghostly light that comes before the sun, all the more ghostly because mist was rising from the meadow they were crossing. They were just coming to the trees at its edge when they heard the baying and barking, approaching fast.

"Into a tree!" Gar told Alea, and turned to face the barking, pulling a sword from under his cloak.

Alea stared; she hadn't realized he had the weapon. Then she shook off her surprise and retorted, "Will you climb, too?"

"Yes, if you do! Then we can throw sticks at them, at least."

"All right, if you promise." Alea scanned the trees quickly, picked one with a low limb, and was about to jump up when the barking burst much louder. She glanced over her shoulder and saw the pack charging straight at them.

Gar wouldn't have time to climb. Fear clamored within her, but she spun and set her back against his, holding her staff up as he had taught her. "You're lost by yourself!"

Gar spat the first curse she had heard him utter, then snapped, "Take a decent staff, then!" His own quarterstaff swung back; she dropped her stick and snatched his. Out of the corner of her eye, she saw him draw a dagger; then the pack was on them.

7

Three dogs leaped at her, one large, dark, and flop-eared; one tan and point-eared; the third smaller and spotted, with long ears and a huge bark. Alea struck in near-panic as hard as she could, the biggest first, then the smallest as it darted at her ankles, making an hourglass pattern with her staff, as Gar had shown her. The middle dog tried to leap in past the staff. She screamed, stepped back, jarred against Gar, and the stick seemed to jump in her hands without her even thinking about it. The tip caught the dog in the belly.

It fell, scrabbling in the dirt, plainly trying in vain to breathe. The other two leaped away and held their distance, barking furiously. She slid both hands to the end of the staff and slashed it in what Gar had called a roundhouse swing, cracking the skull of the big dark dog. It fell, and the little one ran, howling.

But half a dozen more dogs surged around her, snapping and barking. In a panic again, she struck upward and caught one under the chin. Its head snapped back with a nasty noise like a branch popping in the fire; it cartwheeled away and fell.

Instantly the others were on it, biting and savaging. Alea stared a moment, appalled, then realized she had a chance. She stepped forward, swinging roundhouse-style again, and cracked one dog's head, then another and another. They fell—unconscious or dead, she didn't know and didn't care.

Then, suddenly, the three remaining were running, amazingly fast, howling as they went. She stared, unbelieving, then felt a surge of elation such as she had never known. They had tried to kill her, and she had won!

But there might be more of them. She whirled to look past Gar.

He stood, still crouched, sword and dagger still raised, panting and glaring. Alea looked where he did, then turned away, choking down nausea. "What . . ." was all she managed.

"I killed several and maimed one," Gar told her. "They ran when they found out I wasn't going to be easy meat. When the one with the broken leg caught up with them, they turned on him."

Alea forced herself to stare at the sight.

"Don't look," Gar said anxiously. "It will sicken you."

"I have to face the world as it really is, bad as well as good!" Alea snapped. "If I'd done that all my life, I might not have been so stunned when they cast me into slavery!"

Gar was silent. She sensed a queer mixture of admiration and disapproval in him, but that only made her more determined to watch. She stared for a minute or two before she turned her back, hand pressed to her stomach, bent over and fighting nausea.

"Yes, it's ugly," Gar agreed.

She looked up in surprise and saw the concern in his face.

Perhaps it hadn't been disapproval she had sensed, only fear for her delicate feelings. Well, she was determined that they wouldn't be delicate any more!

She turned back for another glance, then turned away again. "Poor beast. I know how it felt."

"I hope you never will," Gar said, his voice low, "but I know what you mean."

"Do you really?" Alea looked up at him sharply, but saw the gravity of his gaze and realized that he did. She looked away. "Thank Heaven people aren't such traitors!"

"Aren't they?" Gar said with contempt.

Alea's head snapped up to stare at him, amazed to find that he, too, felt bitterness. She backed away, suddenly wary again, even though something within her told her that if she had cause for bitterness, he might well have it, too—but cause or not, it made him dangerous again.

Gar straightened up. "Quickly, let's find that tree before they work up enough courage to come back."

This time he gave her a boost before she could turn it down, catching her by the waist and swinging her high. She cried out in anger but caught the branch and swung herself up, glaring down at him. "Don't you ever do that again!"

"Only if it's a matter of life and death," Gar assured her, "and it well could be now." He handed his staff up, and she took it automatically. Then he leaped high, caught another branch, and swung himself up on the other side of the trunk from her. Somehow, he had managed to make his sword and dagger disappear again.

"We should go higher," Alea said.

"If they come back, yes." But Gar was scowling at the pack, staring at them with a somber intensity. Alea gave him a peculiar glance, wondering what was wrong with him—but the dogs suddenly broke off from what they were doing and ran howling away across the meadow, back the way they had come. When they had disappeared into the dark line of trees on the far side, their howling died away, and Gar said, "I don't think they'll return."

"What scared them?" Alea asked, wide-eyed.

Gar shrugged. "Who can say? If they were someone's pets, I might be able to read them, but I haven't had any experience with wild dogs." He turned to her. "Did any bite you?"

His words triggered awareness of an ache. Alea looked down, amazed to see the blood on her ankle. "I didn't even notice it!"

"That happens in a fight sometimes." Gar dropped down and swung his pack off. "Tell me if you see them coming back." He took out a small bottle and a bit of cloth, pulled the stopper, then poured a little of the liquid onto the cloth. He turned to dab it on Alea's ankle.

She snatched her foot out of the way. "Don't touch me!"

"I won't." Gar sounded exasperated. "Only the cloth will— but I have to put medicine on that bite. It might make you sick otherwise."

"Only if you put the same stuff on your wrist!"

"Wrist?" Gar looked down at his left hand, amazed. "So they did get me!"

"A wonder we each only had one," Alea said. "Will you treat it?"

"Yes, after yours."

"All right," Alea said, "but only the cloth, mind!"

Gar dabbed the liquid on the bite marks, front and back. Alea cried out; it stung!

"Sorry. I should have warned you," Gar muttered. He stepped away, dropped the bit of cloth, and took another from his pack. He poured more medicine on it and dabbed at his own wrist. Then he capped the bottle, put it away, and took out a roll of bandage. "Here. Cover the wound with this."

Alea took it hesitantly and managed to pull her foot up well enough to wrap the bandage. "You seem awfully concerned about these bites. What are you afraid of?"

"Rabies," Gar said, his voice hard.

Alea froze in fear. Dread crawled through her. She had seen people die of rabies, tied down and howling.

"Not really much chance of it," Gar told her. "In the late stages, rabies is pretty obvious. But one of them might have been in the early stages."

"There's no cure!"

"My people have found one." Gar took another bottle from his pack. "They used to have to scratch it into you with a needle, but after five hundred years, they learned how to make it into a pill. We'll have to take one a day for two weeks, but it will protect us against any other bites."

Overwhelming relief flooded Alea. She took the pill and put it in her mouth, then unslung the skin the giants had given her to squirt a mouthful of wine. Gar looked up in surprise as she handed it down to him. He nodded and took it. "Yes, thanks. Pills go down much more easily that way." He squirted a stream into his mouth and bit it off just as skillfully as Alea had; she decided his people's ways couldn't be all that different from her own.

He handed the skin back to her and said, "I think we'd better try to break our trail before we pitch camp."

"How can we do that?" Alea asked, frowning.

Gar showed her quickly enough, and it was very unpleasant. Wading through a cold stream made her ankle hurt even more, and swinging from tree branches wasn't much better.

But she was really surprised when he asked, "What kind of plant here has a really bad smell?"

"That one." She pointed to a broad-leafed weed.

"Then take some and rub it on your shoes," Gar said. He yanked off a leaf, rubbed it on the soles of his boots, then pulled the rest of the leaves and set off, rubbing them on his boots every dozen steps or so.

Alea saw what he was doing and broke off some leaves for herself. There were a great number of the plants—they were one of the worst of the weeds—so they made slow and smelly progress.

Finally Gar pronounced himself satisfied and looked for a campsite.

"There." Alea pointed at a patch of dense underbrush.

"I had in mind something a little less thorny," Gar said.

"It's hollow in the middle," she told him. "See the big trees? There will be room enough there for your fire. Come on!"

Gar looked doubtful, but he followed her as she pushed her way into the thicket, breasting the thorns away with her staff. Gar followed, using his sword as she used the pole, and sure enough, there was a rough circle ten feet across in the center with two big trees, one of them with low branches.

"For a village girl, you know your woodcraft," Gar said with approval.

"You learn such things when you want to find places to be alone and safe from other children," Alea told him. "Someone else has been here before us." She pointed at the blackened stones of a fire ring.

Gar grinned. "So they have! How nice of them to leave us a site. Well, I'll find a stream and fill my bucket."

Alea frowned up at the trees and the patches of sunlight

that filtered through. "The sun's well up," she said. "Maybe we ought to make do with the waterskin."

"It's full enough," Gar agreed. "We'll find a stream tonight."

In a short while, he had boiled water and was brewing tea. They ate their usual dinner—biscuit with some roast wildfowl left over from the morning before. As they ate, Gar said, "It's a good thing you wanted to learn how to use the staff."

"I knew it would come in handy," Alea said drily.

"It will, and we'll keep up the practice."

She smiled, amused that he was careful not to call them lessons, careful to hide the fact that he was teaching and she was learning—but she appreciated the courtesy. Once again, she was amazed that a man could be so considerate of a woman. "It's a little late for practice, lad."

"Tonight, then," Gar said. He scoured the plates and cups with sand, stowed them in his pack, then sat down by the fire. "It will take me a while to relax enough to sleep. I'll take first watch."

He always did, and he always had a different reason. Alea smiled as she climbed the tree. She paused on the third limb, thought it over, then said, "I'll climb high tonight, lad."

"Please do," Gar called up. "If those dogs find us, I might be coming up there too, and fast."

Alea lashed herself in on the sixth limb—it looked to be the last that was thick enough to be secure. Exhaustion hit her like a tidal wave, and sleep claimed her.

They found Alea a new staff and practiced every evening before they began their night's hike. Finally Gar said, "You're skilled enough with the weapon now. But what will you do if someone catches you without it?"

A chill went through Alea. "Run and hide!"

" 'Catches you,' I said. What if someone has you by the throat?"

"No!" Alea stepped back, hands coming up to defend. The mere prospect horrified her.

"If they do, you put your hands together, thrust them up between his arms, and push them wide to the sides and down in half-circles—and you do it as quickly as you can." Gar demonstrated on thin air. "That will knock his hands away. But how do you keep them from coming back?"

Alea stopped backing, staring in amazement. "How?"

"Catch his wrist and his shirtfront as you pivot in to put your feet between his, and your back to his front with your hip out, crouching down." Again, Gar demonstrated. "Then straighten your knees as you bow and pull on his arm and shirt, and he'll go sailing over your hip to the ground—if you do it all together in two movements, and do it so fast he can't stop you."

Alea frowned, imitating the pantomime. Gar told her how to do it better, then better and better. Finally she said, "I'm fairly sure I'm doing it right—but how can I tell?"

"There's only one way," Gar said, his face wooden. "You'll have to try it on me."

Alea recoiled. "No!"

"Just as you say." Gar nodded courteously. "I'm perfectly willing to be your practice dummy—but you don't have to try it. Still, as you said, it's the only way to tell if you're doing it right."

Alea stood, tense and wary, watching him.

"It would be too bad to try it on a man who won't *let* you throw him," Gar said, "and have it fail."

Alea shuddered, plucked up her courage, and stepped forward. "No touching, now!"

"None," Gar promised. "You touch me, but I won't touch you."

It was a nice distinction, since her hips rammed into the tops of his thighs as she straightened her legs, bent, and pulled on his arm and tunic front—but she had to admit the contact was only for a second. He sailed over her hip and landed on his side, slapping the earth with his extended arm a fraction of a second before his body hit, then rolled up to his feet and bowed to her. "Well done. If you can take a man by surprise with that, it will put him down long enough for you to run."

"How can I be sure it will surprise him?" Alea countered.

"By doing it very fast, and hoping he hasn't learned it himself." Gar spread his arms. "Try it again, even faster."

Alea eyed him warily, then suddenly spun in, grasping his arm and tunic front, and threw him again—and again, he slapped the earth full-armed and rolled up to his feet, nodding. "Very good, and enough for one night. But you'll have to learn more than that."

She did. They practiced every evening. The more she learned, the more bodily contact it required—her bottom against his hips, his arm across her chest—but he was always very impersonal about it, even cold. As the days passed and she gained skill, Alea was amazed that he never made any sexual advances, not even mild overtures. She wondered if there might be something wrong with him, but from the occasional admiring glances she caught when he thought she wasn't looking, she decided it couldn't be that. The glances did make her feel good, but when he never even hinted at anything more than companionship, she began to feel insulted. Relieved and safe, but insulted.

So Alea kept her distance, walking ten feet or so behind Gar, though when loneliness seized her, she came up even with him, still six feet away, to talk a little. Every evening, before they started their night's travel, Gar gave her a lesson in unarmed combat. Then they practiced with the quarterstaff. Every morning, they pitched camp and prepared to sleep for the day. They talked across the campfire—Gar knew how to build them so that they gave almost no smoke, so Alea didn't worry about them attracting hunters. She stayed across the flames from him, but they could still talk. Gar seemed curious about everything in the world, curious to learn everything about her, but Alea always turned the conversation away from herself and back to the world of men, dwarves, and giants.

She was amazed to find how much Gar didn't know. She asked about himself and his past, and he answered readily and at length, turning answers into stories and filling the stories with humor. He seemed to take it as a personal triumph when she laughed. But somehow, when she tied herself to a trunk for the night and thought back over what he had said, she found he had really told her very little.

"You spoke of runaway slaves among the outlaws to the north," Gar said one morning. "How many slaves are there who *haven't* run away?"

Alea was again amazed at his ignorance, but told him, "I'd guess there are half as many slaves as there are free people, between the ones who were born of Midgarders, and the dwarves they bring back when they fight off a border raid."

"Or commit one," Gar said thoughtfully.

"The Midgarders, do the raiding?" Alea asked, shocked.

"What would the dwarves have that we—I mean, the Midgarders—would want?"

"Dwarves," Gar replied. "More slaves." He raised a hand. "I'm sorry, I don't mean to insult your people—but human nature doesn't change much."

"They're not my people! Not any more." But Alea was surprised to find that she still felt the urge to defend the Midgarders. They didn't deserve such loyalty, of course. No doubt Gar was right—it was they who started the raids, not the dwarves. "Do you think they're the ones who start the raids on the giants?"

"Sometimes," Gar said, "on the excuse that they're keeping the giants from raiding *them*. Do they bring back giant slaves?"

"Of course not!" Alea said. "Who could keep a giant? That would be far too dangerous."

Gar nodded. "Bullies, then. Do many slaves escape?"

"Not in my village." Alea was fighting the urge to defend her people from the charge of bullying, so she answered absently. "Maybe three or four in a year. But we hear that a great number of slaves do try to run away, all across the country. Every week, the crier calls out the news the messenger brings him from the baron, and there's always at least one tale of a slave who tried to run away but was caught and brought back. Usually two or three such."

"Each one a separate tale?"

"Yes." Alea frowned, wondering what significance he saw in that.

"Told in full and gory detail, no doubt," Gar mused. "What happens to slaves who are caught?"

Alea shuddered, remembering scenes she had watched and thought were right. "They're beaten at least, then usually maimed in such a way as to keep them from running off again." She remembered how Noll had hobbled afterward. He'd been a child with her, but had stopped growing early. She wished she could apologize to him now, for all the taunts and insults she'd hurled at him. Of course, all the children had. . . .

"You were enslaved, too." Gar made it a statement, not a question.

"You know I've said it," Alea said, her voice harsh. "I was sentenced to slavery a week after my father died. The headman confiscated everything we'd owned, house and lands and cattle, all Mama's jewels, even their clothes." Tears stung her eyes. "The ruby brooch she loved so—I pinned it on her dress when she lay in her coffin, but the headman made the sexton take it off and hand it back to Papa. I didn't understand why, then. I'd never seen anyone do that before. . . ."

"You were probably the first one who ever tried to send a treasured object with the dead," Gar said gently.

"Perhaps I was. I never paid that much attention at anyone else's funeral, only went through the motions like everyone else, cried a bit if they'd been close friends—not that I had many of those, after I turned fifteen and grew so much." Alea's voice hardened. "At least *their* friends came to their funerals. Papa lived almost a year after Mama died, but he never really seemed to notice much of what went on around him. I don't think he wanted to live without her." Her eyes filled with tears, but she blinked them away angrily; she would *not* show weakness in front of this man! Or any man. Any woman, either, not now; she couldn't trust anyone now, they all smiled like friends, then turned on you. The funeral came rushing back into her mind, the coffin propped on trestles in the big keeping room of their farmhouse, drawn curtains making the room gloomy in daytime, candles burning to either side of Papa, herself wearing her black dress, the same one she had worn not a year earlier, for Mama. The neighbors came up in a steady stream, gazing gravely down into the coffin, some with lips shaping silent prayers to speed his spirit to the gods and keep it from walking, some muttering a few words of farewell to an old friend, then turning to murmur a few words of sympathy and condolence to her before they moved past to take a cup from the sideboard and drink to the dead. Alea thanked each one in turn, very mechanically, barely thinking about the words, so amazed, so daunted by the sense of loss, of aloneness, that she felt scarcely alive herself, and knew she couldn't believe any of the offers of help.

"So all the neighbors came to see him off to Heaven." Gar's gentle voice intruded, made the darkened walls seem thinner, let her see through them to sunlight and leaves, perhaps even the hope that she hated now. "That meant the whole village, didn't it?"

"Yes." Alea wondered why Gar had said "heaven" instead of "Valhalla"—though everyone knew Valhalla was in the heavens, of course. "Even one or two enemies he'd made, the ones who hated him for having built more and earned more and having a few lovely things, even they came. I was touched—for a week. Then at the trial, I saw the gleam of triumph in their eyes, and I knew they'd only come to crow over the ones they'd envied."

"I'm sure most of them meant it when they gave you their sympathy," Gar said softly.

"If they did, they changed their meaning quickly enough! I should have realized they were lying!" Again memory seemed more real than the present, again Alea saw all the old familiar faces filing past, faces arranged in lines of sympathy, but all so formal, so distant, that they made her feel like a stranger. She expected it in the Wentods, was surprised to even see them there—they'd been her parents' worst enemies, and their children the most poisonous in their insults once she started to grow too tall. But come they did, and even made grave, polite comments as they filed by, Vigan Wentod and his flint-faced wife, and all six of their brood, only the youngest two still unmarried and at home. Polite, yes, but as distant as though a wall stood between them.

The other neighbors weren't quite so far removed, but enough, enough, as though they were talking to a stranger. Alea had been numb inside, though, so dismayed and disbelieving that she never stopped to think what it meant. She sat there mouthing automatic thanks, her lips shaping the words by themselves without her mind's help, and all the while tears stung her eyes, barely held back, as they did now. . . .

"We all need to weep now and then," Gar said, his eyes on the flames. "It does no harm, as long as it's not in battle. One must let the tears fall to relieve the overflowing of the heart."

He turned away from her, and she let herself weep, grateful to him for leaving her a share of privacy. When the worst of it had passed, she rubbed her cheeks with a sleeve and went on. "I was used to being treated as something of a monster, after all, so their reserve didn't seem all that odd—but Alf!" Her voice hardened again. "He's more than a head shorter than me now, but he wasn't when I was fourteen and he sixteen, when he . . ." She caught herself. "Well, he made noises of sympathy as he ushered his wife past, but he looked back to give me a leer that made my blood ran cold, as though he were claiming me for his own again the way he did the night before his wedding, whether I wanted it or not. I didn't understand it at the funeral, I only turned away and tried to hide my shivering, tried to put him out of my mind—but a week later, when I stood before the village council in the meeting hall, and saw him standing there with his hot eyes, drying his palms with a square of linen, I realized what that look had meant. He intended to have me again, and for longer than a week or two this time! I had just been an amusement to him fourteen years before, another conquest, and one that he knew he'd never have to marry, for I was already too tall, and too plainly still growing! Now, though, he meant to claim me as a servant for his po-faced little wife, as a nurse for their horde of brats, then in secret make me do by force what he had persuaded me to do willingly fourteen years before. I made up my mind then that I would sooner kill myself than be his whore. Any one else's I thought I could bear to be, for that was the life the Norns had plainly spun for me—but not his!"

Some remote part of her was appalled, was demanding that she stop, be silent, not pour out her heart to this stranger whom she had known for a scant three weeks—but he was the only one she was sure would really listen now that her parents were gone, and the words came almost of their own accord, words that shaped another memory, the village hall's brightness drenching the funereal keeping room and washing it away, leaving only the sight of the headman sitting gravely at his table with the gavel in his hand to remind everyone that the law smote with the force of Thor's hammer. The baron's steward sat beside him to make sure they didn't deal too lightly with a woman who was halfway to being a giant, and would probably birth only real giants. Neighbor or no, childhood friend or not, she was an abomination in the eyes of the gods and must be spurned with contempt.

Behind the hardness of their eyes, though, Alea saw the

fear and, looking out at the villagers gathered on benches facing the headman, she saw that same fear reflected in all those faces, fear hardened and sharpened into hate. How could she have failed to see it all these years? Surely they had hidden it behind false smiles for her father's sake, but how could she have failed to see it?

Alf's glance was not only whetted with fear and hatred, though, but also hot with lust and avarice. A quick look told her that; she turned away, shaken, hoping against hope that the headman wouldn't award her to him.

8

―⟨⟨⟨⟨⟨⟨⟨ ♪ ⟩⟩⟩⟩⟩⟩⟩―

Alea Larsdatter, have you a suitor?" the headman in-
toned.

Alea reddened, but bit back the hot words that came to
her tongue. She had to be respectful here; she was in great
danger, and a wrong step could hurl her into a lifetime of
misery. "No, Master Senred, I have not." As though he didn't
know, as though everyone in the village didn't know! But he
had to force upon her the humiliation of saying it herself,
loudly and publicly, didn't he?

Senred harrumphed and puffed himself up with self-
importance. "If you were married or betrothed, it would be a
different matter—or even if you had a suitor. . . ."

He paused, seemed to be fishing for words, and Alea was
surprised to realize he might feel badly about what he
was doing, might be hoping that some young man would step
forward to bid for her hand even now. None would, of
course—no boy could be interested in a woman so tall and
broad, so dangerously close to being a giant and likely to pro-

duce giant offspring. But Senred almost seemed to be hoping one would!

The baron's steward stepped into the breach. "If you had a husband, Alea Larsdatter, there would be no difficulty, for of course he would inherit your father's house and lands with you."

Alea fought for patience, even lowered her gaze and joined her hands at her waist to appear demure. "I am twenty-eight, sir, and my father made me his helper in all matters of caring for the farm, even as my mother trained me in the care of the household. At the very least, I must make his ghost proud by looking after myself, and by managing his holdings!"

"A woman manage holdings? How foolish!" the steward scoffed.

Even Senred scowled. "If your father taught you such unwomanly things, Alea, he offended both the community and the gods!"

Alea stared into his eyes and felt her stomach sink. He really meant it!

Then the outrage flowed, and she had to lower her gaze to hide it—but she couldn't stop the trembling.

"I know it is a fearful matter," Senred said, his voice soothing. It would not have been if he had known why she had trembled!

Even so, the steward didn't like such gentleness. "No woman can protect a steading, so no woman may own one—and especially not a woman who may yet breed up giants among us! Turn a steading near the border of Jotunheim over to a giant's brat? Have a giant's outpost in our midst? We can never allow it!"

"I am not a giant!" Alea cried, tears starting to her eyes. "I am a good Midgard woman! You cannot take my father's steading from me!"

"The baron can do whatever he wants," the steward said, his voice iron. "The steading must go to those the baron can trust!"

"There is no justice in this!" Alea blurted out, and the tears flowed. "There is only cruelty! All I have left is . . ."

"How dare you accuse the baron of cruelty!" The steward was on his feet, catching Thor's gavel and slamming it on the table. "The baron shall do what is right and just!" He looked out over the room. "Who among you most hated her parents?"

The room was quiet, everyone staring at everyone else, thunderstruck.

Then Vigran Wentod shoved himself to his feet. "I despised the man. What right had he to so much rich land, so fine a barn and house?"

Alea cried, "He built them with his own . . ."

"Silence!" the baron bellowed, pounding with the gavel. "The steading is yours, worthy man! The woman too is yours!" He glared down at Alea. "How dare you say the baron is cruel!"

"Because it is true! To take all I have and give me to those who hate me? What can be right in that?"

"It is right to make you an example to those who would resist the will of the baron and the gods!" The steward's face purpled. "It is right that you should be be taught to obey and submit! You are half a giant and a willful, rebellious woman besides! If you do not learn to obey, you might turn on your neighbors, beat them, even slay them! Surely the only place left for you in this world is as a slave!" He glared at Vigran. "See that she learns to submit!"

"Oh, my lord, I shall," Vigran purred, and Alea felt the chill of doom.

At least Alf hadn't won her. There was that much triumph, at least.

It was little enough.

Birin, Wentod's wife, had a round face that turned sour every time she looked at Alea, and she looked at her as soon as they came into the Wentod house. "Take the broom and sweep, slave! Then dust, and see you break nothing!"

Alea bit her tongue and bowed her head, blinking hot tears from her eyes as she took the broom from the corner and began to sweep. The urge was strong to strike Birin with the stick and jam the bristles into her mouth, but Alea reminded herself that this must be what the gods wanted, since it was the fate the Norns had spun. If she swept well here on earth, she might die to sweep in the glory of Valhalla until Ragnorak. She closed her ears to the gloating chuckles of Vigran, his son Silig, and his daughter Yalas as they watched her wield the broom. She tried especially not to look at Silig; he was nearly twenty, as tall as his father, though nowhere nearly as fat, and the way he looked at her made her skin crawl.

"Can you not get it all in the dustpan?" Birin snapped.

Alea bit her tongue again; the women knew the sweepings couldn't all slide into the dustpan on the first brooming! She set the pan at right angles to the line of dust and swept.

"I marvel your mother did not teach you how to do it properly," Birin sniffed.

The criticism of her mother sent the blood roaring through Alea's head, and she stood rigid a moment.

Birin's hand cracked across her cheek. "Sweep, you lazy slut! No tarrying here!"

The pain of the slap dazed Alea, as though she were waking from a dream of life into the torments of fire. She bent to the sweeping again, her work blurred by a haze of tears—but she realized Birin's game now: to goad her into reason for beating! After all, they had promised the baron's steward they would teach Alea to obey and submit!

Vigran sat heavily in his huge chair by the fire. "Unlace my boots, slave."

Outrage flamed through her, but Alea remembered their game and went to kneel in front of her new master, unlacing his boots.

Birin's hand cracked across her cheek. "I did not give you leave to stop sweeping, slut!"

Anger almost got the better of her then, but Alea rose and took the broom again.

Vigran leaned back and swung a kick into her buttocks. "You've only unlaced the one!"

Alea lurched into the wall. Anger spread a red haze over the room as the teens' laughter rocked around her. She pushed herself away from the wall and swung the broomstick at Vigran.

It took him by surprise, cracking across his pate—but the other three roared in anger, and Silig leaped forward, slamming a fist into her belly, then another into her cheek. Yalas was there an instant later to slap her left cheek, then Birin her right. By that time, Vigran recovered and surged to his feet, bellowing in anger and swinging a huge fist to strike again and again.

So the day went. She could do nothing right, of course,

and try as she would, they managed to goad her to anger twice more, beating her each time. The last time, Birin told Silig, "Tie her hands to the post!"

"No!" Alea screamed, panic tearing within, but father and son dragged her kicking to the pillar that held up the ceiling-beam, and Vigran held her hands fast, chuckling, while Silig bound them.

"Bare her back, Yalas," Birin directed. "You men look away!"

They didn't, of course; they watched with hungry eyes as Yalas tore open the black dress, the only good dress Alea was ever likely to have again. Pain tore into Alea's back with a smack; she cried out once in sheer surprise, then clamped her jaw shut and refused to let out a sound as the willow wand struck again and again, and the men's laughter gained a hungry note. Her very silence must have angered Birin even further, for the blows became sharper and sharper. When they finally ceased, Birin panted, "Loose her!"

They did. Gasping to keep down her sobs, Alea turned to see Birin's right arm hanging while she massaged it with her left, glaring at Alea as though the pain of so much swinging of the willow wand was her fault.

She swept until the floors were spotless, she peeled and chopped in the kitchens, she drew water from the well and hauled it to the kitchen, she cooked their dinner and served it in spite of their carping and criticizing of every mouthful—though Alea knew it was better than Birin could do!

Then she had to scour, wash, put away, be scolded for doing it wrong and be beaten once again. She had to haul the scraps to the hogs and was allowed to brew a little gruel for herself.

Finally, tottering with fatigue, she went out to the barn, as

Birin had told her to go sleep there. Despite the pain in her back, belly, and face, she managed to climb the ladder and collapsed into the haymow to let the sobbing begin.

The sobs grew louder and louder until she was almost howling with grief and hurt. How could her parents have left her to this! How could her father have dared die and leave her! And why, oh why, had the Norns spun such a doom as this for her? Why had they let her be born, if this was all she was for?

Alea bit her lip and tried to force back her tears, force her body to be pliant and unprotesting. If this was what the Norns willed, if this was her doom, then she could only submit to it without complaint, accept it without protest. She would try, she would really try. . . .

But she knew she would fail, that she would scream protests, even fight. A brief, lurid vision flashed in front of her, of Vigran grinning all the wider because of her resistance. She forced the picture away, shuddering and sobbing, ashamed and angry at herself for being so willful, so contrary, willing herself to accept without complaint what the next night might bring—but the anger at her father blazed up, for dying and leaving her to this!

It was a blaze that subsided to ashes in minutes, though, for she remembered how worried he and Mama had been that she had no suitors, was not married. She remembered how impatient she had become with them for insisting that she should accept whatever match they could make for her. She'd thought they had been cruel at the time, but now, now she understood and, understanding, cried herself to sleep.

The Wentods made her cook all the meals, sweep and dust, beat the carpets, feed the livestock, even hoe the kitchen garden. The worst was having to go with them to help spread lurid lavender paint over the lovely wood panelling of her parents' house, the same paneling that she and her mother had so lovingly waxed every month. The only blessing was that Birin didn't want to move into their new house until she had redecorated it to her own taste, every bit of which screamed offense inside Alea.

Birin stayed to supervise, so Silig and Vigran couldn't do anything there, and Alea began to realize why the woman had made her go sleep in the hayloft, instead of an ash-filled corner on the hard tiles of the kitchen hearth.

She still couldn't accept her fate meekly. She broke down and screamed protest at Yalas and Birin, even struck at them. She knocked them down of course, for she was so much bigger and stronger—but their cries of fright were enough to bring both men, and she couldn't beat off all four of them.

So she tried to do as she was ordered in silence, for the gods and for fear of their blows—but try as she might, grit her teeth as she might, she knew she couldn't simply lie there and let it happen, not the next night, or the next. She decided that she'd rather be dead.

So when dusk fell and she went out of the house, she didn't go to the hayloft, only ducked around the barn and, with it between herself and the house, went out across the barnyard, forcing herself to run as well as she could in spite of the aching of her bruises, trying to ignore her weariness. The trees along the stream seemed to open their branches to embrace her, and she fled into their shadows. There she had to slow down, to pick her way through the darkness, but she waded the stream till it led her into the wood, and her first night of freedom.

When the world began to glimmer with the coming dawn,

she was able to find a cave under the roots of an oak, and pulled herself in to munch the handfuls of berries she had gathered as she went. Soaked and shivering, she curled herself into a ball and prayed for death. But she blessed the Norns for her birth near the border; one more night and, with good fortune, she would be out of Midgard and into the strip of wasteland that separated her birthland from Jotunheim.

She knew she should have submitted to the fate the Norns had measured out to her, and fell asleep praying apologies to them for her failure—but she knew she couldn't even try any longer. If she'd been born the daughter of a whore, it might have been a different matter; she might have grown up knowing that lot in life and able to accept it. But she had been the treasured daughter of a loving couple, and the sudden plunge into humiliation and degradation was more than she could bear. Even now she felt dim traces of outrage through her exhaustion, but they didn't last, for she fell asleep.

"I shall never be a shield-maiden in the hall of the gods now," she told Gar bitterly. "If my soul survives this life at all, it will go only to torment and misery."

"I can't believe that," Gar told her, "and I can't believe your doom could be so far from your weird."

Alea lifted her head, incensed. "What do you know of my weird?"

"I know that you're a woman of spirit, daring, and courage," Gar told her, "and those qualities do not fit a doom of meekness, and submission to the cruelty of others."

She stared at him with wondering eyes. "You cannot mean the Norns had another doom in mind for me!"

"I mean exactly that," Gar answered. "If you have read your weird at all, you have read it badly."

"Oh, have I indeed!" Alea exclaimed. "What weird would you read for me, then?"

The admiration flashed in his eyes—almost, she would have thought, worship. Then it was gone, masked, but only masked, she knew it was there, would always be there, and she sat shaken to the core, even though there had been nothing of desire in it.

"I don't know you well enough to guess your weird," he told her, "but I do think you have the courage and strength to try to move the world, if you had a lever long enough with a place to rest it—and the Norns have led you to a man who is considering doing just that."

"What?" Alea asked, aghast. "Moving the world?"

"Changing it, at least," Gar said, "changing it to a world of peace, in which no one will be allowed to debase another human being as these Wentods tried to debase you." His eyes gleamed with admiration again, though he managed to mute it. "They would have failed, you know. No matter how long and how hard they tried, they would never have managed to break your spirit. You are too courageous, too determined—and, way down deep, you still respect yourself too highly."

Alea stared at him, feeling the blood drain from her face. "I'm not like that," she whispered, "not like that at all. I'm only a woman."

"What do you mean, 'only?' " Gar asked, with a wry smile. "Every woman moves the world a fraction when she bears and rears strong children—and every woman has access to a depth of timeless power that men can only dream of, the power of the void, from which women bring forth Life."

Alea found reason for indignation; it gave her a hold on herself again. "Not all women are witches!"

"No, but all women are magical." For a moment, Gar

smiled into space, reminiscent, and Alea felt a stab of jealousy. She scolded herself for it on the instant—it was no concern of hers, which women he had enjoyed! She had no interest in him at all, other than as an aid to survival!

Then his gaze returned to her, and he became grave again. "There have been women who have changed the world far more directly, and as greatly as any man. When you say that you could not submit to degradation, you are also saying that you have integrity and strength of character. No one of such courage should have to submit to such exploitation. No one of any kind should."

Her heart fluttered, but she hid it with a jibe. "Would that be part of this new world your peace would bring us?"

"I certainly hope so," Gar replied.

She was startled by the notion, then regarded him narrowly. "You can't change the whole world overnight, you know."

"No, but I can make a start," Gar told her, "though it will probably take a lifetime. Offhand, it seems to me that the dwarves, giants, and slaves have common cause."

Alea frowned. "How so?" Then she stared. "You mean they all hate the Midgarders? No!"

"You don't hate them?" Gar asked evenly.

"Well . . . yes, for what they've done to me, and more for what they would have done if I hadn't run, or if they catch me," Alea said slowly. "But as a giant would hate them? My own people? No!" However, she remembered how gentle, almost sympathetic, the giants had been to her, and felt a qualm of guilt.

"What of those who haven't escaped?" Gar asked. "What of those who have been caught and brought back?"

"After the way they've been punished, they won't have

spirit enough left to hate anybody." Alea shuddered at the thought of the lifelong punishments that awaited her if she were caught, then turned her mind away from the worst of them. She wouldn't remember that, she would not! "Anyway, what matter if they did all hate the Normals? What good would it do?"

"Yes, what good," Gar mused. "That is the question, isn't it? After all, it's one thing to hate, and another to do something about it."

Alea looked up, shocked. "Do something about it? What?"

"Make a change, of course." Gar smiled. "But for that, the dwarves, giants, and slaves will have to join together."

"That's impossible," she said flatly. "How can they league when they're leagues apart? The giants are in Jotunheim, to the west of Midgard, and the dwarves are in Nibelheim, hundreds of miles to the east! The slaves are in between, sprinkled throughout Midgard, seldom out of hearing of their masters! How could the three nations even talk to one another? Besides, they wouldn't if they could, for they fear and hate one another too much for any but the harshest speech."

"There's always a way." Gar smiled as though he already knew of one, though he only said, "I have to admit I don't know what it is yet, but there's always a way to set people talking."

"How can you say that when you don't even know these people?" Alea cried.

"I can say it *because* I don't know them," Gar replied. "I'll have to learn much more about them before I'm willing to admit there's no way to set up dialogues between them—and I suspect that once I do know them, I'll be able to think of a way to induce them to band together."

Exasperated, she scoffed, "You think you can do anything you want, don't you?"

Gar turned grave. "No. There are many, many things I can't do, and I know it. They're the things that ordinary people do every day and don't even think about. Sometimes they don't even realize how much satisfaction those mundane, common things give them."

Alea stared at him, at the sudden bleakness of his face, and felt the guilt rise, and with it a surge of tenderness that surprised her, a yearning to fill that inner void that she suddenly sensed in him, to comfort this huge, capable man who seemed all at once to be powerless, defenseless, tossed about by the gales of chance.

But that sudden rush of feeling scared her, shocked her; she forced her heart to hardness, so that it wouldn't be hurt.

"If I can't do those everyday, human things, though," Gar told her, "I'll do the odd things I can—and some of them are very odd indeed."

Fear of her own tide of feeling made Alea's voice harsh. "How will you do them?"

"I won't know until I've talked with people of all three nations," Gar said.

"What then?" Alea challenged him. "Even if you can make them talk with one another, what can you do?"

"Yes, that *is* the question, isn't it?" Gar stood up, shouldering his pack. "After all, there's no point in trying to make a change if you don't know what change you want to make, is there?"

Alea stood up too. "What change do you mean?"

"There's only one way to find out," Gar told her, "to ask them. Let's find a dwarf, shall we?"

One morning when they pitched camp, Alea frowned up at the graying sky and said, "It feels as though we've only been walking half the night—but we've been hiking northward for six weeks now, and the nights should be growing longer again."

"Nights become shorter as you go farther north," Gar told her. "We've come more than three hundred miles, so we've lost an hour or two of darkness."

Alea transferred her frown to his. "You must have traveled a great deal, to know that." Envy sharped her tone.

"Oh, yes," Gar said, intent on the fire he was lighting. "A very great deal."

The tilt of his head couldn't hide the bleakness in his face, and Alea's heart went out to him as she realized the cause of his traveling. What could have happened to make so huge a man lose his home?

Any number of things. She had begun to realize just how ingenious people could be when it came to meanness and cruelty. She spoke a bit more gently. "If we've lost darkness, at least we've lost people, too. It's been ten days since we've seen a Midgarder band, and eight since we've seen a giant."

He had been fishing in a stream, quietly and alone, but they had heard a deep voice from a nearby grove calling in a mother's tones, with a lighter voice, a mere baritone, answering. Even so, Gar and Alea had stepped farther back into the shadows of the trees before they moved past, as silently as they could.

"It has been peaceful," Gar agreed. "I think we could even begin traveling by daylight."

The words sent alarm through Alea, but kindled a longing too—to be able to see more than a few yards ahead! To see an enemy that might be coming! But caution prevailed. "There are still the dog packs and the pig herds."

"The dogs find us by night, too," Dirk reminded.

"Strange that the hunters didn't." Alea frowned. "We've only seen three bands, setting out on the day's patrol or pitching camp, and they never looked our way."

"Something else on their minds, no doubt."

Alea glanced at him suspiciously; his tone was too casual. But there was no way he could have anything to do with the minds of Midgarders, so she let it pass. "You mean any band coming this far north won't be looking for us?"

"Not likely," Gar agreed. "Don't mistake me—we'll have to be even more watchful than we have been—but I think we can start traveling by daylight. We'll have to, if we want to march more than four hours a night."

"True," Alea said reluctantly. "We'll have to slumber when the sun does."

"We'll have to shift our sleeping schedule bit by bit," Gar said. "We've been awake six hours, to judge by the stars, so let's nap for an hour or two, then walk till mid-afternoon and see how long we can sleep,"

"That could work," Alea admitted, "but we'll be starting very early tomorrow."

They rested for a while, eating a light meal, then set off again—but they had only been walking a few hours when they met the giant band.

9

There were eight of them, and two of the giants were balancing the ends of a pole on their shoulders. Slung from that pole was an ox. Each giant carried a bow or spear in addition to the axe at his or her waist.

"Run!" Alea caught Gar's arm.

"Oh, I think we're far enough north that there's no danger of their mistaking us for spies," Gar said easily. "We have come into the North Country, haven't we?"

That brought Alea up short. "If you're right about our having come more than three hundred miles, yes." She wasn't sure, actually, but she'd heard that the border of Midgard was three hundred miles or so to the north of her village.

"Well, we've met giants before, and they were peaceable enough—as long as we were. You're right, though, it might be better for you to stay hidden until we're sure." Gar started to angle toward the giants.

Resentment flared into anger, and for a few seconds, Alea glared at Gar's retreating back with pure hatred. How dare he make her feel so small! She ran, caught up with him, and snapped, "If you're not afraid of them, neither am I!"

The warmth and admiration of the look he gave her quelled the hatred utterly. "You have courage, Alea, and that's more important than being fearless."

She managed to glare at him anyway, uncertain whether or not she was being complimented. "You seem awfully sure that they won't try to kill us!"

"Not quite sure," Gar replied, "but if what you've told me about the North Country is true, I think they'll at least be civil."

"So it will be my fault if they attack?" Alea demanded.

"Oh, no. It will still be my fault." Gar grinned. "After all, you would never be as foolish as I."

Alea had to work to keep the resentment and anger going. Then she had to work to keep her fear from showing, as they came onto the same trackway as the giants.

By the gods, they were huge! But when they saw the travelers wading out of the grass onto their road, they halted, and the two bearers laid the dead ox beside the track. No one drew an axe, but every right hand rested on a belt by the axe-head, and every left hand moved bow or spear a little to the fore.

"Hail!" Gar held up a palm, imitating the giants' accent as well as he could. "May your road be smooth!"

"May your road be soft," a woman in the front rank of the giants said. By her gray hair and lined face, they could see she was the oldest present. "Where are you bound, strangers?"

"To Nibelheim," Gar answered. "We dare not cross Midgard to go there. I am Gar, and this woman is Alea."

Alea stared. A woman, be spokesman for a hunting band?

"Have we come into the North Country?" Gar asked.

"You have indeed." The giant frowned. "Do you not know where you are?"

"No, for we've never been here before, and have only rumors to guide us," Gar said. "What lies before us?"

"Moor with outcrops of woodlands, and a broad river," the Jotun said.

"There is a ford a day's journey north of this track," one of the men informed them.

"We heard a dog pack in the distance," a younger woman added. "They did not come near us, though."

"I don't wonder at that," Alea muttered.

"But why do you not dare go through Midgard?" the spokeswoman asked. "Are you renegades?"

"You could call us that," Gar said slowly. "We are escaped slaves, who dare not go back."

"Too tall for the Midgarders, eh?" The woman nodded. "We've heard of that. You don't look much taller than most Midgarders to me, but I hear they have very little patience with a few extra inches."

"Oh, you may be sure of that," Alea said, her voice almost a whisper.

The giant woman's gaze focused on her, frowning, and Alea felt her blood go cold. "What did you say, lass?" the woman asked.

"I said, 'You may be sure of that,' " Alea answered more loudly, "and I'm a grown woman, not a lass!"

"Gently," Gar hissed. "Don't start something I can't finish."

But the giant woman inclined her head in grave apology. "Your pardon, young woman. To us, all Midgarders look much the same, and you're young enough that I couldn't say whether you were fifteen or thirty."

Alea could only stare, thunderstruck by such courtesy in a person of authority.

Gar's elbow in her ribs jarred her out of her trance. "Accept her apology," he muttered.

Alea gave herself a shake. "Your pardon for my sharpness, Great One—and I thank you for your courtesy."

The woman smiled gently. "Call me by name—I am Riara. You sound as though you're not used to it."

"I'm not," Alea said shortly. Then the desire for sheer fairness made her jerk her head toward Gar. "Except in him. His name is Gar, and I'm Alea."

Gar looked down at her, pleasantly surprised, and might have said something if the giant woman hadn't spoken first.

"A pleasant meeting, Gar and Alea." Riara's face creased with a smile. Then caution returned as she asked, "Why do you wish to go to Nibelheim?"

Gar turned back to her. "We have spoken with giants, and found that most of what the Midgarders teach their children about your folk is false. Now we wish to talk with dwarves, and learn if there is any measure of truth in that set of tales."

"Well, we do not know the tales, so we cannot judge of that for you," the giant woman said, frowning.

"We know the dwarves, though," one of the men said. "They are as good a folk as we, though their ways are not ours."

"Still, you have the right of it in that you must see for yourselves," a third giant said. "Beware, though, for the dwarves will."

"Will beware of us?" Gar nodded. "Well, they might, if they have fought the Midgarders as long as you have."

"You do not sound like a Midgarder, though." The older woman eyed him with suspicion.

Alea spoke up. "It is because he tries to speak as you do."

"I do that," Gar admitted. "I thought it a sign of respect."

"And a slighter chance that we might misunderstand you?" The older woman smiled, but it was only a quirk of the lips. "Speak as you would without such effort."

"Why, then, this is how I sound," Gar said, without his imitation Jotunish. "Can you understand me clearly?"

"Aye, but you still do not sound like a Midgarder," the woman said, "nor even like the woman who accompanies you."

"That's because I'm from far away," Gar said, glibly but truthfully. "I came into Midgard as a friend, and was forced to my knees and enslaved within minutes."

Alea stared at him in surprise.

"It would seem your companion has not heard of this," the giant woman said.

Gar shrugged. "There was no reason to tell her. She has troubles enough of her own."

"But I asked." The giant nodded. "You must have known nothing of Midgard indeed—or you must be a mighty fool."

"A fool I am," Gar returned, "for I believe that giants, Midgarders, and dwarves can learn to live with one another in peace."

All the giants shouted with laughter, and the sound struck Alea and Gar as a physical sensation.

When she could bring her laughter under control, Riara wiped her eyes and said, "Foolish indeed! We giants might live as friends with the dwarves, but the Midgarders would never cease to attack us both! Don't mistake me, they would cheerfully enslave all of Nibelheim if they could—but I would not call that living in peace."

"No, nor would I," Gar assured her. "Of course, you might choose to enslave them."

The last chuckles cut off as though by the blow of an axe, and a giant rumbled, "That is not our way."

"Even if it were, there are too many of them," Riara said.

Gar didn't look convinced.

But Riara nodded. "You must indeed be from very far away, if you know so little of the Midgarders—and so little of us. Nay, come home with us, wayfarers, for if you insist on going ahead with your folly, you might as well have a night or two under a real roof—and you surely must learn something more about Jotuns."

Alea stared in amazement, then stepped back and a little behind Gar out of fear.

Gar, though, only looked surprised. "We are honored, good woman—but dare you trust Midgarders among you?"

"Only two of you, and so small?" Riara waved a hand to dismiss the notion. "Be our guests, strangers, and let us show you that giants are not monsters."

Fear made a taste like metal on Alea's tongue, fear made her belly clench, nearly cramp, and she could have screamed with frustration when Gar gave a courtly bow and said, "How good of you to offer—and what a mannerless churl I would be if I declined! Thank you, thank you a thousand times for your hospitality. We will be very pleased to accept."

"We will be pleased to have you," Riara said, smiling. "Come with us, then."

But Alea seized his upper arm in a grip so hard and unexpected that it made him wince. "How can you feel safe among people so much bigger than yourself?" she hissed.

"I am supremely conceited," he whispered back.

She glared at him, knowing it wasn't true.

"If you'll excuse me a minute," Gar said to the giant woman, "my companion needs a word in private."

Riara nodded, her face stolid. "Of course. Step aside; we'll not listen." And she turned to discuss the event with her friends. One or two glanced at Gar and Alea as they moved a few paces away, but they turned back to the conversation resolutely, determined to honor privacy.

"You may be able to fight a dog pack," Alea told Gar angrily, "but you can't fight a whole village full of giants!"

"Oh, I can fight them," Gar told her. "I'll lose, but I can fight them. Still, I don't think I'll have to. Even if they do become angry with us or try to imprison us, there are always ways to escape."

Alea scowled, suddenly aware that there was something he wasn't telling. "How can you be so sure!"

"If I can escape from a Midgarder farm," Gar told her, "I can escape from a giant's pen. They're not even used to trying to keep people in."

"How do you know that?" she asked suspiciously.

"You heard them yourself—they don't take slaves," Gar told her. "Besides, they look to be the kind of people to whom hospitality is sacred. Still, I can understand your reluctance to spend a night among them. I can escort you to a safe hiding place, then go back to follow the giants' trail to their village."

Alea felt a sudden determination not to show the slightest sign of fear in Gar's presence. "What you do, I'll do! But by all the gods, you'd better be right!"

Why on earth should he have given her such a shining look? She could almost have sworn he was proud of her stand! But all he said was, "I chose better than I knew when I asked you to travel with me. Let's go be good guests to generous hosts, then."

He turned away, and Alea followed, only a pace or two to the side, wondering why her knees felt weak. It must have been her fear of the giants. She found herself hoping that none of them would find her pretty.

The first sign that they were coming to the village was a dozen giants leveling the earth of the roadway with six-foot-wide rakes, then spreading sand over it, then levering slabs of rock two feet thick and six feet square into place on top. Riara and her party hailed them, and the giants grinned and waved back, then stared at the two guests and clustered around, gesturing and bombarding them with questions. Alea shrank back, she couldn't help it, but Gar grinned widely and answered every question and asked a number in his turn. He seemed very interested in their system of roadwork, and Alea could have screamed at him in frustration—but she saw his strategy quickly enough; in minutes, the road crew were discussing construction techniques with him, and not the viciousness and prejudices of Midgarders. In fact, they seemed to accept him as an equal, and not even all that much of a stranger.

"How did you manage to make them friends so quickly?' she asked as Riara led their party onward.

"Masons welcome one another everywhere there are people," Gar told her.

Alea frowned. "I didn't know you were a mason."

"Well, not that kind," Gar admitted, "but I'm interested in everything." He looked up at the nearest giant. "Where is that road going?"

"Back to Jotunheim," the big fellow told him. "We're only a colony, you know, up here in the North Country. Things were getting crowded back home—we could see the smoke of three other villages on the horizon."

"Yes, definitely time to look for more elbow room," Gar

agreed. "But your colony must be doing very well, if you can spare the time to build a road."

The giant shrugged. "We enjoy building. When we have an hour or two free, we like to use it to make things of stone."

They had obviously had quite a few hours to lavish on their village. Gar and Alea's first sight of it was a huge wall twenty-five feet high, and all of stone. It stretched out a quarter mile to either side. She stopped and stared. "Do you call this a village?"

Orla, the young giant woman beside her, shrugged. They had become acquainted while they were walking, and Alea was amazed how quickly Orla had put her at her ease. "There are only a few hundred of us living here—but we do need more room than you. . . ." She stopped abruptly, leaving the word hanging, and Alea had just time enough to realize Orla had kept herself from saying "Midgarders" before the giant woman hurried on. "You would think that, if we're only half again as tall, we'd need only half as much room—but it isn't like that, any more than my being half again as tall should mean I'm only half again as wide." She grinned down at Alea. "I'm more than twice as wide as you, as you can see, and I need four times as much space."

"And four times as much, when you have hundreds of people. . . ." Alea shook her head in wonder, staring at the massive wall before her. "To us, that would be a town, and a big one!"

It seemed even bigger as they went through the gates, the hunters waving and joking with the sentries who leaned over the top of the wall, and the gate-guards who stood at its foot. They walked, and walked, and walked—the wall was twelve feet thick, or more!

"Is it solid all the way through?" Alea asked, wide-eyed.

"Of course!" Orla answered. "How else could it hold the weight of an army of giants?"

"An army? Where?" Alea darted fearful glances all about as they came past the wall and into the town.

"Here." Orla tapped her chest, grinning. "And, there, and there." She pointed at the other hunters, then at the houses, then swept her arm to include the whole village. "All about you! We're all the army, everyone sixteen years and older—if we have to be. We can't understand how you . . . how those Midgarders can afford to waste people who could be soldiers by making them slaves!"

"Looking at you, I can't understand it either," Alea agreed.

But she wasn't looking at Orla, she was looking all about her at the giants' village.

All their buildings were of stone, real stone, though the older ones were built of irregular field stones set cleverly together. The newer ones were of quarried stone, so closely fitted that she didn't even see room for mortar. They were each of only one story, though—she was amazed all over again at the thought that fifteen feet from ground to rafters was only one story! But there was only one course of windows, their tops on a level with the door's, so it had to be only one—and for a ten-foot giant, surely that wasn't too much room. The roofs were thatched, and she suspected there was timber beneath the straw—but there were no second floors. She wasn't surprised—she wouldn't have wanted to try to build a floor that would have held the weight of half a dozen of these people, and would have wanted even less to be in the room below them. Why, such a chamber would have needed so many pillars that it would have seemed a granite forest!

The houses were set wide apart, with sheep cropping grass around fruit trees. For a village, it was open and roomy—but it must have seemed almost crowded, to the giants. Alea was amazed by the room, and the richness of so much rock—she had seen very few stone buildings in her life, only the temple, the village hall, and the earl's castle. All the others had been of wattle and daub—but here, even the poorest giant had a stone dwelling!

If there was a poorest giant. All the houses looked to be pretty much of a size, with one great building looming over the rest—the village hall, no doubt—and the people all wore very similar clothing, tunics with cross-gartered bias-hosen, all dyed in bright colors. What a contrast to her own dun-and-gray hamlet! But looking at the women, she realized she need not have worried about lustful young giants—all of them were like Riara, Orla, and the other female hunters. She had assumed that any who went hunting would be rougher than most, more sturdily built—but she saw that all the giant women were as thick in limb and body as Riara and the women of her band. If there was any difference between men and women, it was that the men had heavier faces, as though they'd been hewn from blocks of granite by a mason with a dull adze, while the women's faces seemed dainty by comparison. On the road, Alea had thought Riara looked like a section of tree trunk with the bark left on—but next to the men of her age, she seemed almost delicate. The women had breasts and broader hips, of course, though the difference seemed slight when all had such mighty limbs and the men's chests were so heavily muscled. Alea was certainly far too frail for their notion of beauty. The giant women made her feel petite and dainty for the first time in her life, and she very much appreciated it.

She realized that the only reason Rokir and Jorak, the two

pubescent outcasts, had desired her was because they'd been raised as Midgarders, with the shorter people's ideal of prettiness. Of course, they'd also wanted to use her as a target for revenge on the people who had cast them out, perhaps even their own mothers.

The thought gave her a chill, and she forced it aside, made the effort to turn her attention to the amazing sights about her again. She was fascinated to see that the women were no shorter than the men—but the giants varied so much in size that it didn't seem to matter. Most were ten feet tall, or thereabouts, but some were only nine feet, some eleven, and a few twelve feet tall, or nearly. Some of the women were shorter than some of the men, some were taller, and nobody cared.

They were all massive, though, very massive, and Alea wasn't surprised to see that the pathways were only earth, but packed so hard she doubted even a flood could turn them to mud. When the clay bore the tread of so many feet with so much weight upon them, it probably packed as hard as brick.

Then she saw a Midgarder and cried out in surprise and fear, ducking behind Orla.

"What? Is someone trying to hurt you?"

Alea looked up and was amazed to see Gar standing there, arm out to support, hand out to comfort, though he didn't touch her. Only a moment ago, he'd been talking to a man half his size!

"No one's trying to hurt her," Orla assured him, and reached down to touch Alea's shoulder, ever so lightly. "No one will. What frightened you, friend Alea?"

Friend! Alea stared up at her wide-eyed, caught between delight and fear. "The Midgarder—he mustn't see me!"

"Midgarder?" Orla frowned. "There are no . . ."

"There." Gar jerked his head toward the middle-aged man who was approaching, face all concern.

Orla looked up. "Oh, you mean Garlon? He's no Midgarder, he's my father."

Gar and Alea both stared.

Garlon slowed, nearing them, and smiled. "It's true enough, young folk. I'm a giant, despite my inches—or lack of them—because, you see, I'm the son of two giants!"

"It's quite possible," Gar said, wide-eyed. "Recessive genes don't always link up."

Alea turned to him in irritation. "What nonsense are you talking?"

"Rude nonsense," Gar told her, then to Garlon, "My apologies, goodman. I shouldn't have stared, but you took me quite by surprise." *After all,* he reflected, *it's one thing to see them in orbital photographs, but quite another to meet them and find they have names.*

"I don't mind at all," Garlon said, holding out a hand. "We're not used to visitors, you see, and especially not ones from Midgard, so we don't think to explain in advance."

Gar shook his hand. "So giants sometimes have Midgard-sized children or grandchildren?"

"Yes, and sometimes smaller—I've four of my own children, and Orla is the only one who's a giant."

Orla nodded. "My sister and my younger brother are a little shorter than you, and my older brother is almost short enough to be a dwarf."

"There are even a fair number of dwarf children born to each generation," Garlon explained, "but when they're grown, they generally band together and travel to Nibelheim, looking for mates."

"Isn't the North Country dangerous, though?" Gar asked, frowning.

Garlon grinned. "Our children are a match for any dogs or pigs, stranger, I assure you of that—if there are enough of them."

"Fascinating," Gar said. "But the most vicious predators walk on two legs, not four."

"You mean the bandits cast out of Midgard, and the hunters who track them?" Orla grinned. "Giant brothers and sisters escort the dwarves, so they always survive the trip. Then the giants born of Nibels come back with them, to seek mates here—though truth to tell, they often find them on the trip, among one another."

"It must be hard to say goodbye to a child forever," Gar said to Garlon, face somber.

"Oh, they manage to send messages home with the rare travelers who happen by," Garlon assured him. "The North Country isn't an absolute waste, and there are caravans of merchants now and then. Even bandits think twice about attacking a hundred well-armed dwarves, or a dozen giants."

"Or sixty of both together," Orla amended.

"Amazing," Alea breathed. "They never told us any of this at home!"

"No, because they wanted you to believe we're monsters, or at least completely different from you," Garlon told her.

"Of course," Gar said slowly. "If Midgarders knew that you have children their own size, they'd have to think of you as people, like themselves!"

"Indeed they would." For a moment, Garlon's disgust showed, but he hid it quickly. "Then, of course, they'd have no excuse to go on enslaving one another, or driving out the ones who grow too big." He looked up at Orla. "How was the hunting, daughter?"

"Good enough, Father," Orla swung a game bag off her shoulder and down to him. "There's a dozen geese and eight partridges in there, and the other hunters did as well or better."

Garlon staggered under the weight of the bag, but bore up bravely and turned away. "Come, let us show this bounty to your mothers! Strangers, will you dine with us tonight?"

Alea stared, surprised by the invitation, but Gar said, "We'd be delighted. How kind of you to ask."

"I think the whole village may feast on the common, Father," Orla said as she fell in beside him. "Together, we managed to fell an ox, but I'm sure you've seen that."

"I have indeed, and that's reason enough for feasting tonight," Garlon puffed. "I'm glad you had a good day." He beamed up at Orla with pride. "I wondered when you chose Dumi as your goddess when you were so small, but you've proved true to her in every way."

Orla blushed with pleasure, seeming to expand a little with her father's praise, though he only came up to her bottom rib.

Gar frowned. "Who is Dumi?"

"The goddess of the hunt," Orla told him. "Don't you learn of her, in Midgard?"

"No, we don't," Alea said. "Tell me of her!"

"Well, she's a virgin goddess," Orla said, grinning, "but I don't intend to imitate her in that, at least not forever. I think I'll have to go visit relatives in Jotunheim, though."

"I suppose you will," Garlon sighed, "but there are half a dozen young men here who are worthy of you, Orla, hard though it is for me to admit it."

Gar smiled. "I thought no father ever thought any man was good enough for his daughter."

"Well, I do have to strive to keep an open mind," Garlon admitted.

"All the young men here are very nice," Orla sighed, "but none of them makes my heart beat any faster."

Alea stared at her. "What has that to do with marriage?"

Orla stared back. Then her face darkened with anger. "By the goddess! Those Midgarders only give you a choice between two kinds of slavery, don't they?"

Gar said quickly, "Do I take it that a woman can live with respect and comfort here even if she doesn't marry?"

"Of course!" Garlon said in surprise. "What loving father would make his daughter marry a man she doesn't love, just to have a living?"

"True," Alea said bitterly, "but if that is so, Midgard is filled with unloving fathers." She sent up a prayer of thanks to Freya that she had not been so cursed.

Garlon scowled, but before he could say anything, they came out between two houses to the village green. Giants were clustered around with a liberal sprinkling of smaller people, watching two huge young men wrestling, stripped to the waist and shiny with sweat.

Orla slowed, her eye gleaming. "Let's watch for a little while, Father."

"Why, as you wish, child," Garlon said, giving her a sly look.

They moved onto the grass and stopped twenty feet from the wrestlers. Alea saw why Orla was interested—even she felt a tremor of response inside her at the sight of those huge muscles sliding beneath burnished skin, even though the men were blocky and lumpy by her own standards. She found it interesting that they had very little body hair, even though they had thick and luxuriant beards. Perhaps they shaved. . . .

Gar watched with great interest as the two men grappled, then sprang apart, panting, then sprang together again. Suddenly one giant went shooting up into the air, sailed back, and landed with an impact that shook the ground. The crowd made noises of approval, but Gar almost shouted with delight. "Well thrown! Deftly done!"

The thrown rolled and rose up, but the victor turned to Gar with a grin. "Many thanks, little man. I'm surprised you could see what I did. I didn't know Midgard paid any attention to wrestling."

"I'm not your average Midgarder," Gar told him.

"Then perhaps you'd like to try a fall or two," the young giant said.

A slow grin spread over Gar's face. Alea turned to him in a panic, but before she could say anything, he had stepped forward, casting away his cloak and slipping out of his tunic. "Why, thank you! I'd love the exercise. What are your rules?"

10

For one, we don't allow people like young Skorag to wrestle when there's so great a difference in size!" Garlon protested, hurrying forward.

"Difference in size? I'm only nine feet tall, Goodman Garlon, and your guest must be seven!" the young giant protested.

"Seven, and a few years older and more experienced than you," Gar told him. He stepped close and dropped into a wrestler's crouch. "Someone say 'go.' "

"Go!" rumbled a dozen voices.

"Orla, stop them!" Alea cried. "Gar will be squashed!"

"What can we do, when the young bucks are so determined to impress us?" Orla sighed.

Alea turned to stare. Could that really be what was pushing Gar into this fight? But why would he want to impress her?

Skorag shouted and slapped at Gar—and the smaller man swung in to tangle the giant's legs somehow. Skorag lurched forward; Gar pulled on an arm, and the young giant fell.

The crowd shouted with delight and surprise. Other giants stopped what they were doing to look up, then came to see what was going on.

Skorag climbed to his feet with a savage grin. "Not bad, little fellow! First fall to you—but I'll take the second."

"Toss me if you can," Gar taunted.

Skorag did. Alea didn't see exactly how—she only saw Gar cartwheeling up into the sky, and cried out in fright.

Orla's arm clasped her shoulders. "Don't fear, little sister. They . . ."

Laughing, Skorag caught Gar as though he were a baby, then tumbled him to the ground. "You were lucky the first time, stranger!"

Gar rolled to his feet—right under Skorag, as the giant bent into his wrestler's crouch. Gar turned his back, seized Skorag's forearm, and pulled the giant down on top of him—except that somehow he stayed on his feet, and Skorag went tumbling.

"Lucky twice," Gar noted.

Skorag grunted with surprise and climbed back up. "There must be some skill in you, I'll grant you that!"

"Your turn," Gar said.

Skorag slapped at him, yanked his arm away from an attempted grab, caught a knee with the other arm and tossed Gar into the air. Alea cried out again, pressing tight against Orla's side, but Gar seemed to bounce to his feet, grinning. "Neatly done! Have you thought of trying this?" He swung both hands down on the other's shoulders, pushing hard, leaping into the air—but Skorag swept a hand up to push Gar's heels high, laughing. Gar landed on his back, but somehow he still had hold of Skorag's hand, and the giant's laugh turned into a grunt of surprise as he went flying over Gar, balanced on the smaller man's heels, to somersault ten feet past Gar's head.

He rolled up to his feet, laughing. "I didn't look for that one! But can you see this coming?" He swept Gar up into a bear hug, which the smaller man slipped out of as though he were greased—and tripped over the foot Skorag swung up as his right arm swept around to push Gar over.

Gar dove and somersaulted, coming up to his feet, still grinning—and Alea stared, dazed by the glow that seemed to emanate from him, compounded of sweat and energy and sheer delight in physical contest. She heard Orla's breath hiss in, and knew the bigger woman was experiencing the same stab of feeling that resonated deep inside. *Why, Gar's handsome,* she thought, amazed. Why had she never noticed it before?

Then Gar caught Skorag around the neck with one hand, the other on the giant's arm, but Skorag had caught him in the same hold, and for several minutes, they strained against one another, each shifting his weight to counter the other's twisting, each striving for an advantage, an opening. Muscles bulged under sweat-shiny skin, virtually frozen, giving time for contemplation, and the two women stared, spellbound,

Suddenly the sculpture erupted into movement, and Gar spun out like a dancer's skirt, flying ten feet to land on his side. Alea shoved her fist into her mouth to stifle a scream, but Gar pushed himself to his feet, still grinning, and went back toward Skorag, feet wide apart, crouching as he walked.

Garlon stepped forward. "Enough, enough, young men! Gar, you have fought bravely, and we're all amazed that you could throw a giant three times—but he has tumbled you five, and will widen that margin if you persist."

"He will indeed," said a ten-foot giant with a grizzled beard, stepping forward to lift Skorag's hand. "Hail the winner!"

The crowd shouted their approval.

"And hail the Midgarder who managed to give him a real bout!" the giant cried, raising Gar's arm.

The shout turned into a roar.

Skorag grinned and lowered his hand, holding it out to Gar. Gar took it, grinning in return, and bowed. Surprised, Skorag imitated the movement. Then both turned away, to catch up their tunics.

Alea broke from Orla and ran at Gar, crying. "You idiot! You fool! My heart nearly stopped every time you struck the ground!"

"Did it really?" Gar stopped with his tunic about to go over his head, his eyes meeting hers—and for a moment, those eyes were all there was in the world.

Then Alea turned away, feeling her face grow hot, and said, "Of course! What would happen to me if anything happened to you?"

"I think that's the second best reason I've ever heard for two people to protect each other," Gar told her, then stepped closer and spoke softly. "But the bout was good strategy, you see. They'll welcome us more warmly now."

Alea thought of her sudden bond with Orla, but only said, "You didn't say what the best reason was."

Gar was looking off to the side, though, and grinning. "I thought your friend didn't find any of the boys here very interesting."

Looking up, Alea saw Orla talking with Skorag, and saw the extra inch to her smile, the gleam in her eye, as the giant woman tossed her head, chin tilting up, even though she was six inches taller than Skorag. He moved a little closer, his own grin widening as he looked up at her, saying something they couldn't hear.

"It would seem both of us have succeeded in our purposes," Gar said, "Skorag and I."

"Oh? And your purpose was only to gain greater acceptance by these overgrown boys, was it?"

Gar gave her a heavy-lidded glance, but quickly looked away and said, "Well, there might have been an ulterior motive." Then he froze, staring. "Is that what I think it is?"

Frowning and vaguely disappointed, Alea followed his gaze and saw one of the stone houses with a straight line slanting upward toward a nearby tree, shining in the late afternoon light. "It's a cord running up to a branch—but why?"

"Because it's an antenna." Gar yanked his tunic over his head and stepped away to catch up his cloak. "Let's go see what's in that house, shall we?"

Alea started after him, but just then, Orla tossed her head again and turned away from Skorag, who watched her walk away with a very intent gaze. The giant woman reached out to Alea. "Come, little sister! You must meet the women of my clan!"

Alea knew better than to protest—it might seem rude and, somehow, she sensed that she was being honored. But she cast a backward glance at Gar as he strode toward the house with the cord, hoping that he would understand when she didn't follow.

Gar followed his host, remembering his excitement when he and Herkimer had discovered that this lost colony hadn't quite regressed to completely medieval culture.

"What could have sent this colony into back to the Middle Ages?" Gar wondered.

"That happened to quite a few colonies," Herkimer reminded him, "when Mother Terra withdrew her economic and technological support."

"True, but there are usually some signs of a high technology origin," Gar said. "Is there any reason to think this colony hasn't completely regressed?"

"Only some rather constant radio signals, Magnus."

Magnus sat up straight, eyes wide. "Radio? With horned helmets? Solid state war axes? Just what is going *on* here?"

"Battles, as we know," Herkimer replied. "Most of the radio messages seem to be tactical orders in Terran Standard Language, with a thick local accent—three of them, in fact."

"One for each nation." Magnus nodded. "What about the messages that aren't military?"

"I would have to call it gossip, though perhaps it is news," Herkimer said. "I confess that it makes little or no sense—the voices are discussing events and concepts that are totally foreign to me. Without knowledge of the cultural context, I can make no sense of them."

"Then we need to learn something about their history and the way they live," Magnus agreed, "more than we can find out from orbit. Brace yourself for a wild guess, Herkimer."

"I am braced." The computer sounded resigned; it was basically allergic to ideas that could not be proved by evidence.

"It's possible that the rulers of this society—of one of the three societies, I should say—have managed to hold onto their power by having kept knowledge of high technology to themselves and letting the majority of their people drift back into the Dark Ages."

"They do dress like Teutonic barbarians," Herkimer admitted, "and your hypothesis does account for a medieval civilization having radio. But it does not account for the informal conversations in so many of the transmissions."

"Well, it was a try," Magnus sighed. "Can you tell anything else from the messages?"

"There is an anomaly here," the computer replied. "The

chatty messages are in two accents and use only AM, though they also transmit some military information. The third accent, though, is transmitting in FM, and is communicating only battle orders, with the occasional message that has to do with apprehending fugitives."

"Strange." Magnus frowned. "At a guess, I'd say that one of the three nations doesn't want to talk to the others. Beyond that . . ."

This nation of giants, however, seemed quite ready to talk—in fact, to chatter. As Garlon led Gar into the huge cottage, he saw half a dozen giants sitting at two long tables, one at either side of the room, all of them leaning back in cozy conversation with disembodied voices that rattled from large paper-coned loudspeakers. The giants spoke into microphones as large as Gar's head, but their transceivers were miniature boxes not much bigger than Gar's hand.

He relaxed, feeling suddenly at home in the presence of electronic technology, remembering Fess, his father's robot horse, who had been the inseparable companion of his childhood. Of course, Gar had tried to separate himself from the robot several times, wanting an adventure Fess wouldn't have approved of, but the computer-brained steel horse had found him every time.

It almost seemed that Fess had found him again.

The women were gathered about the firepit at one end of the common. There were several men working with them, skinning out and cleaning the ox.

"That was a good match," one of the men opined.

"It was indeed, Korlan," Garlon agreed. "I was amazed that Gar lasted so long against a giant."

Korlan nodded. "I was proud of my son. He wrestled his best, but was careful not to hurt the little fellow."

"You should be proud indeed," Garlon agreed.

Alea was surprised that he took no offense hearing a man bigger than he referred to as "little"; he seemed to understand that the term was relative.

"Skorag showed good hospitality to a guest, Isola," Riara said to another woman. "You have reared him well."

Isola smiled, pleased. "Thank you, Riara. He wrestles well and is considerate. Now if he would only settle his heart on one young woman, I would count myself a successful mother indeed."

Orla suddenly became very concerned with the bit of hide she was scraping.

Alea watched her, smiling. "If you can find me a knife, I can help."

"Surely, little sister." Orla took a second knife from her belt, glad of the change of subject.

The blade was as long as Alea's hand. She started scraping the hide loose, saying, "This knife must be so small for you! Why do you carry it?"

"For splitting the quills of feathers, to fletch arrows," Orla told her, "and other fine work."

Isola and Korlan lifted the ox high so the others could scrape the hide off the underside. Alea was glad the head, hooves, and tail had been removed before she came, and the spit placed. She'd seen such things done before, but preferred not to.

"This whole generation of young men seems to have grown up healthy and strong," Riara said. "The gods have blessed us."

"I like the chests on them," Orla said; then, critically,

"Some of them have lumpy arms, though. Muscle enough, mind you, but lumpy."

"I know what you mean," said Riara. "I prefer a clean flowing line to the shape, myself."

Garlon surveyed the woodpile and said, "I think we'd better see to splitting some more logs."

"I'll come with you," said one of the other men, almost twice Garlon's size.

They strolled off as Isola and Korlan, with a grunt of effort, hoisted the spit onto its brackets.

"Stand clear," another man told them, then struck sparks into the tinder in the firepit. He blew on it gently; the fire caught and ran through the kindling.

"There should be dancing tonight, Tovaw," Korlan told him. "Are your pipes tuned?"

"I had better check them," Tovaw said.

"And my drum needs a new head." Korlan strolled off with him, sharing a grin.

"I don't like lumpy legs, either," one of the other women said. "Muscles, yes, but not if they're knobby."

"I forged a dozen arrowheads today," one of the remaining two men told the other. "Did you bring home an eagle from your hunt?"

"No, but a large hawk should do as well," the other said. "We had better fletch some more arrows."

They rambled away, but glanced back at the women, then exchanged knowing nods.

"Well, of all the nerve!" Alea cried indignantly. "Leaving us as though we had the plague! Your men are no better than ours!"

Then she realized that Isola was smirking as she watched the men wander off.

"They want us to be free to discuss their merits," Riara told Alea, "without worrying about hurting their feelings."

"Can women hurt men's feelings?" Alea asked, amazed.

The women laughed heartily at that, and Orla said, "Your Midgard upbringing has left you with a great deal to learn, little sister. Yes, we can hurt their feelings as easily as they can hurt ours."

"More easily," Riara said. "Their vanity is so easily wounded, poor souls."

"Sometimes I think they value our good opinion too highly," said another woman.

"True, Sria," Riara said, "but never let them know it!"

That brought another general laugh. As it ended, Alea said, "Their wandering off, then, was only good manners?"

"Well, a bit more, I would say," Sria said judiciously, "but yes, it's a mark of their regard for us."

"And fear of what they might hear," chuckled a fourth woman.

"A giant can face anything but a woman's scorn, Narei," Riara agreed.

"If he cares for the woman," Narei amended.

Alea only listened, wide-eyed. She had never thought that men might fear women's opinions of them—but that did explain why they were so quick to anger.

"You seem to know little of men's better side," Narei told her.

"You might say that," Alea said bitterly. "Mind you, I've seen a few men who did treat their wives gently, but only when they thought no one else was watching."

That brought a storm of incredulous questions and horrified denials.

"Surely they must flatter you when they're courting you," Orla objected.

"I wouldn't know," Alea said, bile on her tongue. "None ever courted me—I was too big."

But Riara caught some sort of undertone to her denial. "None at all?"

"Well, there was one when I was very young, scarcely a woman." Alea had to force the words out. "I didn't realize that he only meant to use me, not to marry me. I learned quickly enough, though, when he went on to another lass."

"He didn't!" Narei cried indignantly.

"You mean he had the audacity to court you when he didn't mean to marry you?" Orla asked, aghast.

"I mean exactly that, though of course I didn't know it until he'd had what he wanted and left me." Even now, fourteen years later, Alea had to fight back tears.

"If any of our young men did that, the fathers and brothers would beat him to a pulp," Isola said darkly, "if we women did not do it to them first."

Alea stared. "Do none of your young men come courting unless they are ready to propose?"

"Not ready, but wanting to," Orla said slowly, "and we, for our part, let them know quite quickly if we don't."

"It's unfair to keep them dancing on a string, like puppets," Riara agreed.

"Of course," Sria said, "they aren't allowed to court until they have proved they can grow a crop, raise animals, and bring home a filled game bag."

"And before a man can propose, he must build a house, though his friends may help him," Riara said, "and keep it clean, inside and out."

"Of course, we have to prove the same," Orla said.

"And that you can cook?"

"Cook?" the giant woman exclaimed, astonished. "Everyone can cook! How else do you think bachelors stay alive?"

"Why, living at home, where their mothers can feed them," Alea said.

The women all laughed at that. When their mirth had ebbed, Riara said, "Fancy a mother letting a grown man stay around the house! No, our young men live in the bachelors' house, and if they haven't learned to clean up after themselves by then, they quickly do!"

"We've heard the Midgarders don't treat their women very well, little sister," Orla said, frowning. "From what you say, it would seem to be true."

"I had no complaint of my father's treatment," Alea said slowly, "but outside the home, the boys were forever insulting me—and, for that matter, the girls were, too."

She told a little of the constant insults and slights she had suffered at the hands of her peers, then told them of her treatment when her parents had died, ending in her few days of slavery—the constant insults, the beatings for minor mistakes and for talking back, and the sexual threat. By the time she was done, she was leaning inside the circle of Orla's arm, fighting back tears, and the women were livid.

"We have heard of such things," Riara said darkly. "Tell us his name, so that we may send word to all the giants to take him prisoner if he comes with a raiding party."

Alea stared in surprise.

"Don't worry, little sister, we'll save you the leavings," Orla said, smiling.

"But . . . but . . . would your own men let you beat him?"

"No grown giant tells another what to let or not, my dear,"

Isola said gently. "But as to our men, we dare not tell them why we want the fellow, or they would grow so angry that they would simply squash him, and that's far too quick a punishment for any man who abuses a woman's love."

"It is indeed," Alea said, round-eyed, "and I thank you for saying it!" She had suspected that many women felt as she did, of course, but had never met any who dared speak it aloud.

When the ox was fully roasted, the giants gathered around, chatting and laughing, bringing wooden plates with slabs of bread on them as wide as Alea's arm was long. They took turns cutting slices off the roast for one another.

Gar came up, eyes shining, but sat down beside Alea without saying a word. Frowning up at him, she could see his mind was still busy with the sight of wonders. She felt the same way, but also felt somewhat insulted that he didn't seem to notice her. "Was it so wonderful as all that?"

Gar looked at her in surprise, then looked rueful. "My apologies—I hadn't meant to be rude. But yes, it is wonderful, when you see it in the midst of a medieval village."

"What is it?" she asked, visions of fairy treasures filling her mind.

"Radio," he answered, "a transceiver—a magical box that lets you talk to people a hundred miles away and more, and lets you hear their answers. Only it's not magical, really, just a very clever sort of machine."

"It sounds magical to me," Alea said, wide-eyed. "No one I've met has ever spoken of such a thing! Well, perhaps in the wonder-tales about the ancestors coming down from the stars. . . ."

Gar glanced at her keenly. "So they remember that much,

do they? I must admit that the giants were surprised that a Midgarder should know about radio."

"Well, you're not a Midgarder, really," Alea reminded him.

"I asked how they knew," Gar went on. "They told me that in the early days, only a generation or two after their ancestors came from the stars, the first giants grew so big they scared the Midgarders, and the smaller people drove them out, village by village, all along the western border—but villages were tens of miles apart in those days, so they went about in small bands, not even knowing there were others like them."

Alea stared in surprise; she'd never heard the tale from the giants' side.

"One band, though, stumbled across the remains of a cabin made of a shiny material the Ancestors used, a sort of way station for wanderers who might become lost in the wilderness. It had food and drink stored away, and fuel for heating—but most wonderfully of all, it had a radio. They were sick with loneliness, so they listened to the Midgarders talking to one another. They tried to talk, too, but once the Midgarders knew who they were, they refused to answer. The ancestors played pranks on them anyway, starting conversations, then revealing that they were giants—and learned how to use the device. Then, wonder of wonders, another band of giants answered! They found several radios they could carry with them, and by using those, they were able to find one another."

"So Jotunheim started because of radios?" Alea asked.

"As a nation instead of dozens of small, scattered bands, yes. Once the first two bands had joined together, they were able to search for others. They set about studying the books in the way stations and learned how to make radios of their own. Then bands of explorers went out with transceivers. Some died, but they called back to tell what was happening to them every day, so the ones who followed them were able to avoid the dangers, or be ready to fight them off."

"Packs of wild beasts?" Alea asked.

"Some. There were whirlpools and quicksands, too, and mountain trails prone to rockslides. But most of the explorers found other bands of giants and gave them radios, then fell in love and brought home wives and husbands. With radios, they were able to set up periodic meetings, and the separate bands were able to join together to become a nation. They were also able to call up soldiers to fight when they saw a raiding party coming, and the radios helped them mightily in coordinating a battle—one reason why the giants have managed to survive when they're so badly outnumbered. Then they answered a call seeking someone to talk to, and found it was a dwarf. Now they trade their labor, building stone walls in return for dwarf-made radios. They can build their own, but they say the dwarves make better."

Such cooperation went against everything Alea had been taught about the other nations. In a desperate attempt to hold onto one of her childhood illusions, she demanded, "They trade, even though a few giants have always known how to make these radio things?"

"*Everyone* does!" Gar exulted. "They have schools, actual schools!"

Alea frowned. "What are schools?"

Gar sobered, staring at her. "Don't your peo— Don't the Midgarders have schools for at least some of their children?"

"If they did, would I ask what the word meant?" Alea asked impatiently.

"A school is a building where children, and sometimes adults, are taught how to read and write and . . . oh, all sorts of things. How do your leaders learn?"

"The barons have scholars come to teach their sons," Alea told him, "and any boy who wants to be a priest goes to live in his village's temple. But buildings just for learning? What a waste!"

"Scarcely that," Gar said, "though I can see it's one of the ways your barons keep their power. The hatred they teach you is another—if they can keep you angry about dwarves and giants, no one will think to be angry at the barons."

"Angry at the barons?" Alea stared, scandalized. "But that would be wrong, that would be . . ." She ran out of words as she realized what he meant.

Gar read her eyes and nodded. "None of your people could even think of speaking against the barons, could they? That might make you weaker if you had to fight off a giants' raid. But the giants' government doesn't worry about holding onto its power—there aren't enough of them. They *are* the government, all of them, and they can't afford to waste a single person's talents. Their schools teach all the children, girls and boys, and new giants, outcasts from Midgard, at night. They learn how to read and write, how to use the number-language called mathematics, and all sorts of other things about how to make and build, things I learned under the names of chemistry and physics. They learn literature and history, too—what they know of it."

"Well, everyone knows how to tell stories." Alea was clutching after familiar words.

"Yes, but I think the giants learn a number of stories Midgarders don't know," Gar told her. "The giants do know where the Midgarders found the names for the gods, though—the giants, and the dwarves."

"I could have told you that," Alea told him archly. "We all have to learn the Ring Cycle. In fact, we all grow up singing it, or at least the best of its songs."

"Wagner's Ring Cycle, yes," Gar said, "but the giants tracked those stories back to their source: the sagas, the *Nibelungenlied*. It makes a difference."

"What sort of difference?" Alea asked, but Orla came to hand them each a filled platter, and stayed to talk, so Alea didn't have her answer until after dinner, when the giants began to tell stories and sing songs. She heard the original versions of some of the tales of her childhood, and her eyes grew bigger and bigger as every difference sank home. By the time Orla found beds for them in a guest house, her brain was whirling so much she could barely remember to say, "Thank you."

That whirl in her head may have been the cause, or perhaps it was so much rich food after living on journey rations for two months. Perhaps it was both put together, and the harrowing experiences of her parents' death and her own enslavement—but whatever the cause, Alea dreamed that night, a dream such as she had never had before.

First there was darkness, as there always was behind her eyes at night, though Alea was never aware of it—she simply fell asleep, dreamed, then woke. This time, though, she did become aware of the warm, velvety blackness, and knew when it turned cool and smooth. Then she saw the white dot appear, a dot that expanded most amazingly until she realized that it was a face rushing toward her, a face with no body, turning and turning, its long white hair and beard floating around it. She began to feel fear when the face filled her vision; it reminded her of the baron's steward at her trial, and she was afraid she was looking at Odin himself, but she couldn't have been, because Odin only had one eye, and this old man had two.

"Don't be afraid," the face said. "I am the Wizard, and I have come to tell you about the Way."

11

Alea was a little reassured, but only a little, so she lashed out from simple fear. "How dare you come into my dream without my asking you!"

The face smiled, but said gravely, "Pardon the intrusion. If I did not think the Way would benefit you, I would not have come."

That helped a little. "The Way? What Way?"

"The Way of Virtue," the Wizard told her.

"I've heard talk enough about virtue," Alea said hotly, "and it was nothing but mealymouthed excuses for one person to give in to another. If you're going to tell me I must lose in order for someone else to win, you can swim back into your whirlpool right now!"

She waited, trembling, for the lightning bolt to strike, for the earth to open up and swallow her, but she was absolutely determined not to let this threatening old man see her fear.

Instead, he disappeared—but in his place was a glowing disk with a long S-curve down the middle. One tadpole-shaped half of it was red, with a small yellow circle in the middle of the fat end. The other half was a yellow tadpole, nested against the first, with a small red circle inside.

"This is the Great Monad," the Wizard's voice said, "the great whole. The yellow and red shapes stand for opposites."

"What opposites?" Alea demanded.

"Any opposites," the Wizard answered. "Male and female, darkness and light, day and night, hot and cold, order and chaos—or giant and dwarf."

Alea had a premonition that she wasn't going to like what she heard, but she felt she had to know. "Which color is which?"

"Let us say the red stands for the giants, and the yellow for the dwarves," the wizard's voice said. "Each has the seed of the other within it—the yellow circle in the red, the red circle in the yellow."

"Even as the giants give birth to dwarves," Alea said, "and dwarves give birth to giants." She felt a sudden chill. "But where are the Midgarders?"

"They are the line between the two," the Wizard answered, "the hub out of which both grow, and which grows out of both."

"Even as the seeds of both giants and dwarves are within the Midgarders!" Alea felt a rush of relief, but dread followed it instantly. "You said *all* opposites. Which is good, and which evil?"

"Neither," the Wizard said firmly. "Evil comes when the two are out of balance." The disk began to rotate slowly. "As the wheel turns, the male principle grows greater, and the female smaller. When the midline is mostly male, there is too much order—in government, a wicked king, whom all must obey. No one can choose anything for himself or herself, and disobedience is punished by torture or death. This is evil."

Trust the men for that! Alea thought.

But the disk continued to rotate, and the yellow shape took up less and less of the disk, the red more and more. "When the female principle grows greater and the male lesser, there is chaos. Everyone must forge weapons and build strong walls, for his neighbors may turn on him at any minute, to try to steal all his belongings, as well as his food, his wife, and his children. Bandits infest the countryside; the barons care nothing for their people; the kings are too weak to protect the peasants. This, too, is evil."

"Then good is a balance between the two?" Alea asked doubtfully.

The wheel steadied, male and female taking up equal amounts of its circle.

"Yes, balance is good," the Wizard replied. "In government, there is a monarch, or a council, or both; there is order, but every person is also guaranteed freedom to choose, even as the giants do—freedom to make most of their decisions for themselves."

"And men do not exploit women!"

"They do not, nor do women torment men. Neither seeks to rule the other; each finds his happiness in trying to bring the other joy."

"It sounds pretty," Alea said bitterly, "but how often does it happen? And how long can it last?"

"It happens rarely," the Wizard answered, "though it can be achieved by constant trying. For the Wheel wants to turn, you see; holding it in balance takes effort, constant effort. Harmony is an accomplishment, not something that happens by chance."

Alea thought of Gar, but her thoughts slid away from him. "Are you saying that the Midgarders could make peace if they wanted to?"

"They could," the Wizard answered, "but the giants and dwarves also could bring that peace to them. Each is necessary to the happiness of the others, you see, because they are all parts of one great whole."

"You cannot mean the only way to be happy is for all three to make peace! The giants and dwarves will, I'm sure—but the Midgarders feed on their own hatred! They would die rather than give up their wars!"

"You must find a way," the Wizard said. "You must all find a way, for the happiness of the giants depends on the Midgarders, and their happiness depends on the dwarves. Each one's happiness depends on the other's. To be happy yourself, you must make the others who depend on you happy, too."

"The Midgarders will never believe it!"

"They must learn to, or drown in their own hatred," the Wizard said inexorably. "You must all co-exist in harmony, or you will tear your world apart, tear one another apart, and all end in misery."

Alea shuddered with the chill his words brought.

The disk began to revolve again. "The Wheel turns," the Wizard said. "If you risk your happiness on gaining power, you will be doomed to sorrow, for dominance is constantly changing."

"But the ones who have power make everyone else miserable! The only way to be happy is to have that power!"

"If you have it, you will someday lose it," the unseen Wizard insisted. "The only way to be sure you will be safe is to embrace the whole, male and female together, giant, dwarf, and Midgarder in harmony."

"But how can we ever convince the Midgarders of this?" Alea cried in anguish.

"Tell them the tale of Thummaz," the Wizard answered. "See that it spreads throughout Midgard."

Alea frowned. "Thummaz? Who is Thummaz?"

"A god of whom your ancestors did not tell you," the Wizard said. "The giants know it, though."

Alea stared, outraged at the thought that her ancestors might deliberately have withheld the key to happiness. "Did they know of this Monad, our ancestors?"

"It was not their way of thinking," the Wizard said. Then his tone became stern. "But never forget that is all it is—a way of thinking. This mandala is a guide to clear thought, a device to help you think—it is not truth in itself. Assign the colors as you will, but never forget it is you who assign them, that the Wheel is a thing drawn by people, and that there is a great deal of life that cannot be explained within it."

"It explains enough," Alea said, trembling. "How shall I learn the tale of Thummaz?"

"Ask the giants." The mandala turned back into the face of the Wizard, hair and beard swirling about him as he turned away, receding, growing smaller as the darkness spread inward again.

"Tell me yourself!" Alea demanded in anger.

"It is theirs to tell." The Wizard's voice had become smaller, more distant; he was only a small white circle in a field of blackness turning velvety again, only a white dot; then the darkness swallowed him up, turned warm and embraced Alea, comforting her, drawing all the anxiety out of her, relaxing her, lulling her to sleep again.

The sun rose in a clear sky, but the mist rising from the village green made the giants' houses seem indistinct, unreal.

Nonetheless, giants came forth, their steps slow, speaking little, avoiding one another's eyes, but drawn to the firepit like moths to a flame. Isola knelt there, feeding the flames, building a fire that heated a cauldron into which she crumbled herbs. The giants sat about the fire, hands held out to the warmth, some shivering in spite of it, all looking somber, waiting, waiting for the water to boil. . . .

Waiting for someone else to start speaking.

"Your village makes a man feel very safe," Gar told them all. "I dreamed such dreams as I never have."

Everyone looked up at the word "dreams," but only Gorlan said, "Did you, stranger! And what did you dream of?"

"Of an old man—at least, of his head and face," Gar said. "He called himself the Wizard of the Way, and told me about a thing called the Great Monad."

"Why, I had such a dream!" Skorag said in almost desperate hopefulness.

"I, too," Orla said, meeting his gaze. "He told how men and women are both parts of one whole."

"And giants and dwarves!" exclaimed Korlan. "It was a circle, like this!" He took a stick from the woodpile and scratched the mandala in the bare ground by the firepit.

"Why, even so!" said Riara. "But in my dream, each half had a seed of the other in it."

"Yes, like this." Korlan drew in the small circles.

They compared notes, voices growing more and more excited as it became obvious they had all dreamed the same dream. Only Gar sat silently watching, but his eyes glowed.

"What magic is this?" Isola asked. "Never before have we all dreamed together!"

"It is good magic, whatever it is, if it shows a way to peace and harmony!" Riara said fervently. "Is there a family here that has not lost at least one son or daughter in war? If this dream can stop the Midgarder raids, I will bless it to the end of my days!"

"If we can send word of this among the Midgarders, it might," Gorlan said, frowning. He turned to Gar. "How can we do that?"

"Leave that to the Wizard of the Way," Gar said. Everyone gave him a sharp look, but his eyes told them that he wasn't joking.

"Surely the Wizard was only a dream," Skorag protested.

"Was he?" Gar asked, then looked around the assemblage and raised his voice. "Did no one dream of anything else?"

Silence answered him.

Alea plucked up her nerve and said, "The Wizard told me to ask the giants for the tale of Thummaz."

"You do not know it?" Riara asked in surprize.

"It's not one that's told in Midgard," Alea returned, "just as the story of your Dumi is not."

"Well, the two are joined," Isola said, frowning. She looked up at Orla's father. "Gorlan, you brought your harp."

"I usually do, when the village eats together." Gorlan swung an instrument around from his back; it looked like a squared-off D with horizontal strings. He began to pluck chords from it.

"Korlan, you are the best singer of the men," Isola told her husband. "Sing with me."

Alternating lines, often in question and answer, they sang a story—of the handsome stranger-god Thummaz, who came across the mountain to the foot of Bifrost, the rainbow bridge, and crossed over it to Valhalla. He came before the gods, and they saw that he was more handsome than any but Baldur. The young women thronged to him, but jealousy sprang up among the men. Loki played on that jealousy and fanned it to white heat, then spread a rumor that Thummaz had spied upon Dumi while she was bathing.

Now, anyone should have known that was false, for Dumi was a huntress and very skilled with the bow; moreover, she guarded both her virginity and her reputation very shrewdly, and any man spying upon her would have been dead before he could tell of it. But the men kept their tales from the women's ears and went out to lay an ambush for Thummaz, even as Frey invited him to hunt.

Loki took the form of a deer and bounded away from them. Thummaz and Frey went chasing after, and Thummaz rode too fast, leaving Frey far behind—but the buck abruptly disappeared, and the gods fell upon Thummaz and struck him dead, then cut his body into six pieces and buried each in a separate part of the world.

When Thummaz failed to return, Frey rode back to bear the news, and the women turned upon the men in fury, accusing them of murder. Even Sigune turned upon her husband Loki, and under the lash of her tongue, he admitted his treachery, but excused it as jealousy over her. The women recognized some truth in this, so they sought no revenge on their husbands and suitors, but only turned away from them, sorrowing.

Dumi, however, felt the need to restore her honor, because the story Loki had made to arouse the gods' jealousy had been fashioned around her. Even though it was a lie, she set out with her hounds and her hawks to find the pieces of Thummaz's body. Long she searched, but the hawks flew about the earth and brought back word, and a year from the day of his death, she brought the pieces of his body back to the gods.

None had decayed, of course, for this was the body of a

god, not a mortal. Dumi laid the pieces out, joined together, before she summoned the women. They gazed upon Thummaz's beauty and wept—but Dumi appealed to Frigga, Odin's wife, and the two of them together persuaded the Norns to come see what they had done by cutting Thummaz's life-thread so short. They came but, being women, once they had seen, they too were struck by Thummaz's beauty, and wept. They gave the pieces of his life-thread to Frigga, and with it, she stitched his body back together. Then the Norns spun the life-thread for him anew, and the body glowed and rose. Thummaz came back to life, more beautiful than ever before, and set about contests with the other gods, in which he proved that he was stronger and quicker than before he was killed. He forgave them then, and begged Dumi to marry him, but she knew her weird and refused him. Sorrowing then, Thummaz left Valhalla, to wander the world in search of a woman he could love as much as he loved Dumi, but who would love him in return.

"Why, this is to say that what has been torn apart, will be stronger and more healthy when it has been knit back together!" Alea declared. "No wonder the Wizard wanted you to tell it to me!"

The giants looked at one another in wonder.

"The small one speaks truly," Riara said. "The myth tells us that the nations of humanity may be rejoined into one, and will be stronger and better for having been sundered, then rejoined!"

"No wonder the tale isn't told in Midgard," Alea said bitterly.

"Perhaps there is another reason," Gar said. "Where did your ancestors learn this myth?"

The giants exchanged glances. Riara said, "They found

old books, and searched out the eddas and the sagas, as we
have told you—but I think they may have made that tale
themselves."

"Or taken it from another book," Gar said. "It sounds like
one I've heard that comes from lands far south of the home
of the Aesir—as do Dumi and Thummaz."

They looked faintly surprised, but most of the giants nodded. "You come from far away indeed," Riara said "and we
have no reason to doubt you. Surely, though, the source of the
myth matters not."

"Indeed," Gar replied, "and I will guess that you have tales
of Frigga and Freya and Idun and the other goddesses, tales
that have grown among you here, and were never heard in
your ancestors' home in the stars. This is your world, after
all, and myths have grown here to fit it."

"Do you say that stories take on lives of their own?" Korlan
asked, frowning.

"They most definitely do," Gar said, "and I've learned that
no border and no army can keep out a myth."

When the sun was well up and the giants had talked through
the meaning of the Great Monad to the point where all could
accept their dreams, Gar rose. "I must thank you all for your
hospitality, but I must also be on the road again."

Alea rose with him, saying, "I thank you, too." Then to
Riara and Isola, "I will never forget what you have taught me."

The giant woman looked down at her with blank stares,
then smiled. "I'm glad of that," said Isola, "but I didn't know
we had taught you anything."

"You have taught me that women deserve respect," Alea
told them, "and that may change my life."

The women stared in surprise, and Orla said, "Then I am

glad indeed you stayed the night with us." She held out a sack scarcely bigger than her hand, but Alea had to strain to hold it up when she took it. "There is cheese and bread there," Orla told her, "and some smoked pork, as well as some slices from last night's roast."

"Ale," Garlon said, handing a huge wineskin to Gar. "If you can't trust the water, you can always trust this."

"I shall drink all your healths with it," Gar promised as he slung it over his shoulder and turned to Alea to ask, "Will you join me in the toast?"

"Of course!" Alea exclaimed. Then, quickly, "Though I won't drink as much as Orla would."

The giants laughed at that, and Gar with them.

"The dwarves have far-talkers, too," Korlan said. "Shall we call and tell them you are coming?"

"Thank you, but I'd rather you didn't," Gar said. "Midgarders might be listening, reason out what paths we take, and set an ambush for us."

Alea's blood ran cold at the thought.

"Our ancestors began to use the fartalker three hundred years ago," Korlan said, frowning, "and never since the first days have we heard them talking on our kind of device. There is another sort that we use for listening to them, but we do not talk—we know they will not answer. It only works near the border, anyway."

"Within line of sight." Gar nodded. "I suspect they use FM, while you use AM—far better for long distances. Still, if you listen to their talk, they may be listening to yours. A giant army might take the chance, but two of us alone would not."

"Even as you say." Korlan didn't seem surprised at the idea. "Still, at least take this." He held out a rolled sheet of parchment half as long as Gar's torso. "It is a letter to the dwarves, telling that you have been our guests, and good guests. It should bring you safely to Nibelheim without need for a fight."

"At least with the dwarves," Riara reminded them. "Midgarder hunters and bandits are another matter."

"And I do not think the dog packs and pigs know how to read," Garlon said, grinning. "Take care, my friends, and may your road be safe!"

"Thank you all, thank you deeply," Gar said, looking around at them with glowing eyes. "I shall remember you all my life with happiness. I hope that we shall meet again some day."

"Until then, fare well," Korlan rumbled.

"Aye, fare you well," Orla said, holding down a huge hand to Alea.

Somehow, though, the smaller woman found herself hugging the young giant around the waist, burying her cheek in the rough cloth of her tunic and fighting back tears. "Oh, fare you well!" she gasped.

Orla stood amazed a moment, then put one huge hand gently against Alea's back. "We shall see one another again some day, little sister. May Dumi guard your journey."

"May Frigga guard your staying!" Alea gasped, stepping back.

Then, finally, they were walking down the road out of the village, turning back now and again to wave to the giants, some atop the walls, some standing outside the gates, hands raised as though in blessing.

"I wish we could stay," Alea said around the lump in her throat, "but I know we can't."

"No," Gar agreed. "We aren't really giants, after all."

"Tell that to the Midgarders!" Alea said bitterly. She welcomed the return of her bitterness—it dried up her tears.

"More to the point," Gar said thoughtfully, "tell it to the Jotunheimers. Why were we welcome here, when the giants near the border didn't even offer us a night's lodging?"

It was a good question. Alea thought it over for a moment, then guessed, "Perhaps because it *was* near the border, and they couldn't trust anyone who might have been a Midgarder?"

"A good reason," Gar said, nodding. "It also might be that here in the North Country, where villages are few and far between, folk depend on one another and grow hungry for the sight of new faces."

"Human life is cheap in Midgard," Alea said, relishing her bitterness, "but it's dear, here in the North. Is that what you mean?"

"Something like that, yes," Gar agreed. "Now, if only their stories could make the Midgarders realize the value of human life, too. . . ."

Alea interrupted, impatient with him. "You have an uncommon amount of faith in the power of stories!"

"I believe there is goodness inside most human beings, though in some, it is buried quite deeply," Gar returned, "and a really good story can reach that goodness."

" 'Most?' " Alea caught the qualification and returned it. "Not all?"

"I have met a few people in whom I couldn't find any trace of goodness," Gar said. "I think something may have gone wrong inside them even before they were born—but whatever the reason, whatever was good or humane in them had been burned out."

Alea shuddered, and hoped she never met such a person. Then it occurred to her that perhaps she already had.

They turned their steps eastward, across the top of Midgard toward Nibelheim. They began each day with combat practice, and Gar showed Alea how to deal with two antagonists attacking her at once. It was rather clumsy, since he had to jump about trying to take the places of both, but they practiced day after day until Alea could run the drill smoothly and without thinking. Then Gar showed her how to deal with three, then with four.

"What do I do once I have all four down?" she asked him.

"Run as fast as you can," Gar told her. "You can take them by surprise once, but a second time, they'll be ready, cautious, and canny."

Alea went cold inside at the thought. "All right, I'll run. What do I do if they follow?"

"Hide if you can, fight if you can't. Choose the best ground you can before you're completely exhausted," Gar told her, "ideally, a place so narrow they can only come at you one at a time. *Then* fight—but only if you have to. Remember, the woman is always at a disadvantage, so run if you can, and fight if you can't."

Alea decided she had also better pray to Dumi.

Gar had begun to teach her how to fight five when the bandits attacked.

They were walking through a birch forest. The trees were wide apart, with little or no growth between them, so they could see a fair way around themselves. The bandits took them completely by surprise, dropping from boughs and leaping out from behind the few thick trunks with bloodthirsty howls.

"Back to back!" Gar snapped. "Run if you get the chance!"

"Run to where?" Alea cried.

Then the bandits were on them.

She heard cracks and howls behind her, and grunts of pain from Gar, but she could scarcely pay attention because of the swinging quarterstaves with grinning, lascivious, unshaven faces behind them. A staff swung down at her from the left; she parried it with the tip of her own, but the impact nearly wrenched the stick from her hands and left them aching. She didn't have time to worry about pain; she kicked the man in the knee as she fended off another strike from the right, then swung the end of her staff into the stomach of the man charging from the front. She reversed, spinning the top of her staff up to block his stroke, and a strike from the left sent pain through her head, making the world swim about her. She fell to her knees, heard shouts of triumph, and swung her staff up to the left, felt it jar against something that shouted in pain, then swung it above her head to the right. Another man grunted, and the world stopped swimming long enough for her to see three attackers writhing on the ground around her, but a fourth and fifth stepped over them. She struggled to her feet, holding her staff up to guard, still unsteady—and the bandit to her left swung like a windmill. The two staves met with a sound like a thundercrack, whipping Alea's staff out of her hands to bounce away across the ground.

The bandit on the right shouted victory and stepped in, his staff swinging around at her belly.

12

A lea seized his leg the way Gar had shown her, digging her
fingers in and pushing. The man fell, screaming. She let
him go and turned to the other man, who charged her full tilt,
swinging his staff down to choke her. She fell back, catching
the staff and drawing her legs up, then pushed hard with her
legs as she pulled with her hands. The man went somersault-
ing over her head with a howl of surprise, letting go of his staff.

Alea used it to push herself to her feet and looked about
her, wild-eyed and panting—and saw all five of her assailants
on the ground, three curled around pain and moaning, two
struggling to their feet.

Run! her panic screamed inside her—but it screamed in
Gar's voice, and one glance showed her that he was still beset,
whirling his staff one-handed, half a dozen outlaws on the
ground before him—but another half-dozen still confronted
him, and two had bows. If either of them gained a shot at his
back, he was dead.

She couldn't leave his back unguarded. She turned to face

her attackers, her back to Gar's, even though every sense of caution within her screamed at her for a fool.

The two who managed to struggle to their feet stalked about her, staves up and ready, bruises purpling on one man's face, both breathing hard and glaring harder. Her heart went faint; she remembered Gar saying, *The second time, they'll be ready.* But she held her ground, on guard and waiting—and waiting, and waiting. Neither man seemed eager to strike. Finally she realized that each was waiting for the other; *then* he would finish what his partner had begun.

At last they thought to look at one another. Both nodded, and they turned to Alea, sticks swinging back.

They were wide open. She lunged, stick straight out, butt jabbing one in the belly. He doubled over in pain, mouth wide in a shout he had no breath for. She snapped her whole body back to guard, turning to the last attacker. He froze, stick high, then realized he was unguarded and yanked his stick back in front of him.

"Hold!" a voice shouted, and it wasn't Gar's.

Her attacker froze, still on guard, but looking relieved.

Alea risked a glance behind her, turned back in time to see the bandit raising his stick to strike. He saw her eyes and froze—but she had seen a man with a sword, shield, and iron cap facing Gar and looking indignant. He was almost as tall as Gar. The shortest of them was as tall as Alea.

"We struck you with a dozen, and you've beaten down ten of us!" the bandit chief exclaimed in injured tones. "How in Hela's name have you done that?"

Alea shuddered at his invoking of the Queen of the Dead.

"Not by Hela, but by Thor and Dumi," Gar said, sounding mild. "I'll be glad to teach you. If you'd like another lesson, swing!"

There was a pause. Panting, Alea locked glares with the bandit—but two of his mates staggered to their feet with the aid of their staves, giving her poisoned looks.

"No, I'll seek a more peaceable way." The bandit leader sounded as though he would dearly have loved to beat Gar's brains out, but was forcing himself to be placating. "No one's ever proved himself so strong a fighter as you—and I've never seen a woman fight at all!" He didn't sound happy about it. "Except a giant's woman, that is."

"Aren't we giants?" Gar asked, still mildly.

"No, but we're a far sight better than the Midgarders!" the man said, with such bitterness that it startled even Alea. Then he forced his voice to mildness. "Come home with us and pass the night as a pledge of peace, for we must honor a fighter like you."

"Why, thank you," Gar said smoothly. "We'll be pleased."

Alea stepped back so that her shoulders jarred against his, leaned her head back, and hissed, "Are you mad?"

"Yes," Gar hissed back. Then to the bandit leader, "I need some guarantee of our safety. What's your name?"

"Zimu," the man said warily. "Why?"

"Because I'm a wizard, and once I know your name, I can use it to work magic that will hurt you."

Alea spun to stare at him, then looked quickly at Zimu—but the man was glaring at Gar with anger and fear. Then she remembered to look back at her opponent, but he was busy staring, too.

"I'll give you some chance of evening the odds," Gar told Zimu. "My name is Gar."

The bandit leader relaxed, still frowning, "Then I can work magic against you."

"If you're a wizard, yes." Suddenly Gar's voice took on a

weird tone and the rhythm of an incantation. "Zimu, Zimu, tell me the names of your men!"

Zimu's eyes glazed. "There's Bandi, Cuthorn, Dambri . . ." He gestured at each as he spoke the name, listing the whole dozen before one of them shouted, appalled, "Chief!"

Zimu shook himself, his eyes clearing, then glared at Gar. "How did you do that?"

"If you have twenty years to learn, I can teach you," Gar said, "*if* you have the talent. Well, I can be sure we'll be safe among you now. So thank you for your invitation, Bandi, Cuthorn, Dambri. . . ." He chanted the list of names. Even the men who were only now staggering to their feet looked up in alarm—to find Gar looking straight at them as he spoke their names. They shuddered and looked away.

". . . and Zimu," Gar finished. He gave a slight bow, seeming to lean on his staff. "We'll be glad to dine with you."

"Well, then, you're welcome," Zimu said with poor grace. "Woman, gather wood as you come! We'll need a big fire if we're to celebrate guests."

Alea stared at him in outrage. No giant would ever have spoken to a woman like that!

"She gathers no wood, and carries only her own pack." Gar's hand hovered over her shoulder, and only the two of them knew that he didn't really touch her. "She is my shield-maiden."

"I don't see any shield," Zimu growled, eyeing them suspiciously.

"She is herself my shield," Gar explained.

Alea had to fight the impulse to look up at him in surprise, and scolded herself for the warmth that spread through her at his words.

"You had better treat her kindly," Gar went on, "for when

she dies, she will become a Valkyrie, and if you lie dead on a battlefield, she'll ignore you if you've treated her ill."

Alea knew he was only making up a story, but still her heart leaped. To become a Valkyrie when she died! But surely all Gar's teaching couldn't accomplish that.

The bandits kept their distance as they led the way deeper into the forest. It gave Alea a chance to step closer to Gar and hiss, "This is the height of stupidity! In their own camp, they can beat us senseless and do with us as they will!"

"They won't dare," Gar whispered back, "and I have to learn what the outlaws are like, how they live, if I'm to have any hope of bringing peace to this land."

Alea stared at him for a full minute, then said, "You really mean it, don't you? You're actually going to try to free the slaves and make peace!"

"I really do," Gar said gravely. "A person has to have something to do in this life, after all, some reason to live, and this is mine."

"What's the matter with a wife and children?" Alea jibed.

"Only that the wife is so obstinate she refuses to be found," Gar answered. "The children are difficult to manage without her."

Looking into his eyes, Alea saw a bleakness and a hunger that made her look away. "Can you really protect us against them?"

"Oh, yes," Gar assured her, "as long as I stay awake—but what's more important is that I have them convinced that I can."

"How can you do it?" Alea demanded.

"It's a talent," Gar whispered frankly, "but it takes training too. I think you might have some of the gift. Stay with me long enough, and you might learn how."

Alea stiffened; if she hadn't known Gar better, she would have thought it was a proposition rather than an invitation. As a matter of fact, she reminded herself, she *didn't* know him well enough—and there might be less danger away from him than with him, after all. She decided to think seriously about leaving him to wander alone.

She had plenty of time to consider it, though.

The bandit camp was only a broad clearing deep in the birch forest, cluttered with debris among the score or so of bark huts that stood about it in no particular order—giant white half-balls, reminding her of puffball toadstools on a damp morning. Looking more closely, she found they were covered with birchbark—over long bent poles, she suspected. She wondered if such dwellings could really keep the rain out and the heat in.

There were women moving about that village, tending near-naked children, hauling water, chopping wood, and mending the huts. The older girls were bringing in baskets of berries. There were a dozen men lounging about the camp, fletching arrows, practicing quarterstaff play or archery, or simply talking to one another. As she watched, one man called a woman over to him and handed her an empty mug. She nodded, took it, and disappeared into one of the huts, then came back and handed it to the man. He broke off talking to another bandit long enough to take a long drink.

Alea felt outrage. After the giants' village, where everyone shared tasks, it seemed abysmally wrong to see women doing all the drudgery. Perhaps there was some truth in the notion that the men had to hunt and be ready to fight, but it did seem to be very uneven.

Zimu stopped by a dilapidated hut. "This is your dwelling for the night. We wish you joy of it."

Alea's sense of outrage heightened, but Gar only said, "It will do. Thank you for your hospitality."

"It's our pleasure," Zimu grunted. "We'll eat when the roast is done—an hour or two. When you've settled yourself, you can join us for some beer and talk."

"Thank you. I would like that."

Zimu nodded and turned away, apparently not feeling it necessary to address a single comment to Alea. As soon as he was out of hearing range, she turned on Gar fiercely, albeit in a whisper. "Have you no pride? Giving us a house like this shows his contempt for you!"

"Yes, it does, doesn't it?" Gar said mildly. "So we'll turn it back on him, and have it snug and clean in half an hour— together."

"Can't you ever argue?" Alea hissed, exasperated. "Do you have to find a way to agree with everything I say?"

"That," Gar said, "or find a way to make what you say agree with me. Think, my friend—what will they say when they see me working with you?"

Alea started a sharp retort, then caught herself, eyes widening. Slowly, she grinned. "The men will tell themselves you're not much of a man, but their bruises will tell them otherwise. And the women . . ." She left the sentence hanging.

"The women will be scandalized," Gar finished for her, "but they'll be thinking about it for weeks afterwards. They won't dare try to talk these brutes into sharing the work, but they'll cheer for anyone who comes to make these bandits learn to farm."

"Farm?" Alea stared blankly. "What crops could grow in so short and cold a summer as this land sees?"

"Barley, oats, cabbage, and half a dozen others," Gar told her, "and wild pigs and oxen can be corralled and bred."

"How will you talk the men into that?" Alea challenged. "More of your stories?"

"What else would men like this listen to?" Gar asked. "Come, let me show you how to take bark from a birch without killing the tree."

Working together, they swept out the hut, patched it, brought in beds of bracken, and started a fire in the central pit under the smoke hole. As they worked, Alea was very much aware that first one, then five, then a dozen men were staring at them, muttering indignantly to one another. She smiled to herself and kept on working. Out of the corner of her eye, she noticed the women taking quick glances at them, trying not to be seen watching—but she knew they were storing away the picture of man and woman working together.

It took a little longer than the half hour Gar had predicted, but the pig on the spit over the village's central firepit was barely half-cooked by the time they were done.

"I should come with you to talk to the men," Alea told Gar, but kept her voice low.

"You could," Gar agreed, "but it might be more important for you to talk to the women. I expect they want to scold you for letting a man help you."

"Well, that's one way of showing envy," Alea said, grinning. She found herself looking forward to the contest.

"You might want to explain it by telling the women the story of Dumi," Gar said. "I'm sure they haven't heard it."

"And then, of course, I would go on to the story of Thummaz?" Alea asked, with irony.

"You might," Gar said. "I should be telling it to the men about the same time. I wonder how we'll dream tonight?"

Alea stared up at him. "You don't mean the Wizard is following us!"

"He might have gone before," Gar said, "but I don't think these outlaws would have been so quick to attack us if he had. Let's see if we can prepare the way for him. Good luck with the women."

"And you with the men." But Alea couldn't help an anxious glance after him. He might be only a friend, but he was indeed a friend, and all she had.

Most of the women were as tall as Alea, three or four a little shorter. They had gathered around a stream-fed pool ten yards from the cooking fire, watching older children turn the spit and chatting in low voices. The conversation gelled as Alea came up; she walked into silence. She decided to take the bull by the horns and looked down at the pool. Someone had widened the stream into a circular basin and paved it with rocks. "How pretty!" she exclaimed. "How clever of your men to make this for you!"

Some of the women stared at her as though she were insane, but others gave shouts of laughter, quickly smothered. One said, "Whatever possessed you to think the men did this, girl?"

Alea bridled at the term—she was clearly old enough to be an old maid, so calling her "girl" was showing contempt. But she kept her temper in check and said, "Those rocks must have been heavy to haul. Don't tell me they left you to carry them yourselves!"

Several of the women lost their laughter and glared at her instead, but the one who had spoken only sneered. "Are you so weak you can't lift a rock, girl?"

"I think I might." Alea leaned on her staff to call their attention to it, though she doubted the men would have said anything about her using it on them. "But why should I, when I have a great hulk like Gar to haul them for me?"

"Oh, your man," another woman sneered, "if you can call him that. How much man can he be, if he does a woman's work?"

The men suddenly broke into angry shouting. The women looked up, eyes wide in fear. Alea felt it too, but forced herself to turn slowly, looking with curiosity only.

Two of the men were on their feet, the rest shaking their fists at Gar, but he only sat, watching them, and when the shouting died, he went on talking calmly. "Why are you so surprised? Dumi was a goddess, after all. Of course she was an excellent archer!"

"Not as good as the men," Zimu said stubbornly.

Gar shrugged. "If you can hit the bull's eye, how can you be better?"

Alea turned back to the women, looking as smug as a cream-fed cat. "He's man enough to fight all your men to a standstill—and you know he did, or they wouldn't have invited him to stay the night."

They did know; their gazes were angry, but they slid away from hers.

For her part, Alea was surprised to realize she felt proud of Gar. "I'm as big as any of you, and bigger than any Midgarder."

"Midgarders!" the oldest woman said with disgust. "Puling little things! The men are right—we're much better than they are."

The other women chorused agreement, and the oldest, a woman in her forties, said, "You're right in that, Elsa—and as the men say, we're even better than the giants, those great lumbering hulks!"

Anger kindled in Alea, partly at the thought of these semi-slaves ranking themselves better than Riara and Orla, partly at women being so ready to be cowed. "Oh, is that what the men say?"

Elsa frowned at the edge to her tone. "Aye, it is, and true! What Sigurd says is right—we're a new breed come into being, better than any of the other three, and you should be glad of it, girl, for you're one of us, too!"

Alea shuddered at the thought of being such a slave. "So you know what your men think. Do you know what you think?"

"We agree with the men." Elsa glowered, then asked the older woman, "Don't we, Helga?"

"Why not, if they're right?" Helga answered, but her glare was on Alea. "We're bigger than the Midgarders and stronger, and smarter and more nimble than the giants!"

"I've met the giants," Alea told them, "and stayed the night with them. Believe me, they're just as smart as we are, and gentle to boot!"

The women stared, scandalized. "The giants? Gentle?"

"To us, and to their women," Alea replied. "The giant women do all that the men do, and the men do all the tasks that the women do. I didn't hear any fighting—they talk things out until they agree. I never once heard a giant man give orders to a giant woman."

"Well, of course, when you're that big and strong . . ." Helga grumbled.

"The giant men are bigger and stronger," Alea reminded them, "but women are precious to them. They need to win their favor—and keep winning it."

Helga looked surprised, then calculating, but Sigurd said, "What if a man did give one of them an order, and she refused it? What then?"

"Aye!" said Elsa. "If the giant men are so much bigger than the women, how could she save herself?"

"None of their men would ever lift his hand against a woman," Alea said positively, "but if he did, the other men would knock him flat—and if they didn't, the other women would."

All the women looked surprised, then excited—then crestfallen. "If the women banded together to defend one of their own," Sigurd said, "wouldn't the men come in a gang to thrash them all?"

"Here, perhaps," Alea told them. "In Jotunheim, no."

"But their women know how to fight!"

"A woman can learn." Suddenly, Alea was aware of the pain from her bruises all over again, even the muted throbbing in her head—but with them, the fierce sense of exhilaration that came with knowing she had fought back and not lost, even if she hadn't exactly won, either. "Believe me, a woman can learn."

The men broke into another burst of shouting, half of them on their feet and shaking their fists. Gar only smiled up at them, interested, not amused, and gradually they quieted.

"The giants aren't stupid," Gar said. "I tested one of them, wrestling, and used some movements he didn't know. By the end of the match, he used them on me. Oh, be sure, they're intelligent enough."

Dambri stared. "You wrestled with a giant?"

"Nothing could teach our men to honor us," Helga said, with total assurance.

"Perhaps you should take your children and all go away long enough for them to learn how much they need you."

"Perhaps they would come after us with sticks," Elsa growled.

Alea sighed and searched her mind for a rebuttal—but when she didn't find one, she remembered that she was supposed to be trying to bring these women peace, not war and possible death. "Tell them it's religious, and make it so. Tell them you need time to meditate the new myth I've brought you."

"What, that the giants are gentle toward their women?" Helga asked, with full sarcasm.

"That's no myth—it's news. The story I've brought you is the tale of Thummaz," Alea said. "It isn't told in Midgard, but I learned it from with the giants here in the North Country. It's about a southern god who came to the gates of Valhalla, to visit. . . ."

They listened at first with suspicion, but it evaporated under the spell of the tale. They listened intently, and when she was done, they relaxed with a sigh of pleasure.

"But what good does this tale do us?" Helga asked.

"It shows you that humanity can only become great if all its parts join together," Alea answered.

Shouting erupted again, all of the men on their feet this time, and Zimu strode up to Gar, planting his fists on his hips, demanding, "How could you possibly put outcasts like us back with the Midgarders? Without our being slaves?"

"By cherishing your children who only grow as big as Midgarders," Gar told him, "cherishing even the ones who grow no bigger than a drawf, and the ones who grow as big as a giant!"

"None of our children will grow like that," Zimu growled, but he sounded uncertain.

The women's eyes all turned haunted at that.

"They can only say that because they don't know the pain and suffering that go into making and birthing a child," Alea reminded them. Her heart ached at the thought of the experience she would never have. "The greatness is in the life, not the size."

The women all turned to her, staring in surprise and relief, but Sigurd frowned. "The men say *we* are the ones who are becoming great—that there's something new in each generation, better than the last, and that we are the best that's ever been!"

Alea frowned. "What of the giants?"

"A mistake," Elsa said promptly. "The gods tried to make a better people, but made them slow in mind and body—and don't even think to ask about the dwarves, those piddling little monstrosities! They're mistakes if ever there was one!"

Helga said, as though that proved it beyond the shadow of a doubt, "So say the men."

"What do *you* say?" Alea asked.

The women stared at her blankly. Finally Sigurd managed to say, "We'll leave that kind of thinking to the men. How to raise the children, what to cook for dinner, that's what women should think about."

"Is it? And who told you that?" Alea challenged.

"Our mothers!" Helga snapped. "They also told us that women who meddle in men's affairs will lose their husbands, and die trying to fend for themselves!"

"A giant woman would live, fending for herself," Alea returned. "Didn't the men say you were better?"

Helga scowled and repeated stubbornly, "The giants are mistakes, and so is your notion of them!"

"The mistakes are in the minds of your men," Alea said tartly. "Humanity is like Thummaz, torn into four parts— giants, dwarves, men, and women. We're sending ourselves to death if we stay apart—but we can be stronger and better than ever if we can pull all four parts of ourselves back together."

"As Dumi did to Thummaz?" Sigurd guessed.

"Even so," Alea confirmed.

Helga leaned forward, hands clasped, her frown one of interest now, not anger. "Tell us more of this Dumi. We haven't heard of her before."

When the girls came to tell them the roast was done, Helga nodded her thanks and stood up. "We'll test it, but I'm sure you're right, Thala. You've been turning spits long enough now."

Mild though the praise was, the twelve-year-old dimpled with pleasure. The women went slowly toward the spit, listening to the men argue.

"But the giants and the Midgarders aren't anywhere nearly as good as we are!" a brawny man almost as tall as Gar was saying. "And the dwarves are so little and weak it's laughable! How could we lower ourselves to join with any of them?"

The other men chorused agreement, with cries of "That's right, right, Lafo!"

"Right as you're big, Lafo!"

"Then the giants must be more right than any," Gar said reasonably, "since they're the biggest."

"Don't play with my words, stranger!" The speaker shook a fist. "You know what I mean!"

"You only think the giants are slow and stupid because you don't know them," Gar told him. "As to the dwarves, they must be smart, or they wouldn't still be alive."

"Prove it!"

"There's only one way," Gar told him. "Visit them."

For the first time, fear showed in the men's eyes.

"Wouldn't we be the fools, though?" another man snorted. "Stupid they may be, but those giants are monsters, too! They'd eat us for dinner!"

Alea almost said the giants wouldn't be able to stand the smell, but caught herself in time.

"Giants eat oxen, Kargi, not people," Gar said. "If they did, Alea and I would be dead now, probably bone meal in a loaf of bread. You've been listening to too many children's tales."

"We've only your word they guested you," Zimu grunted.

"And a huge aleskin," Gar reminded him.

"All right, so you're a clever thief!"

"If we go back to them," Gar said, "will you watch from a distance and see how they treat us?"

"Aha! So that's it!" Kargi cried. "You're the bait, come to lead us into their traps! All this noise about this Thummaz you've told us, is only a ruse to lower our suspicions!"

"A safe distance, I said," Gar reminded him. "You watch from a ridge-top a quarter of a mile away."

"Yes, while your giant friends creep up behind to catch us all and gut us for dinner!" Kargi turned to his mates. "Are we going to let them get away with that?"

"No! Never!" Came from two dozen throats, and the bandits were all on their feat, striding toward Gar, shaking staves and battle-axes.

13

Alea's heart sank, but she stepped up behind Gar, back to back, quarterstaff on guard. The odds were two dozen to one, but she was bound and determined to die fighting, determined that they'd have to kill her, that the pains of battle were the only ones she would suffer.

She didn't even think of surrendering and leaving Gar to die alone. It went without saying that she'd be right back where she was in Midgard, maybe worse.

A bandit ran at her, his face twisted into an ugly mask of hatred, stick high to deliver a crushing blow.

That stick disintegrated, crumbled to dust even as he swung it.

Alea stared, not believing her eyes. The bandit jolted to a halt, staring at his empty hands, just as disbelieving. But other bandits shouldered him aside and swung—and watched their own staves crumble to powder even as they descended. A fourth bandit pushed past them, roaring and swinging a battle-axe—but it turned to rust and struck Alea's staff, shredding away into brownish clumps as it did.

The man stared at her in horror. Then he shouted, "Witch!"

"No!" Alea cried.

Half a dozen men leaped on her, howling with anger and hatred, reaching for her with their bare hands. She swung her staff with maniacal speed, cracking knuckles and heads. Rough hands caught her arms, but she swung a knee up, a man howled, and the hands went away to clutch at his groin as he doubled over. Another man took his place, seizing her by the throat, but she knocked his arms away as Gar had taught her, then jabbed him in the belly with the butt of her staff. Two more sprang in from the sides to seize her upper arms, but she swung the staff with her lower arms as hard as she could, first the one side, then the other, and the men cried out in pain, their holds loosening. She wrenched one arm free, turned to lash out at the other man—and something struck her head, hard. The world went dark, sparks clouded her vision, there was roaring in her ears, and she fought in panic to hold onto consciousness, wildly afraid of what might happen if she lost her hold on the world.

Then the sparks cleared, the roaring softened, and she stared about her at a dozen men lying on the ground. Sick guilt filled her at the thought that she might have killed so many, but she saw that their eyes were closed and looked more sharply.

They were all breathing.

She looked about in amazement. The women crouched back around the fire, clutching children in their skirts, arms up to protect their faces, moaning in terror.

Then a hand came into her vision, palm up. She flinched away, then heard Gar say, as though at a feast-day dance, "May I help you up?"

She took the hand, trembling, and climbed to her feet, looking about her. All the men of the band lay on the ground, unconscious or asleep. She stared up at Gar. "How . . . how did you . . . ?"

"I warned them I was a wizard," he told her calmly. "There were too many of them, though. They would have buried me under sheer numbers, if you hadn't guarded my back long enough."

She tightened her hand on his, stared into his eyes, then looked away from the heat there, and blinked at the women. "I'm . . . I'm sorry. . . ."

"For what?" Helga found her voice, staring as though Alea were mad. "For walking free? For fighting off men who would have raped you, if they'd had the chance? Go along with you!"

"I think we had better," Gar said. "We don't seem to be welcome here any more."

"How could you think to be, preaching such nonsense as you did!" Elsa exclaimed.

But Helga touched her arm. "She told us the truth—women *can* learn how to protect themselves."

Elsa stared at her, then turned back to Alea, and her gaze verged on awe. "That's right. . . . We've seen it ourselves, that much was true. . . ."

"How much else of what she said was the truth?" Sigurd wondered.

"I think we had better leave and let them work out the answer to that by themselves," Gar said softly into Alea's ear.

"Just a moment." Alea advanced on the women, pulling out her belt knife.

They moaned and shrank away, ready to run.

Alea stepped past them to the roast. She carved a huge thick steak and carried it back to Gar, speared on her knife. "Loot."

Gar grinned. "Yes, they did offer us dinner, didn't they?" He tipped an imaginary hat to the women. "Thank you for your hospitality. I'm sorry we can't stay to enjoy it to its fullest. Good night, now."

"Good night," Alea echoed, then marched off into the forest, letting Gar do the catching up for once.

They stopped an hour later at a cave Gar had somehow found in a hillside, where he lit a small and almost smokeless fire. As they waited for the steak to warm, Alea asked, "How did you manage to knock them all out?"

"Magic, as I told you," Gar said.

"The same magic that made their staves crumble to dust?"

"Not quite, but close," Gar told her. "I wasn't joking. Still, I made it look as though I were knocking each of them on the head with my staff. The women won't think it was a spell, and the men will take better care of their weapons in the future."

Alea shivered against a sudden chill that had nothing to do with the temperature of the night. "How did you do it?"

Gar closed his eyes. "I'm picturing an object. Close your eyes and tell me what you see."

With misgivings, Alea closed her eyes—and saw Gar's face. She dismissed it impatiently, thought of darkness, an overcast night sky, saw dark clouds.

Then an image appeared in front of those clouds, murky and misty, but it seemed to gel, to harden, to become clear. . . .

"An instrument of some sort," she said. "It has a pinch-waisted body and a long neck, with one . . . two . . . six strings."

"It's called a guitar," Gar said softly, "and you don't have them in Midgard, nor anywhere else in the world, as far as I know. Yes, that is what I was thinking of. You have the talent to do magic yourself, Alea, though how much talent, I don't know yet. Do you want to learn?"

The answer leaped up with savage eagerness, but she held it back, afraid—of the power of that magic, of the unknown. . . .

But not, strangely, of Gar.

"I'll have to think about it," she said.

"As you will." The words practically purred with approval. "Well, enough of such airy nonsense. Let's see to that steak, shall we?"

As she settled herself for sleep, Alea reflected on her luck, and found herself struggling to believe it. She had found a companion, a friend, who seemed to value her as a person more than as a woman, but there were hints that he appreciated her femininity too, femininity that she'd scarcely known she still had, for the boys of her village had never seemed to notice it once she grew taller than they. Moreover, and more amazingly, he gave her the honor and respect he would have given another man, treated her as an equal, never even seemed to think that she was anything else. He had protected her, hunted for her, nurtured her, soothed her fears, given her more self-respect than she had ever thught to have again—and was now offering to teach her magic!

There was no need of it, she told herself. He was magic enough in himself.

Not that she was about to let him know that, of course.

* * *

She woke with the sun, feeling sluggish, and went to feed the fire, wondering why she felt so lethargic. Gar rolled out of his blanket and sat up as she was hanging the kettle over the flames. She looked at his face and, for some reason, had a dim memory of the Wizard looking rather disgusted.

Suddenly she knew why. "I wonder if the bandits dreamed of the Wizard last night."

"They did," Gar said, with complete certainty, "and he showed them the Great Monad and explained it to them, but they argued with him every inch of the way. The more ridiculous their stand became, the harder they fought."

Alea looked at the fire. "They'd rather die than give up believing they've become supermen, wouldn't they?"

"I think they would," Gar said, with wonder and delight. "How did you know?"

"I talked to their women." Alea stilled, frowning into the fire. "I nearly said 'wives,' but I don't think any of them are."

"Not legally, perhaps, but most of them are in fact."

"The men treat them as housekeepers and whores!"

"That's what the men want to believe," Gar agreed, "but the women have become more to them, much more, and I think they're about to find that out." He looked around, peering upward. "I've become turned around in the dark. Which way is east?"

They had been hiking for another six weeks when the pigs attacked.

The cunning beasts waited until they were squarely in the middle of a meadow with no nearby trees to climb. Then they seemed to materialize from the grass and came squealing from all sides, the boars in the lead. They had gone back to nature in good form, growing tusks and shaggy coats.

Alea whipped about back to back with Gar out of sheer reflex, her staff up and ready. All he had time to say was, "Don't let them near! Scare them if you can!"

Good advice, Alea thought with exasperation, but how was she supposed to do that? She held her stick by the end and swung it in desperation—and saw what he meant. The pigs were shrewd; they saw the staff coming and leaped back from it. But as soon as it was past, they sprang in.

Well, there was a way to deal with that. Alea set up the figure-eight pattern Gar had shown her, and the pigs shied away, then started in, but the butt of the staff came back to crack very satisfyingly over one's head. It stumbled back and fell, and three others fell on it instantly, squealing and fighting for cannibal rights.

But they had stopped the staff just long enough. From the other side, a boar shot in to rip Alea's skirt with a toss of its head. She felt the pain in her leg and screamed in fear-born anger, whirling her staff to crack its head. It stumbled back and fell, but she was paying attention to the left again, and kept the figure-eight going. The pigs shied away, but an old sow grunted, and by Thor's goats, they all seemed to relax and settle down. With a sinking heart, she realized they were waiting for her to tire.

They were right, too. She couldn't keep the pattern going all day. In desperation, she slowed before she had even begun to be winded—and sure enough, two boars sprang in, one from each side.

Alea swung the stick so fast it blurred. It jarred against the right-hand porker and rebounded; she used the energy of that bounce to crack the other across the muzzle. Both squealed and retreated, giving her injured looks as though to say she had broken the rules.

She intended to. She intended to break a lot of rules, especially since she had seen what they had done to one of their own fallen. She slowed the stick again, and two pigs started forward, then hesitated. She slowed the stroke even more, but they only glared at her, waiting.

Behind her, she heard crack after crack mixed with wild squealing, and knew Gar was using the animals' treacherous instincts to the fullest. She was glad she couldn't see what was happening.

The pigs edged away, beginning to look actually fearful. Hope leaped in her heart, and she slowed her staff even more, waiting and hoping.

Then the old sow grunted in anger. A dozen younger boars ranged themselves about her, and a huge old male trotted to the fore.

Alea braced herself; she knew a band nerving itself for an onslaught when she saw one. Her stomach sank as she realized she was staring at her doom, and it had little red eyes that glared—a score of them. She grounded the butt of her staff and waited.

So did the pigs.

Then the old sow grunted, the big boar squealed in rage and charged, and the younger boars galloped past him, echoing his squeal as they closed about in a semicircle, turning inward.

Alea lifted her staff to strike—and heard a voice calling, "Loose!" Feathers suddenly sprouted behind porcine shoulders and in their sides. Four of the pigs fell, but instead of falling upon them, the rest of the pack whirled to face their new attackers. They shot charging away across the meadow, and Alea stared, unable to believe her luck.

The pigs descended upon her rescuers—and Alea's disbelief deepened. The hunters who had come to her help were scarcely taller than the pigs themselves, a dozen men and women three feet high or less, with legs and arms shorter in proportion than her own. There were two of Midgard size, too, with ordinary bows, but most of the dwarves were reloading, cranking back their crossbows for another shot. The pigs would reach them before they could shoot, though, and Alea started after the swine with a despairing cry.

Gar shouted with fright and came pounding after her.

But the dwarves each cried, "Sic!" and the grass exploded with big shaggy dogs, some brown, some tan. Some sprang from the ground in front of the dwarves, some from the sides, and two even bounded at the pigs from the rear—they had lain hidden in the long grass, waiting for their commands.

The dogs fell on the pigs, seizing throats in their own jaws. The pigs turned, squealing in rage and fright, tossing their heads, and two dogs fell back, bleeding. But the rest held their prey fast, and the two bigger hunters let fly with arrows that brought down the old sow and her mate. Then the six smaller folk loosed their crossbows again, and half a dozen pigs fell. Six of the dogs, released of their burdens, instantly turned on another half-dozen swine. The Midgard-sized archers kept their bows humming, and pig after pig died.

Then Gar passed Alea and swung his stick, bellowing. He clipped a boar behind the head, and it fell. Alea slewed to a halt and swung in the same fashion; another pig fell over. A third leaped at her, and she screamed, stepping back and yanking her stick in double-handed to block the monster. She pushed away, hard, and it tumbled. Gar's stick cracked across its skull, and it lay unconscious.

The rest of the pig-pack was galloping away, squealing in terror. Alea stared after them, then looked about her, and saw a dozen pigs lying dead or unconscious with three wounded dogs and one dead among them. She could scarcely believe it.

Then one of the Midgard-sized people was coming toward her, and she raised her stick to guard, all the childhood terrors of the malice and magic of the dwarves coming back, even though this one was only a foot shorter than she.

"Let me see that arm, lass," the woman said.

Alea froze, staring. Whatever she had been expecting, it wasn't concern.

The woman, Alea's age or a little younger, hung her bow over her shoulder and rolled up Alea's sleeve. She pressed the flesh and watched the blood flow. "It seems clean enough," she said, turning the arm, then squeezed harder.

Pain shot through her muscles. Alea cried out and tried to pull away, but the dwarf-woman held her arm fast, even as she turned her head and called, "Mother! I think it's broken!"

One of the dwarves, not even three feet tall, looked up from slitting a boar's throat and wiped her dagger on the long grass. She came toward them, sheathing the knife—at her belt, it looked like a sword. She wore the same clothing as any of the others—belted tunic, leggins, and boots—but looking closely, Alea could see the feminine cast to the features and the unmistakable way the tunic draped over breasts and broader hips.

The older woman reached up to take Alea's arm. "Let me see, Saret."

The younger woman relinquished the arm, and her mother pressed, hard. Alea cried out and tried to pull her arm away, but the mother held it in an iron grip and nodded. "Nay, it's not broken, and there's no vein or artery cut, but the muscle's damaged. It will heal, mind you, but we'll bandage it tightly when we get back to the village. You must be careful not to use it for a day or three." She frowned down at the rip in Alea's skirt. "Show me that leg, lass."

Alea glanced at the men apprehensively. The mother read her meaning and said, "Don't worry, they're all busy killing swine and tending the wounded dogs. They wouldn't look closely in any event, for they know how to respect other people. Up with the skirt, now."

Alea lifted her skirt—and stared. The gash was a good six inches long, and there was enough blood running out of it to make her queasy.

"That, we'll have to see to here." The mother pulled a small bottle and a clean cloth out of a pouch that she wore on a strap that crossed her body. "Clench your jaw, lass, for this will hurt, though not as badly as that wound will tomorrow, if we don't tend it now. Courage!"

She poured fluid on the cloth and cleaned the wound. To take her mind off the pain, Alea gasped, "I am called Alea. What is your name, so I may know whom to thank?"

"I am Retsa," the little woman said, "and this is my daughter, Saret. How did you come here, you two Midgarders?"

"We're not Midgarders," Alea said sharply, "at least, not any more."

Saret looked up, startled, and Alea regretted her tone. "I'm sorry to sound so bitter, but it wasn't pleasant being enslaved, and escaping in fear of my life."

"No, I can imagine it wasn't." Retsa stood up and started

to work on Alea's arm with her bottle and cloth. "Why did they enslave you?"

"For being too tall." Alea tried to keep the bitterness out of her voice.

"We've heard they enslave you if you don't grow big enough, too," Saret said, frowning.

"It's true, and they teach us from childhood that it's right. We don't realize how wrong it is until it happens to us."

Retsa put away her medicine, shaking her head. "We can't understand how folk could so hurt their own children. Lashing out in a fit of temper, yes—it's bad, but we can understand how it can happen. Not wanting to let go of them, that too we can understand—but disowning them, enslaving them? No." She turned toward the main group. "Walk carefully until you're sure how much weight that leg will bear."

Saret came up on her other side, watchful and ready to catch. Alea flashed her a look of surprise and gratitude, then stepped slowly and carefully, bracing herself on her staff. She nodded. "It hurts, but I can keep from limping if I try."

"Go ahead and limp," Retsa told her. "It will do less damage than trying not to. Keep leaning on that staff, though." She watched Alea walk, then nodded approvingly. "It's lucky for you we were near on patrol."

"So you always pace the land on watch?"

"We do," Retsa said, "though we hunt game as well as raiders. We heard the squealing and came on the run. Good for us as well as you, by the look of it, though there's one of us will sorrow for his dog." She looked at the glum dwarf who was laying the furry body on a stretcher. "Canis was a good hound and a better friend. Well, Obon will have to content himself with her puppies."

Alea felt a pang as she realized the dog had died to save

her life, then scolded herself—it was only a dog, after all. Somehow, though, she was sure that to these dwarves, their animals were friends, and close ones. At least the dwarves would show some profit from their rescue—they were already tying the feet of the dead pigs and sliding spears between them to bear them home. "I'll help carry the . . ."

"You'll do no such thing," Retsa said sharply, "not with that leg!"

Alea didn't argue the point, largely because she realized that she'd been assuming she and Gar would go back to the village with the dwarves—but they hadn't been invited, and she noticed that the dwarves who weren't busy with the pigs were still holding their crossbows, and that they were loaded. They weren't particularly pointed toward herself and Gar, but on the other hand, they weren't pointed away, either. For the first time, it occurred to her that they might not be welcome among the small people.

They came up to the main group, and Alea saw that a third of them were women. Only the two bow-carriers were the size of Midgarders—five and a half feet—but the others varied, one scarcely more than two feet tall, others four feet or more. The fairy-tale version of nasty, spiteful Alberich, the dwarf who stole the Rhinegold, and his equally cruel little kin, seemed very far from the reality. The dwarves looked as massive as the giants, though on a far smaller scale. They were also obviously compassionate and concerned for one another and even for these two huge strangers, though Alea did notice a few wary glances. Under the circumstances, she could hardly blame them.

As they came up, one of the older men was saying to Gar, "You have my sympathy for your slavery, and my admiration for your escape, but how does that answer my question?"

"I encountered some giants," Gar told them, "and found that all the Midgarder scare-stories were complete lies. That made me wonder if the dwarves had been slandered just as thoroughly, so I set out to visit Nibelheim and discover the truth. On the way, I was lucky enough to meet this young woman, and we've been traveling together ever since. After we came into the North Country, we stayed overnight with some giants." He drew Garlon's letter out of his tunic. "One gave us a character reference."

The dwarf looked surprised, but he took the letter, opened it, and, to Alea's amazement, actually read it without even moving his lips! In fact, it only took him a few seconds, then he returned it to Gar with a brusque nod and said, "Well, if you're seeking Nibelheim, you've found it, though we're a colony village almost on the border of the North Country."

"We've come out of the North Country, then?" Alea asked in surprise, then bit her tongue.

But the dwarf didn't rebuke her for speaking out of place—he turned to her as though it were the most natural thing in the world for a woman to talk about serious matters, and nodded. "You crossed into Nibelheim some hours ago— not too long after sunrise, I'd guess. We don't expect trouble so far north, but we patrol anyway. We've come across the odd robber band now and again. Mostly, we bring home pork or beef."

The crossbows lowered, as though by accident, and the dwarves began to discuss the event with one another with frequent glances at the two strangers.

"Shall we trust them?" the dwarf asked his fellows.

"The woman has a good heart," Retsa said. "Her name is Alea."

"Welcome among us then, Alea," the dwarf said, with a

nod of the head that was almost a bow. "You too, Gar. Will you be our guests for the night?"

Gar glanced at Alea; with a shock, she realized he was asking her opinion. She recovered and gave him a one-inch nod.

"Gladly," Gar told the dwarf, then turned to Alea. "May I present Master Bekko?"

"A pleasure to meet you, lass," Bekko said. "I take it you've already met Retsa and her daughter Saret." He was obviously saying that for Gar's benefit. "These are Obon, Mala, Robil...."

He introduced the members of the band, each of whom nodded. Alea managed to recognize the nods as signs of greeting in time to return them; so did Gar. When the introductions were done, the big man said, "Since you saved us by killing so many pigs, you must let us help carry them to your village."

"Not Alea," Retsa said quickly. "She has a wound in her leg."

Gar turned to her in alarm.

"Only a scratch," Alea said quickly, but Gar didn't look convinced.

Retsa assured him, "It's more than that, but not bad at all, and will heal in a week. Still, she shouldn't go carrying any more of a load than she has to, at least not today."

Gar seemed somewhat reassured. "Well, I'll carry a balanced load myself, then." Before anyone could object, he strode over to the pile of pigs, took four bound feet in each hand, and came back to Bekko, the two carcasses swinging. "I feel a bit better about accepting your hospitality now."

Bekko laughed, reached up to slap him on the arm, and turned to lead the way home.

The dwarf village stood on a hill above the forest. Their first sight of it was a sort of crown on top of the slopes, one with dark points. As they climbed up to it, they saw that it was an earthen wall with a palisade of sharpened logs slanting outwards.

"We'll bring some giants to build us a proper wall," Bekko said, almost in apology, "as soon as we've made enough radios to trade for their labor."

"How many is that?" Gar asked.

"Twenty is the going price," Bekko answered, "if we can offer a computer with it."

Gar stared down at the man. "You make computers?"

Bekko nodded. "When our ancestors first escaped from Midgard, one band found a metal hut in the forest."

"A *big* hut," Retsa added.

"Very big," Bekko agreed, "but it had to be, for it had a machine in it that was as big as a house itself."

"Bigger," Robil said. "I've seen it."

Obon snorted. "We've all seen it. Every child goes to see it when he's in school."

"School?" Gar asked mildly, but Alea glanced at him quickly, and could have sworn she saw his ears prick up.

"Yes, we have schools, stranger." Retsa smiled, amused. "Children have much to learn if they're to make radios and computers, after all."

"They certainly do," Gar agreed. "What was the big machine?"

"It had wings, so our ancestors were able to recognize that it had flown once. When they read about it later, they found it was a thing called a 'shuttle,' for carrying people and cargo into the sky, to the ship that had brought them from the stars."

"And even a shuttle had a computer." Gar nodded.

"It taught our ancestors to read—in Midgard, the ordinary people had forgotten how, when everything fell apart, and only the priests still knew. Then it showed them how to make radios and more computers."

"It had to teach them a good deal of mathematics and physics first, didn't it?"

All the dwarves glanced at him keenly, but Bekko only said, "That's part of learning how to make such things, yes. Where did you say you came from?"

"Very far away," Gar told him, "but I didn't realize the Midgarders would enslave a stranger. I take it that once you had radios, you started talking with the giants."

"Well, the Midgarders weren't about to talk to us," Retsa said with a wry smile.

"They started using a different kind of modulation, so that we couldn't overhear them." Bekko grinned. "We learned how to make receivers for it. We listen to them now, though they don't know it."

"I wonder if they still listen to you?" Gar said idly, gazing at the sky.

Bekko stared at him, startled at the thought, then exchanged glances with Retsa, then Obon. All had the same wide-eyed look. Alea guessed that they hadn't thought they might be the objects of eavesdropping as well as the listeners.

A sentry on top of the wall called down, "Who are your new friends, Bekko?" In spite of the light tone, his eyes were wary.

"Strangers seeking Nibelheim, Dorsan," Bekko called back. "They have a letter from the giants saying they're good folk, to be trusted."

"Then they're welcome." Dorsan turned to send a warbling call over the village and by the time they came through the gate, a crowd had gathered to meet them with more running up, eager and excited by something new.

Alea looked about her, dazed. She guessed there were a few hundred of them lining the way, and the hunting band had been a good sample of what they were like—most around three feet tall, but some as short as two feet, more as tall as four, a few even taller, with here and there a man or woman as tall as a Midgarder. They all seemed to want to touch hands and be introduced, and Alea's head whirled with the scores and scores of dwarf names.

Finally Bekko waved them away, grinning. "Peace, good friends, peace! These poor big folk can't possibly learn all by our clamor!"

"We do have the impression that we're welcome, though," Gar said, looking a bit frazzled. "In fact, I don't think I've ever had a more ringing reception."

The dwarves laughed and turned away to their work, waving one last greeting. Alea and Gar raised their hands in imitation.

Four dwarves came up with poles to take the pigs from Gar. Looking around, Alea saw that all the swine had disappeared into the crowd.

"There will be feasting tonight," Bekko told them, "partly because of so many pigs brought home."

"But more to celebrate guests," Retsa said. "It's a rare occasion, and we mean to make the most of it. I hope you know some stories we haven't heard."

Alea glanced at Gar, but the big man didn't show the slightest sign that the comment meant anything to him. "We learned some from the giants."

"Oh, those are bound to be old!" Retsa scoffed. "They've

even told us a new one some stranger brought, about a southern god named Thummaz coming to visit Asgard!"

Bekko looked up at a sudden thought. "You wouldn't be that very stranger, would you?"

"I would," Gar sighed, "and there goes my best tale. We'll have to see what else I can remember—perhaps the story of Chang-tzu and the butterfly."

"It has a pleasant sound," Retsa said, grinning. "Come, strangers, let us show you our village."

"There will be dancing," Saret told Alea. "You'll have to show us your dances, and learn ours."

"They may not be very different." Alea looked about her. "So many flowers!"

Every little house had a garden around it. They were made of wattle and daub, with thatched roofs, walls painted in pastels.

"What a lovely village!" Alea exclaimed.

"And so many dogs." Gar looked about, grinning. "No wonder you didn't hesitate to invite us in."

"Well, I wouldn't say we didn't hesitate," Bekko demurred, "but if you're good enough for the giants, you're good enough for us. Yes, we like our dogs, and I think you've seen why."

"Yes, indeed! I can't believe the Midgarders ever had the audacity to attack you!"

"They do, and often," Bekko said grimly. "Even here, so far north, we've had to fight off their raiders now and then, and bandits at least once a year."

"Yes, I've met the Midgarder rejects," Gar said, "the ones who seem to feel they have to persuade themselves they're better than anyone else. It must be quite a shock for them, when you defeat them."

"No doubt they tell themselves it's our dogs who beat them, not ourselves," Retsa said, with irony.

A child was coming out of one of the houses. He was four feet tall, and his mother, a foot shorter than he, came hurrying out holding up a length of fabric. "Please take your cloak, Krieger! It will be chilly this evening!"

"Mother, please!" The boy glanced at the party of hunters, all of whom instantly snapped their eyes away.

"Well, I'm sorry if I embarrass you," his mother said, "but it serves you right for forgetting your coat. You don't have to wear it, after all—you can sling it over your shoulder until it gets cold."

There wasn't even a hint of laughter from the passing hunters, and the boy's embarrassed anger faded. "I'm sorry, Mama. I don't mean to be cross. It's just that . . ."

"Just that mothers worry too much. Yes, I know." The dwarf mother patted the cloak onto his shoulder. "Well, thank you for humoring me, my son. Go now to your friends."

Alea looked around her at granite faces, several of which were obviously fighting laughter. She said to Saret, "Your people are uncommonly understanding, not to tease!"

"Uncommonly?" Saret stared. "Not in Nibelheim, I assure you! Families are far too important to us!"

"Even when . . ." Alea broke off and looked away, embarrassed.

But Saret laughed gently, reading her face. "Even when the child is as tall as any Midgarder? That makes no difference."

"Indeed not." Retsa reached up to take her daughter's hand. "Children are children, after all, and must always be able to come to us for love and support, no matter how big or how old they grow. There's no other way to do it, this task of parenting."

Saret smiled down at her mother and gave her an affectionate squeeze of the hand. Alea had to look away, eyes blurring, for the gesture reminded her of the warmth and love of her own home, and her parents' unswerving devotion, no matter how tall she grew.

"So many wells!" Alea exclaimed. "Every house must have its own! But how can you draw the water out when the well-roof is so low?"

"Wells?" Retsa followed her guest's gaze to the brick cylinder, three feet high, with the slanting wooden roof that seemed to sit right on top of the mortar. There were horizontal slots in its roof, two feet long and an inch wide, each covered by the lip of the one above.

"Why have roofs if they're going to let the rain and cold in?" Gar asked, but Alea looked at his eyes and saw he suspected something.

"Oh, the louvers keep the rain out," Bekko told him, "but they let the light and the air in. Those aren't wells, lass—they're shafts for letting the folk underground breathe and see."

"You have people underground?" Alea asked, her eyes wide.

"Every dwarf village has tunnels for safety," Retsa told her. "If the Midgarders ever break through our walls, we can retreat into our mazes and cave in the entry on our enemies."

"We make our shops there," said Bekko, "so that our work will be safe from robbers and raiders. It's also a good deal easier to keep clean, and dust matters, when you're making such tiny things."

"Clean?" Alea stared. "Surrounded by dirt?"

"We're better housekeepers than that," Retsa said, smiling. "Would you like to see?"

Alea saw Gar's face light up with eagerness, and also saw the motion of his jaw as he bit his tongue. She smiled, amused, and told Retsa, "Why yes, we would."

"Are you sure?" Bekko asked Retsa, frowning.

"If we trust them in our village, why not in our shops?" Retsa countered. To Alea, she said, "You must be careful not to touch anything."

"We won't," Alea promised. "Will we, Gar?"

"Absolutely not!" he averred.

"Well, then, to the mines with you!" Bekko chuckled at his own joke—just as well, since nobody else did. He led them around a little hill covered with grass—but as they came to the front, they found the slope had been chopped off and re-placed with a great oaken door.

"Down you go," Retsa said, and led them into another world, far more like the Nibelheim of the tales.

14

Down they went into darkness, but there was light below. They descended a sloping ramp, but it was paved where the town's streets were not. Then it leveled off, and they found themselves in a mine, shored up by timber—but the wood was smoothed and polished, and the surface between the beams was cream-colored stone. Oil lamps lit the tunnel, attached to the posts. Alea exclaimed with delight, for the dancing flames brought out glints of brilliance from the stone walls. Looking closely, she saw that the blocks were cut into regular rectangles and mortared neatly in place. "Surely the giants didn't do this for you! Even I must stoop!"

"Even as you say—they didn't." Retsa chuckled. "Giants abhor close, tight places. We glory in them. But they did teach us this much of their craft."

"What is that ringing ahead?" Gar stared down the tunnel toward the sound of metal on metal.

"Come and see," Bekko invited.

Stooping to fit a five-foot ceiling, they followed him down

a completely clean, almost antiseptic stone hall. Suddenly it opened out, and Gar stood up with a groan of relief, for they had come into a domed chamber with a twenty-foot ceiling. Lamps lit its walls, but most of the illumination came from a dozen forges placed around the room, with dwarves stripped to the waist hammering metal on anvils. Over each forge was a metal hood with a pipe leading to a central vent.

"This is for ironwork," Bekko called over the din.

The noise quieted amazingly as the smiths caught sight of the strangers. They stared openly, not even trying to hide their astonishment. Alea was interested to notice that some of the smiths were women, wearing only a sort of double halter above the waist; she guessed it was to hold their breasts in place as they swung and bounced their hammers.

"Guests," Retsa called to them. "We'll introduce you all at dinner. We feast tonight, for these strangers led many pigs to us."

"Well, that's one way of looking at it," Saret said, grinning.

"The next chamber is for finework," Bekko said, leading them on, and the hammering started up again. "Gold and silver."

"Why so high a ceiling?" Gar asked as they threaded their way between forges.

"This was a mine at first," Retsa explained, "and still is, below us. Our parents dug the iron out of this stope, then walled it with the very stone they'd had to dig out. Most dwarf villages are built on top of mines this way."

"And when you're done taking out the metal, you make the bracing sure and secure, and turn the stopes into under-ground shops." Gar nodded with a smile of wonder. "Very efficient."

It also struck Alea as amazingly industrious. She was overwhelmed to think of the amount of labor it had taken. So much for the notion of lazy, greedy dwarves who could be stirred to work only by the sight of gold.

"Since we mine iron here," Bekko explained, "we trade with other dwarf villages for other metals."

He led the way through another tunnel and into a second chamber with rings of workbenches, where dwarves sat rigidly erect, sculpting wondrous pieces of ware from gold and silver.

"Why do they make the benches so high?" Alea asked.

"And why do they sit so straight?" Gar seconded.

"If they don't, years of toil will make slabs of muscle and a bend to the spine that will make them look like hunchbacks," Bekko explained.

Alea almost exclaimed out loud, but caught herself in time. To the children of Midgard, dwarves were indeed pictured as slit-eyed hunchbacks. Apparently earlier generations of small people had learned the lessons of posture the hard way.

The third chamber held workbenches with parts the size of a finger joint. The finished work was a rectangular gray block the size of her hand, and she had no idea what it was for—but Gar asked, "Radios?" and Retsa nodded.

The fourth chamber was divided into two separate workshops with a hallway between the dividers. They couldn't go into either one, but they could look through wide windows and see the dwarves at work. They wore white from head to toe, and were making boxes with windows in the front.

"Why can't we go in?" Alea asked.

"Because even specks of dust are too much here," Retsa answered.

"They're making computers," Bekko explained.

Alea didn't understand, but she told herself she would remember this, and some day it would make sense.

She found a few minutes to discuss it with Gar after they came out of the tunnels, and while they were sitting on the village common, waiting for the pigs to roast. The dwarves were gathering slowly, chatting with one another, obviously in a holiday mood. Retsa, Saret, and Bekko had left off being their hosts for a few minutes and were chatting with their neighbors, so Alea could marvel at the contrast between dwarf and giant without worrying about anyone overhearing by more than chance—at the contrast, and the resemblances, too.

"They are both craftsmen," she told Gar, "but each on a scale that befits them. The giants craft walls and towers that are far bigger than themselves, while the dwarves craft things far smaller than themselves."

"Doesn't that fit in with the stories you were told as a child?" Gar asked.

"Why—yes, it does!" Alea said in surprise. "The dwarves were supposed to be wondersmiths, hammering out marvelous things in their caverns—and the giants built huge stone castles."

"I'm sure the giant village we visited would look like a castle to people who never saw the inside," Gar said, "and the workshops we've just seen would certainly seem to be caverns, if you ignored the stonework and finishing that have made them pleasant places to work."

"You don't think the first storytellers had actually been to Jotunheim and Nibelheim!"

"No, I don't," Gar said. "In fact, I think those tales were being told before the first giants were born, and before the first dwarves escaped from slavery. But I suspect all of them heard those stories in their childhood, and remembered them so deeply they may not have thought of them until they'd been exiled. Then, though, the stories came to mind, and they thought that was how they were supposed to behave."

"Could they really pattern their lives after stories?" Alea asked in wonder.

"Haven't the Midgarders done just that?" Gar asked. "And the bandits are quickly making up stories to justify the way they live. Of course, it could be that the giants began building huge houses simply because of their size, and found the work very satisfying."

"And the first dwarves burrowed for safety, accidentally dug up metal nuggets, and found they enjoyed making things of that metal?" Alea nodded slowly. "It could be. Will we ever know?"

"Probably not," Gar said, "but after dinner, I'm going to ask Bekko to let me have some time with their village computer. After that, I'll see if I can use their radio to talk to our friend Garlon to tell him we've arrived safely—and what we've learned."

"He probably knows it already," said Alea, "if the giants and dwarves talk to one another as much as they say."

Then their hosts came back, and the banquet began. There was much talk and laughter, and as much ale as pork, or so it seemed. When they were done eating, the dwarves began to tell stories. Alea listened wide-eyed as Obon told the tragedy of the heroic dwarf Alberich, who agreed to guard the Rhinegold for the Lorelei, and took it down into the caverns of Nibelheim to hide it from the wicked gods of Asgard. But Wotan called on the sly god Loki, and the treacherous two sneaked into Nibelheim and stole the gold anyway. Alberich fought to defend it, and the gods slew him most ingloriously for his loyalty to the Lorelei, and his struggle to keep his promise.

That, of course, was quite the opposite of the tale Alea had learned in her childhood, in which Alberich had been a twisted, power-hungry little villain who had stolen the Rhine-gold and forged from it the Ring that had given him power over all other dwarves. Then Wotan and Loki had braved the dangers of Nibelheim, and the risk of a battle against thousands of dwarves, to rescue the Lorelei's treasure. Alberich had been justly punished for his greed and his crime.

She was so unnerved that when Saret pressed her for a story, all she could say was, "I don't know any you haven't heard," which was true in its way, though the dwarves certainly would have found the Midgarder versions of the stories to be strange—and also insulting. "Ask Gar."

"Yes, Gar!" Bekko turned to the big wanderer. "Tell us a new tale, as you told the giants!"

"Well, there's no point in telling you one the giants have already broadcast to you."

"Broadcast, like sowing seed?" Retsa grinned. "A good metaphor! But surely you know others."

Gar did. He made them laugh with the tale of Chang-tzu's dream that he was a butterfly, and how he wondered ever after if he was really a butterfly who was now dreaming that he was Chang-tzu. Then he held them spellbound with the story of the magical King of the Monkeys, sworn to protect a monk on pilgrimage to the holy land of India, and how he fought three other monsters, brought them to repentance, and made them the monk's servants.

Alea listened as spellbound as the rest, and wondered if she should have him tell her a new story every night.

But Retsa saw through his ruse, and leaned forward, smiling. "So no matter how foreign or threatening a person may seem, he can repent his evil ways and become a friend?"

Gar gained a faraway look, gazing off over their heads, and nodded. "You could interpret the story that way, yes."

Alea was suddenly completely sure he had meant them to interpret it just that way.

So was Retsa. "Even if that person is a Midgarder or a bandit?"

"It's possible," Gar agreed. "In fact, if a robber band's women and children came to ask you for protection from their men, I'd say it would show that they were on their way toward learning to respect dwarves and giants, and that their children would grow up thinking you should all be friends."

Retsa laughed, and all the dwarves joined her. "Well, we won't give up on them, friend Gar," she said, "but for now, we should dance."

Dance they did—it seemed they had only been telling stories to let their dinner settle. Some of the taller men pressed Alea to dance, and Saret taught her the steps. She gave frequent glances to make sure she was never out of Retsa's sight, but with the assurance of the presence of the older dwarf woman, she was actually able to relax a bit and let herself enjoy the dance. She enjoyed it all the more because it had been so many years since a man had been willing to dance with her.

In fact, she was enjoying herself so much that she almost missed seeing Gar go off into the underground chambers with Bekko. She made a mental note to ask him in the morning, and felt sure he would tell her everything he learned from this computer, whatever it was.

Then she put it out of her mind, and enjoyed the dance.

Gar was already awake and sitting by the door, watching the sunrise, when she staggered out to join him, a mug of hot drink in her hand—Retsa had assured her that it would make her head feel better. She sat down beside Gar, took a slurping sip, then glanced up at him, and saw by the glow in his face that his night's adventure had been as rewarding, in its way, as her own. She tried to summon interest and asked, "What did you learn?"

"The history of your world," Gar told her. "It's pretty much as I guessed, only worse."

That brought Alea awake. "Worse? How? Our ancestors came from the stars and started to build a city, but everything fell apart. The people gathered into villages and managed to scratch out a living farming. Then the giants and dwarves started being born."

"That happens when there aren't enough people," Gar told her, "so that, after two or three generations, no matter whom you marry, he's a first cousin one way or another."

Alea stared, appalled. "That happened here?"

"It did," Gar confirmed. "Your ancestors left Old Earth with half a million people—but it would have taken far too big a ship to carry food and drink for so many, so all but the ship's crew traveled asleep, frozen stiff."

"Frozen?" Alea stared, shocked.

"Yes, but it was perfectly safe—they knew how to freeze people and thaw them out safely. There were always a few who died, but only a few, and everyone understood they chance they were taking."

"The Frost Giants," Alea whispered.

Gar nodded. "Perhaps that's where the story started, though these people were all the size of ordinary Midgarders. Apparently one of the crew loved the story of the Ring of the Niebelungs and played it whenever the rest of the crew would let him. Perhaps the sound filtered through the walls to the sleeping people and filled their dreams—who knows?"

"That's not enough to make things fall apart," Alea told him.

"No, it wasn't. But as they neared this planet, a small rock, no bigger than your fist, struck the ship and punched a hole clear through it. The crew patched the hole quickly enough, and didn't think anything more about it—until they started to thaw out the passengers. Then they found out, too late, that the stone had damaged the defrosting computer—the machine that controlled the thawing. They didn't have any choice, they had to go ahead and try to thaw everybody out anyway, but a hundred thousand people died without waking."

Alea gasped. "How horrible!"

"Yes, it was," Gar said somberly, "but the stone had done even more damage than that. It had broken a corner of the ship's furnace, not the part that made it go but the one that made heat and light for the crew, and no one had noticed. The furnace spilled an invisible poison into the stocks of un-born cattle and and pigs and sheep—ova and sperm banks, they were called."

"So their livestock was born dead?" Alea asked, wide-eyed.

"No, but it might have been better if it had. The animals were born, all right, but something went wrong inside of a great number of them, and their meat gave the people who ate it a sickness that killed them in a few days. Half the colonists died before anyone found out why and killed all the infected livestock."

"So there were only two hundred thousand of them left," Alea said, watching his face.

Gar's mouth worked, but his eyes were cold and grim. "Yes, but there weren't enough animals left to feed them all."

"So they fought over the cattle," Alea whispered.

Gar nodded. "When it was all over, only a hundred fifty thousand people still lived, and they all hated one another because of the fighting. They split into rival bands, and after fifty years or so, each of those bands thought if itself as a separate kingdom."

"And they only married people within their own kingdom?" Alea asked.

Gar turned to her in surprise. "You see the answers so quickly! Yes, you're right—it took a hundred years before they started marrying people from other kingdoms, and by that time, the giants and dwarves had begun to be born."

"But why did the Midgarders think they were evil?" Alea pressed.

"Mostly because of a man named Tick, who wanted to rule everybody," Gar told her. "He found the story of the Ring of the Niebelungs that the crew member had made sure everyone knew. He told that story from one end of the land to the other, haranguing the Midgarders and telling them that dwarves and giants were evil, and that they must cast them out and band together, or the giants would pound them flat and the dwarves would undermine their towns. Besides, he pointed out that the giants would eat all the food, and that if the Midgarders exiled them and the dwarves, there would be that much more food for everyone else."

"And they believed him?" Alea asked incredulously.

Gar nodded, his face stone. "Hungry people will believe the most outrageous things, from a man who promises them food—and people who have been living in squalor and humiliation will be very quick to believe anyone who offers them pride and a better life."

"So the Midgarders all banded together into one kingdom," Alea inferred.

"Yes, but they didn't let Tick rule them outright," Gar said. "There was too much hatred between kingdoms for that. He did manage to get them to hold a gathering of barons called the Allthing once a year, though, to vote on the laws and judge disputes, so the kings became scarcely more powerful than any other lord. The Council of Kings sat all year around, you see, and they left their stewards to take care of their lands and people. Through them, Tick taught all the ordinary people to think of themselves as Midgarders, to revere normal size and looks, and to hate the other nations."

"Did he teach them to hate women, too?" Alea asked, her voice hard.

"Close. He taught them that they had to be very strong warriors in order to fight off the giants."

"And men are stronger than women," Alea said bitterly, "so men had to be important, much more important."

"And women were only there to take care of them and do all the drudgery, so the men could fight." Gar nodded. "From that, all the rest followed. It justified slavery—the women alone couldn't do all the hard work, after all—so anyone too tall or too short was enslaved. Anyone who grew to be a giant, though, was exiled, and so was anyone who was so short as to be clearly a dwarf. Many of them died, of course, but the ones who survived banded together and married."

"So we have three separate nations today," Alea said, feeling numb.

"Yes," Gar said. "But remember, only one nation was nurtured with hatred. The other two survived because they learned how to trust one another, and to deserve that trust."

"What of this 'radio' and these 'computers' of yours?" Alea asked. "Did Midgard forget how to make them?"

"Well, somebody there is using radio, at least," Gar told

her. "My guess is that the Council of Kings and the barons have remembered how, so that they can direct battles and listen to the giants' and dwarves' plans. They make sure that no one else learns."

"My poor people." Alea blinked back tears. "So torn apart, so blind! Can they ever be healed?"

"Oh, yes," Gar said softly. "It will take time, it will take a great deal of time—but what one story has torn apart, another can mend."

"But there's nothing I can do about it!"

"Of course there is." Gar smiled down at her, eyes glowing as though she were something precious.

She felt her heart stop for a few seconds and wondered what he saw. "What can I do?" she whispered, then wondered which way she meant it.

"Tell the story of Dumi wherever you go," Gar said. "Tell the tale of Thummaz. What one poet has torn, another can knit up."

"How?" Alea cried, not understanding.

"Because Tick may have taught the Midgarders to hate, but he forgot to teach them not to love," Gar told her, "and his hatred made it all the more important for the giants and dwarves to keep that knowledge of loving alive. If they can love their children who look like Midgarders, they can learn to love the real Midgarders, at least enough to forgive them."

"Perhaps, if the Midgarders can stop hating them." Alea looked out over the village, at Midgard-sized fathers talking to dwarf sons, at dwarf mothers talking to Midgard-sized daughters. "They do care for their children mightily. To tell you the truth, I'm amazed to find that my parents weren't the only ones who cherished their offspring so deeply, even though they were too tall."

"I don't think the dwarves really think of anyone as being 'too tall,' " Gar said, "only as Midgarders, giants, or dwarves."

"So they must learn to think only of people as people?" Alea gave him a skeptical glance. "Very good, if the Midgarders can learn it, too." She knew the giants could.

"It's like Christianity," Gar sighed. "It would work so well, if only everyone would try it all at once. Since they won't, though, someone has to try it first."

Alea turned to him, frowning. "I don't know this Christianity you speak of, but you make it sound as though the one who begins it would be likely to be hurt."

"Not necessarily," Gar said, "but in some matters, such as not striking back unless your life is threatened, it puts you at a distinct disadvantage. It's like love—you have to take the risk of being hurt, if you wish to win the prize of joy."

Alea glanced at him sharply, suddenly wary of what might be an overture, and told herself that the thudding of her heart was only fear—but Gar was gazing out at the dwarf village, calmly and thoughtfully. Piqued, she demanded, "So what risk could these dwarves take? You wouldn't have them march empty-handed into Midgard, would you?"

Gar stated to answer, but Bekko came up to the guest house at that moment, rubbing his hand over his face, his gaze blurry. "Did you sleep well?" he asked politely if indistinctly.

"I did, yes, thank you," Gar said.

"I too." Alea smiled. "And without dreams. Sometimes that's a blessing."

"Yes . . . I dreamed . . ." Bekko gazed out over the village. Other dwarves had begun to come out of their houses, looking equally hung-over. Bekko shook his head, then winced. "I shouldn't drink so much just before sleeping, I suppose."

Alea had an uneasy premonition. "Of what did you dream?"

Bekko only frowned, staring off into space.

"Of a wizard?" Gar prodded.

Bekko turned to stare at him. "You too, eh?"

Gar nodded. "I think your neighbors have, too, from the look of them."

"Did this wizard show you a Great Monad?" Alea asked. "Did he tell you that we could only become better if giants, dwarves, and Midgarders banded together?"

"Something like that, yes." Bekko frowned at her, studying her face. "Has the whole village dreamed of this?"

Alea started to say that she had dreamed of the Wizard weeks before, but Gar spoke first. "I think they have. Did this Wizard tell you that you should be ready to give shelter to Midgarder fugitives?"

Alea turned to him in surprise.

"He did, yes." Bekko nodded heavily. "He said that was all we could do to heal our people for the time being. He didn't say why the Midgarders should be fleeing."

"They'll be Midgarders like us," Alea said flatly, "too big or too small. They'll have been thrown into slavery. If they flee to you, they'll have escaped—but there will be hunters hard on their trails."

Bekko stared at her in surprise. "Is that your own tale?"

"It is," Alea said, voice and face stony.

Bekko seemed to read a lot from her very lack of expression. His voice was gentle. "Did you suffer greatly at their hands?"

"Yes," Alea snapped.

"Greatly enough to make you take the risk of punishment for those who escape," Bekko interpreted. He nodded. "Yes.

I think we could give such people shelter. Not too many in any one village, of course. Perhaps we'll have to build them their own villages, and protect them with our armies." Then he shrugged, turning away. "Of course, I'm only one dwarf, and this is only one village—but I think anyone who dreamed of that wizard would agree with me."

"If you've all dreamed of him," Gar said, "perhaps all of Nibelheim has."

"Or will?" Bekko gave him a wintry smile. "Perhaps indeed."

He shrugged off the whole issue with a visible effort. "Well, there will be time for us all to talk of this in council. For now, the day begins. Shall we see what food there is with which to break our night's fast?"

They left down the winding road that led up to the village, turning back several times to wave to the dwarves who stood thronging the gates, hands raised in farewell, Bekko, Retsa, and Saret at their front. Finally the curve of the road took them in among trees, and they turned away, Alea blinking moisture from her eyes. "How can I feel more welcome among dwarves than among my own kind?"

"Do you mean the bandits we visited?" Gar smiled. "Yes, they weren't terribly hospitable, were they? Besides, we'd seen how well the giants respect their women, and the bandits didn't look very good against them."

"No," Alea said, her voice hard, "they surely didn't."

She looked around at the trees and the empty road ahead, and suddenly felt a bleak despair seize her. To banish it, she said, "Well, we've seen Jotunheim, we've seen Nibelheim, and we've both seen far too much of Midgard. Where shall we go now?"

"Back to the clearing where we met the dwarves," Gar answered.

Alea stared at him. "Why?"

"Because something is waiting for us there," Gar said with absolute assurance.

Alea eyed him narrowly. "What's this? More of your magic?"

Gar looked at her, astounded. "How did you know?"

Alea hadn't, she'd meant it in sarcasm, but wasn't about to let him know that. Let him think she was the mindreader for a change! She kept her face carefully immobile and said, "How else could you know what lies in a clearing miles away?"

"So you guessed." Gar smiled, his gaze warming. "Only it wasn't just a guess, it was deduction—very clear thinking from a few facts."

His gaze was so admiring that Alea had to look away, shaken again. Any other man giving her that look would have been devouring her body with his eyes. Gar was admiring her mind. It was very flattering, and she was glad he wasn't thinking of her figure. At least, she thought she was glad of it.

She needed a change of subject. Not looking at him, she asked, "How can the dwarves so love children twice their size? Wouldn't such offspring remind them too much of the ones who cast them out?"

"You'd think so, yes," Gar agreed. "Maybe, though, the first dwarves were bound and determined not to treat their children the way their own parents treated them—and those children, when they grew up, never thought of not loving their offspring, no matter how big they grew."

"I suppose that makes sense," Alea said doubtfully, "but I suppose I've grown too hard in my heart to believe people do things only out of love, or a determination not to return cruelty for cruelty. Couldn't there have been a more practical reason?"

"Of course there could." Gar's eyes warmed again.

Alea kept her eyes turned resolutely ahead. Then she realized with a bit of a shock that they were walking side by side, and she hadn't even thought of being afraid. How long had that been going on?

"Perhaps it has something to do with the constant danger of those early years of exile," Gar suggested.

"With wild pigs and bandits and wild dogs about?" Alea nodded. "Yes, I can see that people so small would have lived in constant fear. Their only protection would have been banding together, wouldn't it?"

"Yes," Gar said, "and every dwarf lost would make the group that much less able to protect itself. Life probably became very, very precious to them."

"So precious that they cherished every single child," Alea finished. "Perhaps that's also how the male dwarves came to respect their women so well."

"They certainly needed every single pair of hands to be stay alive," Gar agreed. "Gender would have mattered less than number and social skills. Interesting how much stronger and more important the goddesses were in their version of the Ring of the Niebelung, wasn't it?"

So, chatting about safe topics, they made their way off the road, through the trees, and finally to the meadow where the wild pigs had attacked them.

There, Alea halted, staring in amazement and fear, for the clearing was filled.

15

It was huge, it was golden, and it filled the clearing all by itself. It was, Alea thought, like a huge wagon wheel with a great soup bowl upside down to cover the spokes and the hub, and another beneath it. There seemed to be windows up high, there toward the center, and strange lumpy things with holes in them here and there—but what attracted her attention most was the ramp that led up into the doorway that opened in its underside.

Finally she found her voice. "Was this what you knew was here?"

"Yes," Gar told her. "It's a ship for sailing between the stars."

The implications hit her like a hammer blow, but they roused too much fear. She would have to get used to them. For the moment, to hide that fear, she thrust them aside and concentrated only on the anger, the very rightly deserved anger. "Why didn't you warn me?"

Gar was silent.

"Because you wanted to scare me," Alea said, letting the anger show, letting more of it show as she turned to face him. "You wanted me to be afraid, wanted me to run screaming away! Didn't you?"

"I knew you wouldn't run," Gar said. "You've proved your courage time and again. But if you were going to be afraid of me, of what I am, this was the time to learn that. If you were going to turn away from me in disgust and loathing, this was the time to learn that, too."

He was trying to hide it, anyone else would have seen only a granite face, but Alea had been traveling with him too long to be deceived by that basilisk countenance. She frowned, looking more closely, her own fear and anger receding as she stared into his eyes, saw the bitter determination there, the courage to face the truth. Compassion flooded her, and for the very first time, she reached up toward his cheek, almost touched it, held her hand a hair's breadth away. "Why would I loathe you? You, who have fought to defend me, listened to my grief, offered more comfort than I was willing to take! How could that disgust me?"

Relief lightened his eyes, but he was still braced, still cautious, even though he smiled. "Let's go inside, then."

He started up the ramp, but she stared at him, appalled. "Can you just walk away from it? Can you talk to these people about peace and harmony, can you tell me you'll free the slaves, and just walk away and not do it?"

"It has begun," Gar told her, "but it will take a hundred years or more to complete. Come inside, and look and listen at what is happening in your world."

But Alea stood rigid as the implications of that ship came crashing back in on her, no longer to be ignored. "How do you know what is happening?"

Gar turned back, gazing down at her gravely. "Because the dwarves weren't the only ones to dream last night. The slaves in Midgard dreamed of the Wizard too, and he told them to band together, fight their way free if they had to, and flee to the dwarves or the giants, whichever was closer."

"How do you know this?" Alea asked in a harsh whisper.

Gar only gazed down at her, his face drawn, his eyes bleak.

"Because you are the Wizard!" she hissed. "You really can do magic, and you planted that dream in everyone's mind!"

"One for the giants, one for the bandits, one for the dwarves, one for the slaves, and one for the Midgarders," Gar confirmed. "The Midgarders alone refused to believe any of it, or to talk to their neighbors about it. They will, though. They'll remember, and when things start to change, they'll begin to believe. At the very least, they'll tell it to their children as a fairy tale—and the children will remember it when they're grown, when they need it."

But Alea's mind had jumped to the next conclusion. "If you can push dreams into people's minds, you can pull thoughts out! You really are a mindreader, a genuine mind-reader!"

"Yes," Gar said gravely.

"That's how you escaped, isn't it? That's why the bandits ran, all except Zimu! That's why we were able to fight off the dogs, why they ran in fear! That's how you were sure we could beat off the pigs!"

"Yes," Gar said again.

"That's how you knew when hunters were coming! You could read their thoughts a mile away!"

"Yes."

"And that's how you calmed me when we met! That's how you knew what to say! You've been reading my thoughts, too!"

"Only when we met," Gar said, "and only surface thoughts, the things you would have spoken aloud. I did that because I felt sure you would have wanted me to, if you had known me, known that I wanted to help you."

"Never since then?" Alea asked, with ferocious intensity.

"Never since," Gar repeated, very firmly. "I don't read friends' minds—unless they want me to, or would want me to if they knew the need. I don't even read enemies' minds unless there's a good reason."

"How can you say that, when you always knew exactly what to say, how to reassure me, how to comfort me?"

"Because other people have been hurt as badly as you," Gar said, "and wise people have taught me how to care for the wounded heart."

Alea started another denunciation, but caught herself and looked more closely at his eyes. She bit back the retort—that he was one of the wounded ones, too, that he had known how to treat her because he had needed the same care as she, perhaps still did.

But no one had given it to him. . . .

She vowed that she would, that she would think of what she needed and give the same care and compassion to him that he had shown her. The anger vanished, but she remembered something else. "You said I could learn to work magic, too." Her voice quavered.

"You can," Gar assured her. "It will take hard work, and a lot of it, but you have the talent. You can learn it."

To read other people's minds! For a moment, Alea went dizzy with the thought, so dizzy that she stumbled, leaned against something hard. That made her push the dizziness aside, and she looked up to see that the hard thing was Gar's side, and his arm was around her shoulders, his face anxious. "I'm sorry," he whispered. "I should have warned you."

She looked up into his eyes, feeling both drained and filled at once, knew her own eyes were wide as she said, "No. You shouldn't have. You did have to know if I would turn away."

She gathered her nerve and pushed past him, on up the ramp. "Come, then. Let's see these wonders that you say are happening all over the world."

She felt his eyes on her back, felt the heat of his admiration, the depth of his gratitude, but told herself it was just her imagination, that she couldn't be reading his mind yet, he hadn't told her a thing about how to do it, and she went on up into the doorway.

She emerged into luxury she could not believe.

The room was circular, thirty feet across, with one huge window and several smaller ones. Her feet sank into a thick rug that almost seemed to embrace them. It was a deep wine-red, and the moiré satin on the walls was rose. The ceiling was an even darker red, almost black, pierced by holes that bathed the individual pieces of furniture in soft, mellow light, but left the spaces between them dim. There were two chairs with reading lamps next to them on small tables, lamps that wore flat, circular hats with holes in the tops to let the light out above as well as below—but no smoke arose from them! Alea wondered what kind of oil they burned.

The furniture was all large and padded, far more heavily than any she had ever seen. In fact, the whole piece was padded, not just the seat or the back! There were five of them, and another that was long enough to seat three people at once without crowding. Every chair had a table beside it, and a long low table stood in front of the long chair.

There were pictures on the walls, actual oils by the look of them—but even as she watched, one of them changed. It was a landscape of autumn woods, but the leaves were falling from the trees. She could actually see them flutter down, and wondered if, when the branches were bare, there would be snow.

She stood at the doorway, frozen by both the richness of the place and the magic of it.

"Don't be afraid," Gar said at her shoulder. "It isn't magic, not really, and it's certainly something you can learn to understand in a few days."

Alea looked about her and saw that the other pictures were moving, too. One showed fish swimming by, another showed a shepherd watching his flock in a summer meadow (and the sheep were moving as they grazed), and a fourth showed brightly costumed people moving about among huge buildings covered with marvelous and colorful decorations. A boat drifted in the foreground, and the city seemed to have rivers instead of streets.

"It's beautiful," she said.

"Thank you," Gar said gravely. He stepped past her, set his heels one by one in a boot-jack and yanked off his boots, then slipped his feet into soft, backless slippers and went to stand by one of the armchairs. "Come, rest yourself."

"I'm not that tired." But Alea did kick off her own boots and came in slowly, looking about her wide-eyed. She did sit, slowly and at length.

"The chair will adjust to fit you," Gar told her. "Don't be alarmed."

She squealed, for the chair felt like a living thing as it moved under and about her. Then she laughed with delight and stroked the arm. "Is it a pet? Does it have a name?"

"No, it's not alive." Gar grinned. Then that grin vanished

and he said, quite seriously, "But this ship does have a name, and a sort of guardian spirit to go with it."

Alea went rigid.

"It isn't really a spirit," Gar said quickly, "only a machine, like the computers you saw the dwarves building, though much, much more complex. But it does take care of us, and watches over us."

"What is its name?" Alea asked through stiff lips.

"Herkimer," Gar told her, then lifted his head. "Herkimer, may I introduce you to Alea Larsdatter."

"I am pleased to meet you, Miz Larsdatter," the voice said, from everywhere and nowhere.

Alea jumped, then grew angry with herself and tried not to let either the fear or anger show. She said, very evenly, "And I am pleased to meet you, Herkimer. Are you really the spirit of this . . . it seems so strange to call such a thing as this a ship!"

"It is like a ship, at least," Herkimer told her, "for it flies between planets—worlds—as a ship sails between islands. As Magnus told you, I am not really a spirit, only the computer that sails the ship for him."

"And cooks my breakfast, and keeps the ship warm inside, and does the laundry and the dusting." Gar smiled, amused.

"But I will not pick up after you, Magnus," the ship reproved. "I wouldn't know what to keep and what to throw away, after all."

"Magnus?" Alea stared at him. "Is your name really Magnus?"

"It is," Gar told her. "I apologize for having introduced myself to you as Gar Pike—but when I step onto the surface of a world, I use the nickname someone else gave me."

Alea gave him a stony look. "Gar you were when I met

you, and Gar you will remain, at least to me. Why bother using a false name, anyway?"

"Enemies who know my real name may be watching for me."

"But you hadn't been to our world when you first used that name, had you?" Alea said suspiciously. "After all, you said you use it whenever you set foot on a new world."

"Even if I hadn't been there before, enemies might have come before me," Gar explained.

Alea felt a twinge of alarm. "Have you so many enemies, then?"

"Anyone who tries to free slaves and raise up the down-trodden makes enemies," Magnus answered. He sat down in a chair near hers and pointed at the huge window in front of them. "That isn't really a picture."

Alea looked at it. It showed a huge blue and green ball with swirls of white covering most of its surface. "What is it, then?"

"A view of your world, as seen by a sort of magical eye Herkimer left high above us," Magnus said.

Alea stared, completely astounded.

Magnus waited.

Finally Alea asked, "Is it a ball, then? The Midgarders teach their children that the world is a plate, and the sky is a bowl turned upside-down over it!"

"No, it's a ball," Magnus said. "I don't think that's a deliberate lie. Let's call the picture by a magician's word, though—'electronic' instead of 'magical.' We can look at any part of the three nations with it. We can also listen to their radio messages. Herkimer, may we hear the Midgarders?"

Voices cascaded from the screen, sounding tinny and distant. "The giants have formed a wedge! They're smashing through our army as though we were made of paper! In the name of Wotan, send whatever help you can!"

"I apologize for the quality of the sound," Herkimer said; then with a note of disdain, "Their equipment is inferior."

"Forget the quality!" Alea sat galvanized. "Can we see what they're talking about?"

"Of course." The picture of the world went cloudy, then cleared to show a view that made no sense.

"What's *that?*" Alea cried.

"We're looking down on them," Gar explained, "as though we were one of Wotan's ravens, flying overhead."

The whole picture made sense then. She was seeing a town, and the roadway that led to it. Hundreds of Midgarder warriors stood blocking the road, but the giants had simply swerved around them, and the warriors were running to intercept them. Their swords and battleaxes only bounced off the giants' legs, though, and they kicked the smaller men aside without even breaking stride.

"They seem to be wearing chainmail leggins," Gar noted.

Alea stared. "They have never done that before!"

"They have never really raided before," Gar explained, "only fought off the Midgarders' raids. Now and then they may have smashed through to free some prisoners, but I don't think the Midgarders were able to take many giants home with them."

"No." Alea's face hardened. "They killed them where they lay."

"Is this what is happening now, Herkimer?" Gar asked.

"No, Magnus," the voice said. "I showed you the recent past, so you would understand the radio messages."

The radio voices were still squawking at one another in alarm and dismay. The picture seemed to jump, then showed two giants smashing in the side of a slave barracks. The slaves came running out, and the two giants herded them off to the road, where other giants were driving in their own packs of slaves. They assembled all the village owned in a matter of minutes, then turned and strode back the way they had come, the slaves running to keep up, afraid of being stepped on by the giants behind them.

"They're stealing slaves!" Alea cried.

"Of course," Gar said. "Didn't your childhood stories tell you that those greedy giants are always trying to steal everything you own?"

"But that's all they're stealing! Just slaves!"

"Well, after all," Gar said, "from what you've told me, most of the slaves don't dare try to escape. They're sure they'll be caught, and the punishments are harrowing—and very public."

The Midgarders formed up across the road and to the sides, but they were only two ranks deep, and the giants simply smashed through them, kicking and laying about them with clubs. One Midgarder hurled a spear that stuck in a giant's chest; she stumbled, but her fellows to either side caught her arms and helped her to keep striding.

"Body armor," Gar explained.

The giants were past the Midgarders and striding away, too fast for the army to catch up. The slaves began to stumble and fall, so giants caught up half a dozen each and carried them away.

"They stole all our slaves!" the radio yammered. "Who's going to grow our food now? Who's going to tend the cattle and cook and clean?"

"We'll send you enough slaves to get you by," another voice snapped. "There are always more being born, you'll replace them soon enough. Warriors are another matter. How many of you died?"

"Only six, praise Thor! But we have fifty wounded."

"How many giants?"

"None dead." The voice sounded sheepish. "We might have wounded three or four."

"*None* dead? If this catches on, they'll wipe us out! Tell us everything about the battle! We have to figure out a way to stop them!"

The voice began an account of the raid in hesitant tones.

Alea cried, "They could have done this all along! They never had to lose a single giant!"

"No," Gar agreed. "As long as the Midgarders were doing the raiding, they could choose the place and be ready for the enemy, so they could throw spears down from ambush, and giants did die. But the giants were only worrying about protecting their own villages. When the giants do the raiding, they choose the time and place, and nothing can stop them."

"Then they could have been safe for hundreds of years, simply by raiding Midgard so often that we couldn't recover enough to attack them!"

"That's not the giants' way," Gar told her. "You know that as well as I."

"Yes, I do." Alea stared at the picture, her opinion of her own people sinking even further, and her opinion of the giants rising.

"Let's hear AM," Gar said. "What are the giants and dwarves talking about?"

The tinny voices shifted pitch and timbre to those of the dwarves. "Three wheels out first! Hold the tunnel while we gather the slaves!"

"Can you center on them?" Gar asked.

"Playing back," Herkimer said.

"How can he show us what happened in the past?" Alea protested.

"It's like memory," Gar told her, "electronic memory."

The picture jumped, and she saw the earth erupting in the center of a farmyard. It formed a hole four feet across, and armored dwarves poured out of it to take up station around the edges. Taller dwarves, as big as Midgarders and dressed just like them, leaped out and went running to the slave barracks. Others went running to the kitchens.

Midgarder warriors came pelting out, pulling on their armor. Dwarven crossbow bolts struck them down before they could come close enough to swing an axe. Then the big "dwarves" came running, shooing slaves before them, seeming to threaten them with their bows. The slaves leaped down into the hole.

More Midgarder warriors came, but stopped well back from the hole and raised bows, loosing arrows of their own. Spears flew, and a few dwarves fell, transfixed—but the crossbows spewed death, piercing Midgarder armor. The archers fled, unable to match the rate of fire or the penetrating power.

Then the dwarves were leaping back into the hole, all of them gone in a matter of minutes, taking their wounded with them. The Midgarders charged the hole, but skidded to a halt at its edge, then stood around nervously looking at one another. Finally, the oldest shook his head, and they turned away, leaving a dozen to guard the hole.

"A party of women is coming!" the radio barked. "Bandit women, by the look of them!"

"This is the past," Herkimer told them, and the picture jumped again. Alea saw the broad grassland of the North

Country, bordered by its scrubby woods. Twenty-odd women were hurrying across the plain with babies in their arms and children clutching their skirts.

"Dumi would turn away from any who did not help women," a basso rumbled, "and Freya's wrath would strike any who did not rescue mothers. We will send a score of giants to guard them. Tell us when their men come in sight."

The screen jumped, and Herkimer's voice said, "This is happening now."

On the screen, the bandit women were running between the pairs of female giants in a line of a dozen, with the women standing two by two to reassure their smaller equivalents. The bandits came charging pell mell after them, then saw the giants and stopped dead. One giant stepped forward, hands up in a placating gesture, talking.

The voice of the sentry said, "Retsa is talking to them. She is explaining that their women still love them, but are no longer willing to be beaten, or to see their children knocked about, or be commanded to do all the drudgery while the men take their ease. She is telling them they can win back their wives if they learn to treat them well—and if they are willing to be married by a priestess of Freya."

Alea clapped her hands in delight.

"A new source speaks," Herkimer informed them, "with high power, low frequency, and long waves."

Gar frowned. "That sounds like a broadcast designed to reach as far as possible—but how many people have radios in Midgard?"

"I shall search for signs of listeners, Magnus,"

"What's the voice saying?" Alea asked.

"We will join it in progress," Herkimer said.

A voice that sounded for all the world like a Midgarder

spoke. ". . . walked across the Rainbow Bridge, and no one offered to stay him from his quest. Thus Thummaz came to Asgard, He strode into Valhalla and the women of the Aesir exclaimed to one another at his beauty, but the men began to speak bitterly in jealousy."

"There," Herkimer said, and the picture jumped again to show a knot of Midgarders, some very tall and others very short, all dressed in worn and ragged clothing, huddled together around a cooking fire, but there were no gestures, no signs of speech. All heads were bowed, all eyes on a small, flat, gray box that lay on the ground in their center.

"So Loki came up behind Thummaz, and struck him on the head," the voice was saying. "He fell, and Tiw stepped forward with a war-axe, to hew . . ."

"That voice must be a giant's child, Midgarder-sized," Gar said quickly.

"Or a dwarf's," Herkimer responded.

They had meant well, but not quickly enough. Alea had heard the description, and felt a bit queasy. The speaker was making the tale far more detailed than Gar had.

In the picture, an overseer started toward the group of slaves. One of them looked up, spoke a single word, and a hand snaked out to make the radio disappear as the whole group burst into conversation.

"How did they get a radio?" Gar asked, staring.

"It has been three months since we visited the giants," Alea reminded him.

"Shortly after your visit, the giants and dwarves began to discuss the plan by radio," Herkimer told them. "It took me a while to decipher their code, to realize that a 'toe of Thummaz' was a slave and a 'talisman' was a radio receiver—but decipher it I did. The dwarves manufactured hundreds of receivers very quickly—apparently a much easier task than a transceiver—and gave some to merchants to take to the giants, but found ways to give others to slaves all along the western border of Midgard. They passed from hand to hand. Within a year, I suspect there will be at least one in every village."

"Thus it has begun," Gar said quietly.

"What? The peace between the three nations that your stories are supposed to bring us?" Alea rounded on him. "You're foolish if you think that! At the most, the giants and the dwarves may manage to steal most of the slaves, but there will be more born, and more! Besides, their raids will only make the Midgarders' hate burn hotter. They will set their minds to discovering new weapons and new strategies for fighting the giants, you may be sure of that! Then as dwarves and giants are killed in the fighting, they will begin to hate, too!"

"Dwarves and giants have always died fighting Midgarders," Gar reminded her. "If they die in raids rather than in defense, they will at least be able to understand why. Then, when the Midgarders discover that enslaving new people draws giant raiding parties, they will finally begin to exile all instead of enslaving some. Slavery will die out, though it will take twenty years or more. Gradually, they will learn to do their own work, and will have less time to spare for raiding."

"But they will hate more than ever!"

"Yes." Gar nodded heavily. "That will take two or three generations of telling new tales to eradicate—of tales, and of trading with the North Country for the ores and plants and dwarf-made goods that they can't find in Midgard."

"They have always gained such things, by raiding! Oh . . ." Alea frowned, turning her gaze away, thinking. "You really believe the Midgarders will stop raiding, don't you?"

"They will be too busy defending against attacks by the giants and dwarves," Gar agreed, "and within twenty years, they'll have a new enemy, too."

"A new enemy?" Alea looked up, frowning. Then her face cleared. "Of course! We have shown the North Country how to unite, haven't we?"

"Yes, we have." Gar's eyes glowed at her. "The bandit women will never forget how the giants have helped them regain their self-respect, protecting them against their menfolk until the men learn to treat them as the giants treat their women. The mothers will tell that to their sons and daughters, and tell them the stories of Freya and Dumi and Thummaz. . . ."

"And the children will grow up to think the giants and dwarves are their friends!" Alea cried.

Gar grinned, nodding. "Midgard may take a century or more to learn tolerance, but the separate limbs of Thummaz will be gathered in the North Country, and breathe new life into a new people who value all their offspring, no matter their size. Eventually, those stories will be told in Midgard, too—they will begin in Freya's temples, I think. Give it enough time, and even Midgarders will begin to think of giants and dwarves as friends."

"But will the other nations be ready to befriend them?" Alea countered.

"If they tell the tales we've left them and make up as many new ones as I think they will—yes."

Alea leaped up. "Come! I want to go out and see if the world has changed already!"

Gar laughed, sharing her delight, and followed her back down the ramp.

The day had waned as they watched history being made in

the big picture aboard the ship. They came out into moonlight and night, with insects shrilling all about them and the cool breeze filling the land with the odors of living.

Alea drew them in, breathing deeply. "It's in the air already, new life and new ways!" she cried. "We must go out to help it be born!"

Gar saddened. "If you must, then of course you must. But I must go."

Alea whirled, staring at him, feeling betrayed, and deeply. "Go? But why?"

"I'm a catalyst," Gar explained, "something that starts a change but can't really be a part of it. You can—this is your world—but I cannot."

Alea searched his face, not understanding.

"What would I do if I stayed?" Gar asked with a touch of impatience. "Lead a band of giants? Why should they listen to my orders? Why should the dwarves? Oh, I could form an army of bandits, but what good would that do? They will manage their own armies without me, and I wish to bring less death, not more. No, your people can do all that needs to be done by themselves. They have no need of me. There's nothing more I can do here."

Alea caught the emphasis on the word. She repeated it with a hollow sound. "Here?"

"Out there, I can still do some good." Gar looked up, sweeping a hand to take in all the sky. "There, where humanity has settled on sixty-odd worlds that we know about, and dozens more that we don't. There are people living in oppression, being ground down so brutally that you would scarcely recognize them as human. There's nothing more I can do here that you can't do yourselves, but on another world, under another sun, there is work for me indeed."

"But what will happen here?" Alea cried.

"The same things that will happen if I stay," Gar told her. "It will take a hundred years or more with me or without me. I might save a few more lives, speed up the transformation by a dozen years—but I also might not. No, Alea, my work here is done." The bleakness came to his face again as he said it.

That same emptiness settled in Alea's heart. "And me?" she demanded. "What will happen to me? Will you leave me to become some bandit's woman whether I want to or not, or to go to Saret or Garlon and live on their charity for the rest of my life, like a poor relation?"

Gar looked deeply into her eyes and said, "Wherever you go, you will rise to lead your people. You know how to fight now, so no bandit will be able to make you his property without more battle than he is willing to undergo. The dwarves would be glad of your strength, and you know it, and the giants would welcome you as a comrade, now that Gorlan and his kin have done so. You are an exceptional woman, Alea, a rare and remarkable human being, and no matter where you go, people will treasure you."

His eyes glowed as he said it, and she could almost have believed that his mind was reaching out to touch hers. She stood mute, staring back at him, trying to deny the words he said, but feeling a flood of delight and gratitude to hear them spoken.

Finally she could speak again. "People. Maybe people. But can there be one person, one man alone who could treasure me, delight in my presence, cherish me?"

"It may happen," Gar told her, "now."

Her mind screamed, *It already has,* but she buried the words quickly in the darkest recesses of her heart and masked them with a bitter tone.

"It also may not! If you can't do any good here, then neither can I! I haven't belonged here since I turned fifteen and grew taller than the boys! I haven't felt at home since then, not anywhere but in my parents' house, and not even there, now that they're dead!" She remembered the last sight of her old home and shuddered at what Birin Wentod had done to it. In a lower voice, she said, "I have no home anymore."

Gar stared at her.

But Alea stood, feeling numb, listening to her own words echo inside her, and knew that she had finally acknowledged something that she had known as true for months, but had striven to deny.

Gar saw that recognition in her eyes and reached out a hand, smiling gently. But he didn't even try to touch, only swept that hand back up toward the interior of the ship and said, "You have a new home, though, if you wish to take it."

Alea stood frozen, unable to believe the fantastic good fortune that opened out before her. Her soul shied from it, she found that she feared the happiness it offered, the tearing away of all she had ever known and loved. . . .

But that had been torn away already. "Yes," she whispered. "Yes, I want to go with you."

Gar's eyes shone, and he took a step toward her, arms open in welcome.

She still stood like a statue, unable to take the answering step into his arms, the old dread clamoring within her. *Be still,* she told it furiously. She had nothing to fear that way now, and she knew it. There really was something wrong with him when it came to sex, but it was in his mind, and whatever it was, it kept her safe while she was with him—and she had developed an abhorrence for her own people, strengthened by her awareness that many, many Midgarders would want to use her as a target for revenge, once they knew how she had helped Gar turn their world upside down.

Did she really want to be safe that way? From him?

For now, yes—and "for now" was all that mattered.

Still, she stood where she was, didn't reach out, but said, "I'll come. No matter where you're going or what you're doing, it has to be a better life than this."

Now it was Gar who was struggling not to show delight, but she saw it in him, and her heart sang.

"I'm going to the stars," he warned her. "You may not ever be able to come back."

"I don't intend to come back," she said, trembling.

"There will be danger," Gar cautioned, "as great as any you've ever known here, possibly greater. There will be hunger and thirst, perhaps even torture. But if we live, we'll free other people who have been ground down as badly as you were, perhaps worse."

"It's worth the chance," she said, and knew she'd regret it someday. "How can it be worse? This world has become a torment for me already." *Worse, without you in it,* she thought, but kept the words from her tongue and hoped he'd meant what he said, that he wouldn't read her mind. But the thought of freeing other slaves fired her imagination, and she trembled as much with excitement as with fear.

"Don't you dare," she whispered, "don't you dare try to go away and leave me here."

Magnus grinned widely and said, "Now, that would be very foolish of me indeed."

"Separate bedrooms," she said, a touch of her old fear rising.

"Definitely," Magnus agreed, "and separate sitting rooms, too. But we can meet in the lounge when you want to."

"And you'll have to keep teaching me how to fight!" Alea warned him.

"Oh, yes," Magnus said softly, "I surely will."

Alea stared at him, her only real friend, and wondered if he would ever be anything more, if she would ever *want* him to be anything more. He raised his arms again in welcome, and finally she managed to walk.

She walked right around him and on up the ramp, snapping, "What are you waiting for, then? If we're going to leave this world, let's leave!"

She was almost to the top of the ramp before she heard his answer, coming up behind her, filled with suppressed delight: "Yes. Let's go."

Alea stepped back into the wondrous, luxurious room, Gar stepped in behind her. Something whirred as the ramp slid up to close the doorway. She kicked off her boots, jammed her feet into her slippers, and marched across the thick yielding carpet to sit in her chair as though by right, like a queen on her throne. Gar sat opposite her and said quietly, "Lift off, Herkimer."

"Lifting," the disembodied voice said, and Alea stared at the picture before her, scarcely able to believe her eyes, as the trees grew smaller and smaller and the tundra swept in all about them, then shrank away to an expanse of silver in the moonlight with patches of darkness about it that were forest. She was barely able to see little lights that she knew must be villages before mist filled the screen. But it too dwindled, darkness began to show around the edges, darkness that swept in to fill more and more of the picture until the world was only a cloud-streaked ball again, and Alea knew with a certainty she couldn't have explained that the great golden ship had risen into the sky and beyond it, to bear her away to her dreams.